Haven Kimmel is the author of the Number One *New York Times* bestselling memoir, *A Girl Named Zippy*, and the critically acclaimed novel *The Solace of Leaving Early*, which was longlisted for the Orange Prize for Fiction in 2003. She studied English and creative writing at Ball State University and North Carolina State University, and attended seminary at the Earlham School of Religion. *Something Rising (Light and Swift)* is her second novel, and the second part of a planned trilogy.

For automatic updates on Haven Kimmel visit harperperennial.co.uk and register for AuthorTracker.

Praise for *Something Rising (Light and Swift)*:

'Stark yet compelling'   *Vogue*

'You're going to love meeting Cassie Claiborne, the redoubtable girl at the heart of this wonderful coming-of-age story. She has it all – rebellion, grit, compassion, humor, and a perfect eye. Beautifully written, *Something Rising* is a wonder'

SUE MONK KIDD, author of *The Secret Life of Bees*

'What intelligence is here, and what grace, and what unsentimental (and contagious!) love for our messy ways here on planet Earth. Haven Kimmel is true gospel wearing blue jeans; you read her and you are lifted up'

ELIZABETH BERG

D1253517

HAVEN KIMMEL

Something Rising
(Light and Swift)

HARPER PERENNIAL
London, New York, Toronto and Sydney

Harper Perennial
An imprint of HarperCollins*Publishers*
77–85 Fulham Palace Road
Hammersmith
London W6 8JB

www.harperperennial.co.uk

This edition published by Harper Perennial 2005
1

First published in Great Britain by Flamingo 2004
First published in the US by Free Press 2003

A catalogue record for this book
is available from the British Library

ISBN 0 00 717413 6

Set in Berling

Printed and bound in Great Britain by Clays Ltd, St Ives plc

For Melinda

For her children,
Josh and Abby

And in memory of her husband,
Mark Lawrence Frame
1940–2002

Something Rising

(Light and Swift)

Did you ever have a family?

—ALAN SHAPIRO, *Song and Dance*

PROLOGUE

The man standing across from Cassie had nearly a thousand dollars on the line and a pale absence where his wedding ring should have been. He registered on her periphery: his anger, his receding hairline, the slick shirt, the way he leaned against the corner pocket so that she had to look directly at him as she studied the shot. Cassie noticed these things without thought, the same way she could see Uncle Bud behind the bar, drying glasses and keeping his eye on her, without looking in his direction.

The man had left a mess on the table. Cassie paced, dropped her stick up and down on the toe of her boot. On the break he had sunk the six and the two and had cleared the one and three quickly. But he left the four stranded close to the rail and the cue ball downtable, taking a safety. Cassie had to do many things at once—get to the four; sink the four; position the cue ball to take the recalcitrant five; get back down for the seven; release the eight from where it was stranded; and sink the nine—but the whole process felt like one thing, the way walking doesn't feel like a thousand articulated events. Just one event.

Some nights she saw the table as a plane, all four sides extending infinitely, and at those times she couldn't lose. But on other nights, and against opponents like her current one (the Lounge Singer, she'd dubbed him), she fell to earth and used what she could find there. The table was actual and massive, and its borders were discrete. She imagined two protractors joined at the horizontal line, forming a perfect circle, and everything outside that circle was darkness, and all she needed to know was inside. From the ball to the pocket was one side of an angle; from the cue ball to the object ball was the other side. And there, invisible, where the cue and the object met, or would meet: the vertex, her desire. She dreamed sometimes that her whole life was funneled into that point of contact and could be measured in the old ways: acute, right, obtuse, a reflex.

The man across the table had had too much to drink, had bet too much money, and was now showing her his black edge. It was just a look around his eyes, a flush of throat. He thought she'd never take the four, and he was terrified she would. Cassie stopped behind the cue ball, imagined the table flipped into a mirror image, and considered a bank shot. After she'd done her best with angles, the rest was physics. Distance, velocity, and acceleration. The transfer of momentum. And something else: a sensation she'd never understood that caused her throat to close and her heart to pound. She was addicted to the feeling, even though it arrived like heartbreak, with the same thunder and autonomy. The four was too far away, but if she kept her eye on what her opponent couldn't see, the bisections and intersecting lines, the ghosts, she believed she could do it.

She bent so far at the waist that her chin rested on top of the cue, and the lines on the table shifted like a computer design in a war room. The two practice strokes rubbed lightly against the underside of her chin, where she was developing a permanent red line. On the third stroke, a medium shot, the cue ball traveled the length of the table; the Lounge Singer opened his mouth, closed it again. He hadn't expected the backspin, the way the bank happened so fast, sending the four right past the eight and into the corner pocket without a sigh of resistance. The cue ball rolled and stopped six inches from the five, and then it was over. The five, the seven, the eight. She sank the nine lightly, stepped away from the table, and rocked her head from side to side. Her shoulders ached.

Her opponent started to say something, but Uncle Bud filled the doorway like a piece of furniture. "Pay her," he said.

The man reached into his pocket, shaking from the loss, and pulled out a stack of bills held together with a tarnished old clip. His waistband was sweat-stained, and now that she'd beaten him, Cassie had to turn away from seeing him too closely. She took the money, said thanks. He slipped out past Uncle Bud without a word, past the players at the other tables, the regulars who came late and stayed late and seemed to pay attention to no one.

Cassie unscrewed the butt of her cue from the shaft, wiped it down, and put the two parts away as Bud gathered the balls and brushed the felt on the table. When she was ready to go, he walked her to the back door and watched her wheel her bike down the back stairs.

"You going straight home?" he asked.

Cassie nodded.

"He was driving a white Caprice. You see him between here and your house, get off your bike."

"Okay," Cassie said.

"Or else go ahead and knock the crap out of him, I don't care which."

"Okay."

Cassie pulled her cap down over her ears, wheeled out on to the main street of Roseville, where every business was long closed and every resident was long asleep. At the edge of town she leaned into the wind and sped up, past the flat fields of central Indiana, expanses that stretched as far as she could see. She sped down the Price Dairy Road in the complete dark, her headlight casting an arc before her, then turned on to her road, The King's Crossing, which met Price Dairy at a ninety-degree angle. She headed for her house, where her sister, Belle, slept on one line and her mother, Laura, slept on another; and where her father, Jimmy, the vertex, was entirely absent; where there was nothing she could do. No shot to take. No safety.

A light glowed in the trailer at the rear of the property, where her grandfather Poppy had lived with his dogs. Poppy left the light on for her, and the dogs didn't bark. Cassie carried her bicycle up the three back stairs and into the laundry room, took off her jacket, and hung her cue case on a hook. The air in the kitchen was gray with Laura's cigarette smoke. Cassie poured herself a glass of orange juice, leaned against the sink. It was two in the morning, and she needed to get up at six-thirty to be at school on time. Her eyes burned, and she let them close, leaning there against the sink in the silent house. She had always hated school, had hated it until recently, when suddenly the girl who had been expelled six times for fighting, who had flunked every subject in one semester last year (including badminton), began collecting report cards that were different from years past. In this, the spring of her tenth-grade year, she had done poorly in everything but math. Her teacher, astonished, had sent a letter to Laura that said one thing: *She's a natural.*

Part One

The Hammer in Her Hand

THE SPECTRUM OF POSSIBLE OUTCOMES, 1979

On Thursday, in the middle of June, she waited for her father. He hadn't been home for two days, so she got up early, because sometimes he showed up very early and went straight to bed, and then the whole agony of having waited for him to come home was compounded by having to wait for him to get up. He could sleep fourteen hours at a time, hardly moving, she'd studied him. She got out of bed without making a sound, pulled on the clothes she'd worn the day before, didn't bother with brushing her teeth or looking at her hair. There was little left of it anyway, after the episode with the ticks and Poppy's clippers. She got up very early, before Laura or Belle, and crept down the stairs and into the kitchen tinged with morning light, the pale green kitchen that smelled—above and below food, laundry, visitors—of Laura's cigarettes, and took out a bottle of chocolate milk that was made of neither chocolate nor milk. Her favorite drink. She took a banana, too, because bananas are by nature quiet foods, and snuck out through the living room, through the foyer with the two glass cases filled with her dead grandmother's figurines (frolicking baby animals) and out onto the screened porch. The rocker closest to the front door was splintered, the one closer to the road groaned, and in neither did her feet reach the porch. She chose the one that groaned and hoped she wouldn't move. Even this early the air was warm; later a breeze would come up, she guessed, but for now the trees were still. The view from where she sat dazed her with familiarity, the horseshoe-shaped gravel driveway with the holes no amount of dirt or gravel could fill, the yard on the other side of the drive. Nothing in it, just grass. And then her road, the King's Crossing, bumpy asphalt with glass sewn in, in sunlight it shone like diamonds. Across the road a ditch that collected stray papers, detritus, once she'd found a child's tennis shoe, just the one. Beyond the ditch was the fencerow that stretched the whole six hundred acres. To the left of her vision, in the field, was a stand of tall trees—a windbreak—and far to the right was another. Between the stands of trees the corn was pushing up in little shoots, it had been a dry spring, and barely visible to her were the power lines, four gigantic silver men in a row, standing with their hands on their hips, displeased. She knew that if she crossed the field, or rode her bike down to 300 West, also called the Price Dairy Road, and turned left, and got near the power lines, she would hear what Poppy called an infernal hum. The way power speaks. She had no interest in it.

The chocolate milk was gone, the banana was gone, its skin lay bereft next to her rocker. She had hardly moved. When the sun was almost up, the gray burned off, everything that had crouched in the shadow of dawn fully revealed, she knew he wouldn't come, but still she waited. There was nothing else for it; other people pretended to go about their business, whatever business they fabricated, but really they were waiting, if not for him then for someone else. From its spot behind the house, she heard the door to Poppy's Airstream open; the sound carried clearly across the early morning silence, she could almost hear him feel the weather, decide if he needed a hat. He didn't. The dogs clambered down the metal stairs and into the backyard, then rounded the corner of the house, Poppy following.

"That you, Cass?" Poppy asked, shading his eyes and looking through the screen.

"It's me."

His three dogs, Marleybone, Juanita, and Roger, stood or scratched or rolled around Poppy's legs, impatient for their constitutional. Marleybone was Poppy's favorite, the leader of the pack. His fur was a crazy swirl of dark blue and white, he had one brown eye and one blue, his left ear was bent at the tip, and he stood on three legs. He kept his right rear leg lifted off the ground always, had the crazy look of a herder in his eyes. Juanita was a medium-size black dog who shook and mostly kept her tail tucked. There was a painful history on her face, and sometimes, sitting on the porch, looking at the clouds, she would start to shake. Roger had been Poppy's latest acquisition, a wiry little blond dog with a big square head that resembled a cement block. There was mange in his past, but he'd managed to keep the tuft of yellow hair that shot up like a patch of weeds between his ears. Although he seemed to have no legs, so low did he hover over the ground, he could, without warning, leap four feet into the crook of his favorite tree in the backyard.

"You waiting for Jimmy?" Poppy asked. He slipped his right hand into his pants pocket, meaning he was embarrassed.

"Naw," Cassie said, shaking her head.

"'Cause you might find yourself sittin' a long time, if you are."
Poppy dressed carefully every day in a flannel shirt and cotton
trousers, suspenders. He carried a handkerchief in his breast
pocket, shaved every morning, even when he was sick, and kept
his white hair cut short. One of his real teeth, in the back, had a
gold crown, he smelled like Ivory soap and cherry pipe tobacco.
Since Cassie's grandmother, Buena Vista, died two years ago and
before Poppy had begun to collect dogs, he'd moved out to the
1967 Airstream at the back of the property. The world had disap-
pointed him in every imaginable way, but he seemed a happy
man. "Want to go with me? On my walk?"

Cassie shook her head.

"All right, then," he said, and started off down the road.

She waited. It was a fine summer day. Inside the house her
mother and sister began to stir. Cassie imagined them: Belle floating down the stairs in her white nightgown, Laura lighting her
first cigarette of the day, making coffee. Time was and not so long
ago that Belle would have been out here with her, but all had
changed in the blink of an eye; it seemed so to Cassie. On her
twelfth birthday in May, Belle had awakened full of dissatisfac-
tions and resolutions, all of them spoken and written in her notebook then spoken again, and now it seemed that more than two
years separated her from her sister. Something deeper than the
river had carved itself out, Belle on one side. Cassie on the other.

"Don't even tell me," Belle said from behind the screen door.

Cassie tipped up her empty chocolate milk bottle, pretended
to drink.

"Don't even tell me you're out here thinking Jimmy will come
home."

"I'm not," Cassie said, studying the field across the road.

"Did Poppy come by? Laura wants to make sure he got some coffee."

"He's out on his walk."

"That doesn't tell me if he had any breakfast or coffee."

Cassie turned and looked at her sister; Belle's outline behind the screen was ghostly. Her thin arms were crossed over her stomach.

"Edwin will be here soon," Belle said, glancing at her wrist as if a watch were there. But there was no watch.

Cassie looked off down the road, back at the screen door, Belle was gone. She was right—soon Edwin Meyer would appear, because he'd bought the hardware store from Poppy and felt it was his duty to check in every day, and because Edwin and Poppy were best friends in the way that duty binds. In the kitchen Belle and Laura, Cassie knew, were already working out the morning in silences and gestures that operated like a code Cassie couldn't crack. It was another summer day, and all things considered, Cassie lived in a predictable house, and none of it mattered if Jimmy didn't come home. She moved out to the cement steps at the edge of the driveway. She waited.

They came walking down the road with a purpose. Cassie lived in the flattest part of a flat state and could see them coming from a great distance, Leroy Buell and his foster sister, Misty, who lived at the end of the King's Crossing in a tumbledown house with what Laura called a Plague of Relatives. The house was in bad shape, but Leroy's aunt Betta, who was crazy in all other ways, knew how to step outside the front door and throw a handful of seed at exactly the right time, so that everywhere you looked around

13

their house, all along the sagging fence and covering the old walk-ways and right up against the dead trucks and cars and tractors, were *flowers*. No one tended them, no one planted or fertilized, but Laura said the Buell's house was like the virgin prairie, only crazy. Leroy was actually born there, but Misty was an addition, a child taken in a few years ago from the county home who pre-tended she had been adopted, so fiercely did she wish it to be true.

Leroy and Misty sent up the alarm in all God-fearing normal people. God-fearing normal people meant nothing to Cassie, who would happily take their names and kick their asses, as Jimmy was fond of saying. The only way to be safe in the world, as Jimmy would have said, was to be the person other people feared, this is the law of the jungle and among all thinking organisms, and just because we have been given the capacity to imagine it might not be so, or to hope there might be another, more enlightened way to live, is no reason to deny that it is so. *Trouble*, he liked to begin a story by saying, *it is widely known*.

"Going down the river to the shack, cook up a mess of frogs," Leroy said without preamble when he and Misty reached Cassie's horseshoe-shaped yard.

"Build a fire," Misty said.

Leroy had his right thumb hooked in a belt loop of his jeans, which were six inches too short, while his left hand drummed against his bird chest. He was too skinny, his face too long, he breathed through his mouth with a sound like a train in the dis-tance. Misty stood stiff next to him but couldn't seem to stop making noise. This happened in school, too; sometimes if the room was quiet, Cassie could hear Misty two rows over humming the theme song to a television show called *Run, Joe, Run*. She whistled and whispered, snapped her fingers to a hectic beat. But worst of all, Misty was driven toward sound effects, and if she'd been able to hear Cassie think of the faraway train, she would have said: *Chug-a-chug-a-chug-a.* A high wind: *Whoooooooooo.* A catfight: *Yowwwwwl, screeech,* etcetera. Laura would have said there was no future in such behavior.

Cassie gave Misty a good hard look. Her hair was straight as a poker, cut jagged at the edges near her shoulders, and with bangs made crooked by a cowlick. Her teeth didn't meet up right, and she smelled of trapped smoke. Her clothes, a striped shirt too big and blue pants too small, had obviously come from the charity box at the Church of Christ, and Cassie thought it no wonder Misty's parents had decamped for points unknown.

Cassie stood, stretched herself out, then went inside for her backpack, which had been Jimmy's long ago when he had mistakenly thought himself a Boy Scout. This was a mystery to Cassie, how the true nature of a person can be so thoroughly concealed in youth that he does humiliating things. It meant Cassie herself could do them, and later someone would hold out the offending object—a dress, a party favor, an unsent letter—and convict her. She was trying to redeem the backpack. She carried in it a Swiss army knife, a compass, a box of waterproof matches, a second box of waterproof matches, a rain poncho, an old snake bitekit, a small flashlight, a harmonica she couldn't play, a worn guide to dressing field injuries. Now she added a ball-peen hammer—a regular hammer was too heavy to carry—and a small box of nails; boards were always popping loose on the shack, and if she left it to the inbreds and malcontents, as Jimmy called them, the shack would fall down around their ears and they'd go right on sucking the heads off crawdaddies. She also added a second chocolate milk, knowing that everyone down at the river would want it but be afraid to ask; this was the sort of gesture that kept everyone clear about who stood where. Cassie was the person with the chocolate milk and the hammer in her hand, that was all they needed to know.

The three trudged down the road, then cut across the field on Cassie's side, away from the infernal hum of the power lines. "Them new kids is gonna be there," Leroy said. "Emmy Somethin' from Kentucky, and Bobby Puck from up that Granger School that closed."

Misty made a *puck-puck-puck* sound.

"I met 'em already. They was down at the river two days ago when I got there, " Leroy continued. "I says, 'How'd you find this shack? It belongs to us and Cassie Claiborne.' Then that Bobby Puck said something, didn't make *any* sense."

Cassie watched where she was walking, watched for the shimmer of a cottonmouth or the frightened streaking-past of a vole. She could remember when this walk back to the river seemed to take all day. If someone had asked, she would have said the water was miles from her house, but she'd learned it wasn't even a single mile, maybe only a half. As they approached the edge of the field, she recalled an afternoon she and her parents and grandparents had taken a picnic on the bank, and as they'd reached this point, right about here, Jimmy had swung her up on his shoulders and asked, *Do you smell the water?* There had been only that once when they were all together here, walking this path, it was before Buena Vista had gotten sick; and Cassie could see, too, that there was hope and faith in the gesture of a picnic that had somehow gone sorely lacking. If she had tried to plan one, Laura would have scoffed, and Belle would have said she didn't like the river, she couldn't stand bugs, or maybe even nature itself for all Cassie knew. But whatever complaints they leveled wouldn't have much relationship to what they meant, which was: that's all over now.

Cassie smelled the water. As they got closer, she could hear splashing, loud talk, and laughter. A girl said, "You know you're going to kill them."

"I won't! I'm making them happy!"

Leroy lifted a branch and Misty and Cassie walked under. The morning sun hit the water in patches of brilliance; some places were shaded by the tangle of trees overhead. This was a green place, and of ever changing light. The new girl was floating in the river, which was low, in a pair of blue-jean shorts and a Mickey Mouse T-shirt, her arms outstretched and her dark hair floating out behind her. A fat boy was sitting on the bank on top of a five-gallon bucket. Presumably the frogs were in the bucket, and he was making them happy.

"Hark!" the boy called out, waving at the three who were crossing the river on the old log, arms out for balance.

"That's them," Leroy said from somewhere behind Cassie.

"What the hell is a hark?" Misty asked, and then made a *hark-hark-hark* sound.

Bobby Puck was chubby everywhere, even his ankles and wrists and knees. He had a moon face and fine, wavy mouse-brown hair brushed up into a cloud over his head. Cassie could see a mother's hand in that hair. When he smiled, his chubby cheeks rose up and nearly covered his eyes.

Cassie stepped off the log and looked at the two new kids. The river wasn't on Poppy's property, and she had found the shack by accident, but Jimmy would say there are *in-alien-able* rights that govern territory. Years she had been watching her father, sometimes in shadow, and there was plenty she knew about a gambler's face, the reading—like lightning—of options. It all came down, she'd decided, to the size of the stake. How much you could afford to lose.

The boy on the bucket asked, "Are you Miss Cassie?" She nodded. He pointed at the girl in the water. "That's Emmy."

Still floating, Emmy said, "Hey, girl," in an accent with a curve like Buena Vista's, it gave Cassie a cold jolt. She tilted up her chin, waited a full beat.

"Hey." Cassie turned away and headed for the shack; it had been put up and abandoned by hunters at about the time Buena Vista died, and in those two years a lot of stuff had been added to it. Cassie fairly owned it during the summer days, but at night it belonged to teenagers. Someone had dragged an old recliner in, and someone else had brought a mattress. There were pictures tacked to the wall (an elephant being hung in a town square; a toothless woman in sunglasses; a monkey scratching its butt), and lately people had started to bring in books and leave them, old paperbacks creased and dog-eared. Cassie suspected there was more to the books than the plain desire to share literature, since as a group the teenagers weren't what her teachers would call *readers*.

She took off her pack, got out the hammer and nails, and walked around the outside of the shack, hammering down boards that had popped up in the last rain. The hunters hadn't taken the time to make sure the lone cockeyed window actually fit the hole cut for it, so Cassie had chinked in the gaps with river mud. They hadn't put up a doore either, just left a hole for one and hung a sheet of Visqueen in it. When the plastic came down, Cassie cut a new piece and hung it herself, using small tacks that didn't tear. It was important, she thought, to keep the plastic up, to acknowledge the difference between inside and out, else what use was a doorway?

"Light the small sticks, Emmy, we don't have a lot of matches. Did you have these in your pocket when you were swimming?"

"Ooooh, I'm cold now I'm out of the water. The water's warm."

"There's— I tell you, you have to light the small—"

"Did anybody bring a jacket?"

"Emmy's asking did anybody bring a jacket or whatnot?"

Cassie stepped back and looked at the roof. It hadn't been done the way Jimmy would have recommended. Just boards and tar paper. She tried to imagine making the walk back here with a ladder (unlikely), then tried to think of some way to bring a ladder on her bike, but there was no road, only the fields and tree line, and the corn was growing higher. A ladder, a tool belt, some shingles.

Inside, someone had straightened up the books and stacked the empty Mountain Dew cans into a pyramid. A big red candle had been added. Cassie stared at it a moment. The big red candle in the shack was a mistake, as any thinking person could see, and she imagined herself flinging it hard into the river. But taking it away smacked of something Laura preached against, which was Getting Too Thick Into Events. One Never Knows, and sometimes the thing that burns is meant to burn and might be interesting to watch. This set up a jangle in Cassie, truth be told, because no one could say that the shack burnt down was a desirable outcome, or even the shack on fire, interesting as it might be. She walked around inside, periodically stooping down to pound in a nail. A puzzle, the way the nails wanted out of the wood.

"All hail Miss Misty, bringer of fire!"

"Shut up, Bobby Puck, you homo."

"I'm not watching you kill the frogs, Leroy, I'm going over here and also be quiet about it."

Misty said, *rrrbit, rrrbit.*

The book on top of the stack was called *Mr. and Mrs. Bo Jo Jones.* The cover was a photograph, out of focus, of a boy and girl kissing, only one of them was upside down. Mrs. Bo Jo Jones's nose was on Mr.'s chin and vice versa. Taken in profile. *She's sixteen, he's seventeen, a pregnant bride, and her bewildered groom . . . playing a grown-up game with adult consequences.* Cassie picked up the red candle and sat it square on the book; this was surely nothing more than treading the edge of events. She walked outside and around back to take a look at the flat platform she'd built between two gnarled-up trees: it was the first project she'd ever finished on her own. She'd built it in case a flash flood came while they were in the shack, and she'd nailed boards into the tree trunk to make a ladder. The platform was about seven feet off the ground—it couldn't be a biblical sort of flood. She'd come out here and measured and even drawn a diagram in a notebook, then gone back and had Poppy help her cut some tongue-and-groove boards she'd found in the corner of the garage. She climbed up the ladder and stepped on the platform, then jumped up and down. Solid. She knelt down and checked the nails, but they were all snug in, and then she ran her hands over the edge she'd sanded smooth. From here she could see the river slowly moving, and on the shoreline flashes of a white T-shirt. There was a fundamental difference between the shack and this platform, and it could be felt simply by sitting first in one and then on the other, and whatever the discrepancy was made her wonder if maybe she ought not skip putting a new roof on the shack. Below her the fire was just getting going and it smelled good; whatever kind of wood they were using smelled good. A blood scent filled the air.

"You own any guns?" she heard Leroy ask.

Bobby Puck said, "Guns? Are you talking to me?"

Sitting up here, Cassie was waiting for Jimmy but also not waiting, she had let go some. Her own house could be on fire, this was a thing she often considered, and she wouldn't know it until she made the walk back and found the thing in ruins, the trucks and smoke and neighbors watching. She would have no first thought but many at once. Did Jimmy come home, did Laura stay planted where she was, refusing to leave, did Poppy get the dogs out, was Belle out floating around, weeping in the yard in her white nightgown? Beyond that Cassie didn't care, there was nothing she would mourn. Who set this fire?

"Cassie?" Puck was looking up at her from the ground, she hadn't heard him approach. "Can I come up there with you?" He had a very high voice, like a little girl's. As he climbed the ladder, his green T-shirt came out of his shorts, and Cassie could see a white stripe of skin. She looked away. "Oh, this is rather high up," he said, looking over the edge of the platform. "I hope it doesn't make me dizzy. If we were at the tops of these trees we could see my house, it's over yonder as Leroy would say, the opposite side of the river from your house, we could see my dad's blue station wagon in the driveway and my mom's marigolds, my dad has di-abetes. He is a diabetic and never leaves the house anymore, one of his legs is gone and he is now *blind*." Puck leaned forward and whispered the last word in Cassie's ear. She turned and looked at him. Mostly she couldn't abide people who talked too much, and under normal conditions she might have gone ahead and whaled on him. But something in him raised up a loneliness that settled over Cassie like a cloud. "At the Granger School," he continued, holding Cassie's eye, "I was assaulted on a regular basis by ruffians. You remind me of them. When I start at your school in the fall, I'm going to be perfectly silent, in class and everywhere else, so I just thought I'd tell you some things now, that my mom is an aide at the nursing home, and about my dad and whatnot. I don't like sports, I've never gone hunting, I prefer comic books and snacks."

"Puck? Cassie? Want some frog legs?" Emmy called from the shore.

Puck rose, brushed some dried mud from his knees, then bowed to Cassie. "Ladies first," he said, gesturing toward the stairs with a sweeping motion, like the hands of a clock.

She was back home and on the steps by three o'clock. The day had grown hot, and hours to go yet, so she took off her swampy tennis shoes and wet socks and let her feet dry in the sun. Her gray T-shirt said NOTRE DAME WRESTLING TEAM, it was her favorite shirt. Poppy had found it at the dump, back when he used to be a dump crawler, before Laura put her foot down. Cassie missed those days, the great things he'd come home with: a miniature guitar with no strings, a set of rusty golf clubs, a plastic cereal bowl with an astronaut in the bottom. The astronaut was floating outside of and appeared to be larger than his spaceship. All such things Laura dubbed A Crime. But then Poppy came home with a Memphis Minnie album, and when he handed it to Laura, her eyes filled with tears and she turned around and went up to her room and no one had seen her for a whole day, and Belle said

Poppy shouldn't have told her it came from the dump, and Poppy said, confused, Was I to lie?

Cassie's eyes were closed and the world behind her eyelids had gone red when she heard the dogs, not Poppy's dogs who never ran free, but a pack that had been born that winter to a stray down the road. Born in the Taylors' toolshed. The Taylors had no intention of keeping the puppies or of killing them or of having anything to do with them whatsoever, those were Willie Taylor's words to Poppy exactly. Anything whatsoever. A stray who picked us out, we didn't pick her. There were four pups, a brown, a red, a black and white, a black, and they were all hard-muscled, with coats so short they looked like leather, and heads like pigs. Cassie thought of them as the Pig Dogs. They weren't much bigger than young pigs, either. All day long they killed. They killed chickens, ducks, cats, who knew. Once they had run up to Cassie as she walked down the road, and the head of the brown one was completely covered in blood, all the way back to his shoulder blades, still red and wet. No one could touch them. Now they ran toward Cassie with great joy, nearly bouncing, except for the black and white, who was carrying a dead groundhog in his mouth, an animal more than half his size. They were going to leave it in her yard, she could just feel it. Her opinion was that they'd started killing more than they could eat, so they were spreading the carcasses around for fun. The King's Crossing was their game board, and they'd left something on every corner. Cassie stood up and took a menacing step toward them, and they all backed up, tails wagging. They had smart eyes, the Pig Dogs, this was one of their worst features. Cassie stomped, waved her arms, yelled Go on! Git! and the dogs turned one at a time, still sneaky and joyous, and started to run back down the road, except for the black and white, who trotted a few steps farther in and dropped the groundhog, then turned and streaked off after his brothers.

"Cassie, you still out here?"

The groundhog had barely hit the earth, and there was Belle *so soon*, she would take it personally that Cassie had allowed such a thing to happen. Belle stepped out onto the screened porch, wearing a black leotard of Laura's and an old Indian-print skirt, there was a pointedness in her voice that had arrived only in the past two years but seemed to be here to stay. All the way back in Cassie's memory to the place it grew dark and muzzy, she saw Belle with her on a day like this, Cassie at five, Belle at seven, performing their different tasks: one her father's girl, the other belonging solely to Laura. Cassie had her work cut out for her, no doubt about it, being the one to wait and gather clues and wander about the house studying Jimmy's belongings and trying to capture the smell of him somewhere, in his closet, on his pillow. But Belle, maybe, and this was a thing Cassie had only begun to consider, had it a little worse, because her parent was right there and couldn't be reached.

Laura, standing in the kitchen, having a contemplative smoke in her butter-yellow capri pants and white blouse, clothes that came from Somewhere Else and marked her. She wore not perfume or cologne but the oil from a love potion made for her by a Yoruba priestess, oil filled with rose petals and something that looked like whole clove. One brutal fight between Laura and Jimmy started when he called her a *yat*; Cassie had heard yak and assumed her father had been drinking until Belle explained. Bone-thin mother, shoulders slightly hunched, arms crossed loosely over her abdomen, listening to records. She made their meals but didn't eat with them. She smiled, never lost her patience or raised her voice, it was difficult, in fact, to do anything loudly enough or close enough to her range of vision to even get her to turn her head. Bix Beiderbecke with Frankie Trumbauer's orchestra, *Singin' the Blues*. Louis Armstrong, Jelly Roll Morton, Sidney Bechet. One of the only things Laura loved even a smidge about living in Indiana was that one of the earliest jazz labels, the Starr Piano Company and Gennett Records, had been in Richmond. The Friars Society Orchestra had recorded there, and King Oliver, Armstrong, Bix, Hoagy. Laura knew where the building had stood in the Whitewater Gorge, and had driven the girls by on in what was a rare thing for them, a field trip.

This was what Cassie had been thinking of lately, all those injuries of Belle's, all the flaps of skin hanging from her knees, the head wounds bleeding furiously, the falls down stairs, the bicycle wreck in the thorn bush, her slightly chipped front tooth. How could it have been, the two of them side by side and playing the same game, that Belle was always falling? Cassie rarely got hurt. If they walked across the backyard, it was Cassie who found the dead baby bird, the caterpillars and nightcrawlers, she found treasure in tall grass because Belle was looking up. What she was looking for Cassie couldn't say, winged things probably, orioles or nuthatches or bluebirds, or those tiny yellow butterflies that arrive in swarms one day and are gone the next. Belle got hurt, she took her pain in to Laura like a gift, she cried then tried to look brave. There was a demand in her. Cassie thought, but couldn't say (wasn't sure what the words would be) that this wasn't the way to go, Laura didn't like to touch or be touched, she was doing her work *at a minimum* and preferred to be alone. Belle's wounds were akin to getting too thick into events. At eleven Belle started to withdraw from the Great Wide World, as Jimmy called it, she moved inside and became top of her class, at twelve had nearly memorized Edith Hamilton's *Mythology*, which a thoughtful librarian had given her as a gift. Every day she begged for a copy of Virgil In Translation. She had taken to the house and could almost always be found at the kitchen table, under the hanging light with the round shade, and there too was Laura, staring out the window above the sink, and Belle thought she had gotten what she wanted, but Cassie wasn't so sure.

"What's that in the yard? Do you see what I'm pointing at, Cassie? Go on over there and take a look."

Cassie walked across the gravel driveway, periodically stepping on a sharp rock that made her say ow, ow, ow, and through the side door that led into the cool garage, where she picked up Poppy's shovel.

"Do you see the thing I'm talking about, that gray mound over there? Mom's not going to want to walk out here and see it."

The groundhog was lying belly up. He'd been a fat little guy. Cassie studied his face: dead. Also his small, expressive hands, curled now: dead. She put the shovel under him and felt that he'd—

"What is it, Cassie, do you know?"

—been turned to liquid. There weren't bones or organs to offer any resistance. The Pig Dogs had had a time with this one. She got the shovel under his back and tried to lift it; he was very heavy, in addition to being liquid, and he rolled off the end of the shovel and landed facedown.

"I'm going in, I'm not watching this. Take it across the road and over the fence. Drop it *over the fence*, Cassie, so those dogs can't get to it and bring it right back. Do you hear me?"

Cassie got the shovel under his belly and tried to lift him. He rolled off and landed on his back, and that was about all it took for Cassie to see what she was up against. Her shoulders strained and her back began to sweat, It wasn't his weight so much as the fact of him down at the end of the long shovel, and her up at the other end. She gripped the shovel in the middle of the handle, stuck it under the groundhog's back, he was maybe easier to lift this way, but he rolled off and landed on his belly. Simply by turning him over repeatedly, she'd managed to get him a few feet across the yard, so she did that some more: turned him again and again, rolling him like a sausage in a pan. Belly up, belly down. They made it across the road and to the ditch, and putting him in the ditch was no good, Belle would know or the dogs would know. The sun was a violence against Cassie's back, sweat ran toward her eyes. She took off her T-shirt, wiped her face with it, then covered her hands and grabbed him by his paws, his front two in her left hand, his back two in her right. She turned herself sideways, spun around twice, then let him fly, across the ditch and over the fence. At the peak of his flight his back arched like a high jumper's, his chin tilted regally, his arms and legs were loose in surrender. Cassie was, at ten, a child who would have to learn to look away.

Thursday evening, after dinner and a visit with Edwin Meyer and Poppy, a game of Chinese checkers and a bowl of green sherbet, Cassie went out on the screened porch and waited, and Friday she got up very early and went outside and waited.

*   *   *

Saturday morning she woke up and listened; if he was still gone, this would be the longest in a while and would signal nothing good, but then she heard them, the voices that had awakened her. Jimmy and Laura didn't fight about Everything, as some parents did. The tear and scramble of their lives centered around only two subjects, Money and the Prior Claim. The two could be mixed and matched and combined in novel ways. Cassie had hovered for years at the edge of the conversation and could reduce its complex elements to two sentences:

JIMMY: She has a prior claim.

LAURA: Prior to your *children*?

Cassie had written these sentences in her notebook: for her they were no less than Virgil in Translation. She and Belle both wanted to get to the bottom of something, and even if they ultimately knew what it was—lost cultures, Barbara Thompson in a trailer park in Hopwood—they would keep at it. Young scholars. Their parents were having the conversation in the bedroom next door, which was the marital bedroom and contained many mysteries. Laura complained that she hated every stick of furniture in there, the bed they slept in, the dressers and mirrored vanity that matched it, all won by Jimmy in a card game with the Minor Criminals of the Midwest, who were not famous for their taste. The queen-size headboard was tall, flat, and covered with quilted, yellowed vinyl, attached to the frame with brass buttons, brass mostly missing. The dresser and vanity were made of blond wood, perhaps for a blonde woman, which was the opposite of Laura but similar to Barbara Thompson, whose name so far had not been mentioned.

The voices weren't much more than a murmur. Cassie had to get out of bed and creep like a cat across her floor in order to hear what she hoped were the sounds of Jimmy taking his change, his keys, and his breath mints out of his pocket and placing them carefully on his dresser, because this meant he was staying for some hours. Last summer he would sometimes drop in late at night or early in the morning, expecting the girls to be asleep, and deposit with Laura a handful of disputed Money and leave again, that went on for weeks. Cassie heard the loose change land on the dresser top, Jimmy say he was tired, Laura make a sound that was perhaps a word or a cry, and then Cassie knew it was okay to get back in bed awhile. Wherever it was he went—and she didn't believe she'd ever know—her father got very little sleep, he loved to come home and slip into bed in the morning light. She slipped into bed and lay on her back; the sun was coming up on the other side of the house but would reach her soon enough. Her heart pounded, she could see the plaster on the ceiling very clearly, the crack that zigzagged like a fault line from one side of the room to the other. She tried to close her eyes, but they popped right back open.

Last summer Belle had crept into Cassie's room late one night and gotten in bed with her, then wrapped her arms around Cassie from behind the way she had when they were small and whispered in Cassie's ear *Are you very very sad?* In all the great wide world Cassie couldn't imagine another soul who would ask a question like that one and not expect to get beaten up good. Cassie hadn't answered, had just lay there feeling Belle's breath on the back of her neck and trying to think of a true answer. Every day was a vaccination. She missed her grandmother, who had been old and soft, who said few words but who gave to them: she and Poppy had taken them in without a word so long ago, when they had nowhere to live. They'd opened up all the old bedrooms, Buena Vista had gathered up her sewing things and moved them to the attic, and Cassie remembered those years with Buena Vista like a long party where the party is going on inside and no one talks about it. Cassie could still imagine her grandmother so clearly, her white hair curled tight against her head in a permanent wave, the skin on her face that had fallen and kept falling, her watery blue eyes. Buena Vista had been heavy, especially in her legs, and she walked with a kind of back-and-forth Frankenstein gait, and unable to control the distribution of her weight, she had walked hard and made everything in the house shake, especially her animal figurines. She had been just an old woman in a faded housedress, sometimes she even wore her slippers to the grocery store, but something about her had been their hearts' salvation.

Now, lying in bed, her father asleep in the next room, Cassie felt herself swaying back into sleep. *Can you smell the water?* Maybe someday she would tell Belle that she hadn't been, she wasn't sad, she was . . . she almost knew, and then began to dream, there was a wide field, pink and spongy, or maybe it was a desert, there was no sign of anything anywhere, only the vast pinkness all around her, and she guessed she had to cross it, so she started walking.

Laura smoked. Belle sat at the kitchen table doing homework and tearing at her cuticles, her fingernails were already so short they sometimes bled. Poppy came in through the mudroom, "Laurie, have you seen my level?," and Laura said no, she hadn't, and he left again. A few minutes later he popped back in with Roger, who made a mad dash around the kitchen table and back out the door. "Laurie, have you seen my old canvas camp stool?" No, she hadn't.

He left. Cassie wandered from the kitchen to the screened porch, drinking a soda that made her stomach burn, as she hadn't eaten anything all day and here it was almost two in the afternoon. She sat in the rocker with splinters. Finally Belle stuck her head out the door and said, He's up.

Cassie went into the kitchen and casually sat down at the table, picked up Belle's history book, and opened it to the page on Eli Whitney and the cotton gin. Upstairs the shower was running, then it turned off. Jimmy hummed as he shaved. When he came downstairs he smelled sweet, had a swing in his step. Cassie wrote on her palm with her fingernail the things she wanted to talk to him about: a door for the shack, help fixing her bicycle chain, would he toss the football with her, would he figure out how to get a better fence around the garden—the deer were tearing it up. Poppy needed new propane tanks on the Airstream, and there was something else. She tapped her fingernail on the table.

"Stop that," Belle said. Cassie stopped.

"Hey, girls," Jimmy said, sitting down at the head of the table.

"Hello," Belle said, not looking up.

"Hey." Cassie glanced at him, his hair was still wet from the shower and he had some tan across his nose. He'd put on a pressed white shirt, linen pants in a mossy green, one of his thin leather belts. He sat at the table as he always did, with his legs crossed like a woman's, his torso slightly turned. Other fathers looked to Cassie like livestock; Jimmy was how it was supposed to be, a jangly, dancing man. She remembered she wanted to tell him that last week she'd been walking down the road and a fox had bolted out of the tall grass and run right in front of her, she could almost feel him against her skin, and she'd been tempted to follow him. But they move fast.

"Get a some coffee here, Laura?" Jimmy asked.

Her mother turned away from the window, dropped her cigarette in the sink where she'd been washing dishes, filled the percolator with water, slammed it against the counter.

"Whatcha working on there, Bella Belle?"

Belle blushed, tore at a cuticle. "A book report. On *Where the Lilies Bloom*."

"Aren't you— Isn't this summer vacation?"

"I'm just," Belle said, placing her hands over her notebook, "doing it on my own."

"I see. Good book?"

"I liked it."

Jimmy nodded. "Well."

Cassie kicked the chair with the back of her foot until it started to ache.

"How about you, Cass? Having a good summer?"

She glanced down at the palm of her hand, where she'd written her invisible list, then cleared her throat.

"Laura, how about putting a little soup in a pan for me?"

Cassie cleared her throat again—she'd start with the bike chain, she figured—and Laura turned slowly and looked Jimmy up and down, then pulled a pan from the cabinet with a hard rattle and slammed it on the stove.

"And maybe a cheese sandwich." Jimmy looked at Cassie, grinned, shrinking up his left eye as he did so, his bit of a wink. "Man could starve to death in his own home, huh, Cass?"

Cassie thought she might be called upon to betray her mother, it was not at all out of the question for Jimmy to demand such loyalty, but she was spared the request by a block of cheese sailing from the direction of the refrigerator, not its sailing so much as its landing was the distraction. It skidded underneath Belle's papers and came to a stop. The three at the table looked up at Laura. Some very bad things had happened this way, some of which could still be discerned on the ceiling.

"I can see I'm not wanted here," Jimmy said, pushing himself up from the table.

"How *dare* you," Laura said, crossing the kitchen like a storm. "How dare you come home after four days—"

"Five," Cassie said.

"—five days and push me into giving you an excuse to leave again? What in the name of Christ sort of person are you?"

"Mom," Belle said.

"Shut up, Belle, and you shut up, too, Cassie."

"I don't appreciate you talking to me like this in front of my daughters," Jimmy said, pulling himself up to his full height, an inch shorter than Laura.

"Oh, oh, that's rich, too, *your daughters*," Laura said, getting closer to Jimmy's face with every word.

"All I came home for was my stick, anyway." Jimmy turned and walked into the living room, stopping at the coat closet, where he took out his cue case.

Cassie jumped up and ran past him, grabbing her sandals off the porch as she went. She leaped down the porch steps and landed on some sharp rocks, had to make her way down the driveway to where he'd parked, pulled open his passenger door. It was *hot* inside, it was *shocking*. Jimmy drove a 1971 Lincoln Continental with suicide doors and red leather interior, and if they were starving to death or would die without penicillin and the only way to save them would be to Sell The Car, then good-bye Cassie, good-bye Belle. This according to Laura. Poppy reluctantly agreed.

A minute passed. Jimmy had undoubtedly gone upstairs to collect his things, and would come sailing out the front door any minute. He favored a dress shirt that allowed room for an entrance, or an exit, in its graceful folds. He sailed out the door. Laura was right behind him, speaking quickly but not loudly, and she threw something but Cassie couldn't see what it was. Conditions were not ideal, Cassie realized this right away.

Jimmy walked down the driveway, his walk a kind of glide, and pulled his door open. "Get out, Cassie," he said, starting the engine. Boiling air blew from the vents. "Sweet creeping Jesus, it's hot in here."

Sweat poured down her face and in a stream down her chest.

"Get out, Cassie, right this minute."

Laura still stood on the porch but she was hard to see behind the screen.

"Right this goddamn minute, Cassie, I'm not playing."

She turned and looked at him. His long black eyelashes had never worked to his advantage when he was angry, but she could see he really was. Angry.

"GET OUT OF THE CAR."

Another minute or two and he'd see what her point was.

"*Fine,*" he said, his teeth grinding. He pulled the gearshift into reverse as if he wanted to pull it off the column, then backed out so fast stones flew up and hit the bottom of the car, and obviously this wasn't something Jimmy would wish to happen to the Lincoln. He was beyond himself. His tires screeched against the King's Crossing as he moved the transmission into drive, and then Cassie was thrown against the red leather seat, and the compass bobbing around in liquid on the dashboard swung around, up and down.

"Do you see what you do to me, all of you, every last blasted one of you? You make me *hate my life*, Cassie, how does that feel?" Jimmy slammed the lighter into the dash, flipped a cigarette out of the pack in his breast pocket. "I don't know what I was thinking, picking you out at the zoo. I honestly do not know."

Cassie rolled down her window, stuck out her head, let the wind fill her mouth and nose. When she leaned back, Jimmy was smoking, driving slowly, listening to his favorite radio station, Frank Sinatra was singing "Fly Me to the Moon." Jimmy hummed along with him, Jimmy's beautiful voice.

They drove the four miles into Roseville, a town famous for two things: a small candy factory called April and May's, after the unmarried sisters who'd run it out of their kitchen; and a restaurant, Holzinger's, which boasted a large, expensive buffet. Cassie had been there only once, on her parents' anniversary a few years before, and buffet was probably not the correct word. She and Belle had been stunned into silence when they entered. The restaurant occupied four floors: the first was appetizers, the second was breads, the third was entrées, and the fourth was desserts. Cassie had stopped in the appetizer room—the mountain of cold pink shrimp on ice in the middle of a table, the cold silver platter underneath it beaded with condensation, had made her want to run.

Now they passed the Granger School, which was beautiful and looked as if it might fall down, and then the gas station and a flower shop. The main street was tree-lined and shady.

"High suicide rate in Roseville, you know that, Cass?"

Cassie shook her head.

"Oh yeah. I coulda told anybody who asked, and for free, but they hired an *expert* instead."

She doubted it would have been for free.

"County coroner—you know him? Robbie Ballenger?—he suggested it to the county council. Read some article about national suicide rates, saw that ours are as high as an Indian reservation. Don't want that, do we." An old rocking horse and a birdcage were sitting on the sidewalk outside the antique shop. "The Christians are calling for Robbie's resignation. An in-erad-i-cable rule of life, Cassie," he waved his cigarette at her like a stern finger, "do not piss off the Christians, they will throw their stones at you every time."

As they approached the center of the downtown there were fewer and fewer businesses, just empty buildings. An evacuation order. Uncle Bud's sat on the corner of Main and Railroad; it had been a drugstore fifteen years before, a low and long building with a green awning along the front windows. The windows were covered with a film that made them look silver from outside: mirrors. Jimmy pulled into one of the three parking spaces facing the back door. Behind them, on the corner of Railroad and fifth, was a bar called Howdy's. A sign outside advertised fiftycent Miller drafts for and a whole room devoted to darts. Other than Howdy's, everything seemed deserted. A few faded storefronts proclaimed fly-by-night mechanics, flown, and body shops. Cassie had been here once, sent inside Uncle Bud's to fetch Jimmy when Laura was so mad she couldn't get out of the car for fear her legs would explode. The place had held Cassie in an attraction so powerful she could no longer remember the specifics, only the heart-knocking joy. She felt a shadow of it every time she went past this part of Roseville with Poppy, on the way out to the highway and to the strip of stores at the edge of Hopwood.

Jimmy rolled up the windows, reached into the back for his cue. "You're not to bother me."

Cassie nodded.

"I've come here to visit my table and get in some time, not to focus on you."

"Okay."

"And if Bud comes in, who is as you know an old sumbitch, and says you have to leave, then you're going to have to skedaddle and find something else to do."

"Okay."

He leaned over and kissed her on the forehead. His lips were smooth and hard and cool. "You know you're my favorite, Cassie, although God knows that ain't saying much." Stepping out of the car, he pulled his shirt away from his chest, fanning himself witrh it, then looked for the key to the back door.

The door was steel, gunmetal gray, no window. In the back room Jimmy pulled a string, and a bare bulb illuminated the rough wooden shelves covered with boxes of Master chalk, cases of crackers filled with cheese or peanut butter, new balls. On the floor were boxes overflowing with empty beer and soda cans. Against one wall was a line of cues that looked as if they were awaiting surgery. Cassie took a deep breath. This smelled better than anything in her life, better than a Christmas tree, better than the raspberry bush at the edge of the house, tangled with honeysuckle, better than Jimmy's winter coat.

"I'm not going to entertain you, and the rules are the same as when the table was at home, you can't touch it."

Jimmy used another key to open an ugly green door with a frosted glass panel that seemed to have been stolen from a hard-boiled detective agency. They were in the dim main hall. Bud's bar still looked as it had, Cassie guessed, when the building was a pharmacy—a long counter with stools, and a mirror behind it with Rx painted in vivid blue, a mortar and pestle beside it. On the shelves below the mirror were trays of balls and boxes of chalk, mostly battered, and bags of potato chips clipped to a black metal rack. A single jar held dill pickles in cloudy green brine. There were no draft beers or fountain drinks; everything was lined up squarely in a refrigerator with a glass door.

"And I'm not buying you a soda or chips and have you make a mess in here, so don't ask."

Cassie's eyes glanced from surface to surface. She'd never been anywhere so clean and precise. Bud used a big old-fashioned cash register: five-dollars was the last anyone had paid. On the steel counter next to the cash register was a big rectangular book with a grainy black cover, the word ACCOUNTS. The book was centered so precisely on the counter it looked like Bud had used a speed square. A sign on the bar explained that between three and six in the afternoon the tables were a dollar a person per hour, and between six and two in the morning, they were two-fifty. In one corner was a silent jukebox, and other than that just the tables.

"And don't ask for quarters for the jukebox because I didn't bring any." Jimmy had taken out his cue and was screwing the joint on the butt.

Seven tables, five feet from the wall and five feet apart; a light with a green accountant's shade hung over every table. At each end of the room was a rack with ten house cues. A shelf for drinks and ashtrays ran the length of the room, and there were four tall chairs against the wall and ten stools scattered around the room. Cassie wandered around, not quite touching anything, taking in the smell of chalk, beer, cigarettes, while Jimmy used a third, smaller key to unlock the door to the glassed-in room at the end of the hall. Inside the glass room was one table, no stool, no chair. Cassie hovered in the doorway, watched him flip the switch to the light that had formerly hung in their garage.

"Ahhhh," Jimmy said, resting his stick on the toe of his shoe. "There's my best girl." He spread his arms as if making a gift of the whole room to his daughter. "I ever tell you how I came into possession of this table?"

Cassie nodded, she had heard the story many times.

"It's a vintage Brunswick, this one. Built in 1884, probably in New Orleans; moved with a family to Alabama and eighty years later was back in the Big Easy, where one James Claiborne happened to win it in a game that went on so long God wished me luck and went on to bed." Jimmy lit a cigarette. He bent and studied the length of the table, looking for wear on the felt. "I hauled it in the back of a borrowed station wagon to the boardinghouse where I was staying—oh, don't worry, it was a Christian boardinghouse for Christian men. The slate, rails, legs, pockets, rack, sticks, and balls, the whole shebang, I reassembled it in an abandoned tobacco warehouse on Tchoupitoulas, the key to which I happened to find upon my person after another difficult game. In an old hotel, that one. *Spooky*." Jimmy rested his cigarette on the small shelf against the wall, not in the ashtray provided but on the shelf. There was a series of dark stripes in the wood, as if he'd placed burning ash there on a number of occasions. He ran his hand along the shining hardwood of the rails. "There was a single missing part, believe it or not, and I found it in a Brunswick repair shop on Frenchmen Street. It's a civilized town, Cassie, that has a Brunswick repair shop. It's long gone, just like old Jimmy Claiborne. I'd bet I'm still talked about, though. If I were a betting man."

He didn't say the table was walnut, but Cassie knew. The legs were ornately carved and the pockets woven leather. It was four feet by eight feet, the measurement Uncle Bud called True. The slate had been flawless when Jimmy won the table, and remained so; Bud changed the felt, made of fine wool from somewhere in the Netherlands. Wood spun and dyed by virgins, Jimmy said. Cassie wished he would go on, she wished he would tell the story of the light, too, which she had studied for hours. The glass was deep red and imprinted with black Chinese characters, and red silk fringe hung like liquid from the bottom of the shade. She wanted to hear Jimmy say the words *Colorado* and *mining town*, which she'd long ago written in her notebook.

But he said nothing more. His cigarette sent up a ribbon of smoke against the wall. Cassie watched him rack the balls (they came from Belgium, and he would have no others), knowing she was invisible to him. She watched as she had hour after hour, sitting on a kitchen ladder in the garage. The one ball was the yellow of a sunflower; the two was the same shade as the Indiana sky on a flawless summer day, Cassie had often had the feeling they had been made for her, or that they represented, at the very least, the possibility of something beautiful. At night sometimes, unable to sleep, she would imagine the balls spread out across the green table under the red glass of the lamp: someone had stepped on a box of paints and let them fly. Ruined paints on new grass.

Jimmy stood at the foot of the table and, using a house cue left propped in a corner, took two practice strokes (never one or three), then sent the cue ball crashing into the gathered tribe. All fifteen balls careened around the table, and the four and the thirteen fell. He was practicing straight pool, even though he'd been saying for years that the days of the great straight players were over, and that the money was now on 8-ball for hustlers and 9-ball for professionals. Cassie didn't know which he was. Jimmy moved around the table quickly, as if on a preordained path. When the table had been at their house, all those years, she had watched Uncle Bud and many other men play against Jimmy, and she knew her father had a strange and specific style related to his restless grace; he bent at the knees instead of at the waist and didn't sight down the cue as if down the barrel of a gun. In deep concentration, he made his bottom lip so thin it vanished. She would have never told him or anyone, but she had missed this table fiercely, and even after spending her whole life with a man to whom objects gravitated and then were lost—things that came and went like the stray men Jimmy invited to dinner and a game, who would never be seen again—she had not understood what had happened, how the table went missing and ended up here at Bud's.

She had been standing in one spot, watching her father, FOR so long that when she heard another key rattle in the ugly green door, she awoke as if from a dream. Uncle Bud stepped in, gently closing the door behind him. As he passed the glass room where Jimmy played, Bud barely gave him a glance, and there wasn't the comfort of old friendship in the look, either; Jimmy rarely earned such a thing. Uncle Bud had been Jimmy's childhood companion, they had a long history. And there WERE a few dark moments in the past two dark years when Bud had stepped into their house in Laura's name, had roughly set things right.

He was tall and dense, with arms the size of hams, and an enormous head on a thick neck. Bud kept his hair, which was going gray, cut so short he looked like he'd gone missing from some secret branch of the military, and he dressed in T-shirts and blue jeans and motorcycle boots and wore a wide belt with a Harley-Davidson buckle. But he didn't own a motorcycle. There was a wide gap between his two front teeth and his eyebrows sprouted wild. He had a tattoo of Donald Duck on his forearm, the origin of which he would not discuss, and he had formerly smoked cigarettes but had given them up for cigars; Cassie liked the smell. On the whole Cassie faced the world of men with the wariness of the repeatedly betrayed child—Poppy was the only man she trusted—but long ago she had taken to Bud and felt safe in a room he was in. He kept his distance from her.

"Cassie," he said, surprised to see her. "What are you doing here?"

She shrugged.

"Well, come help me carry these boxes up front."

The cases of soda were heavy, but in Bud's arms and against his stomach, they looked like matchboxes. As she passed the glass room for the third time, Jimmy stuck his head out. "Keep her workin', Bud. That's why I had children, although I thought they'd be sons."

Bud ignored him.

Jimmy came out and sat down at the bar. "Give me a cold something." He turned to Cassie, winked. "I ever tell you how I came into possession of that table?"

Bud sighed, stopped at the refrigerator door as if he might not open it.

"Okay, okay. I may have mentioned the adventure a time or two. Let me say that I stole so much from that man that night, pretty much everything he held dear, that if we'da kept it up, I woulda left with one of his kidneys."

Bud relented and got Jimmy the beer.

"I'm back at it," Jimmy said. "Bud, if she bothers you, send her scootin'."

Cassie watched him go, accepted the cold Coke that Bud offered her. "You want to play, Cass? I've got some bookkeeping to do."

"I can't. I'm not allowed."

"Who says? Jimmy? This is *my* pool hall, those are *my* tables, including the one he's playing on which he keeps insisting is his." Bud shook his head. "Nothing to be done about him." He took a tray of balls off the rack and dropped a cube of chalk in the middle. "He never taught you to play?"

Cassie shook her head. "But I've watched a lot."

"I know you have. Jimmy loves an audience. Well, come here, then."

Bud took down a house cue and examined its tip, then chose another. He said ferrule, scuffer, shaper, mushrooming. He put the cue in Cassie's hand. She had sometimes snuck Jimmy's cue out and looked at it, but there was a space that Cassie had never crossed between contraband and the legitimately held thing. She crossed it. The cue felt more formidable than she would have guessed, heavy at the bottom like a weapon and delicate at the top, just a stem. Bud showed her how to rack the balls for 8-ball, 9-ball, straight pool, which she already knew, then taught her the difference between an open and closed bridge, then taught her how to sight and where to hold the cue with her rear arm. He said head spot center spot foot spot corner pocket long string foot string center string head string. Kitchen. Head rail side rail foot rail side rail, and for the next four hours, as they lined up shots and hit them, he said a thousand things that Cassie fought hard to remember. When the tip of the cue strikes the cue ball, the forearm of your rear arm should be at a ninety-degree angle to the floor. Play begins here. This is a foul, and this is a foul, and this is also a foul; one of your feet must remain on the floor at all times. This is a mechanical bridge and there is no shame in using it. Chalk your tip before every shot but not until your opponent has missed because it's rude not to wait. A slice, a thin slice, an impossible slice. The ghost ball, or phantom ball, the ghost table acting as a mirror. Bank shots and combinations and the massé and jumps. Sharking. Speed of stroke, hold the cue lightly, deadstroke. How to will deadstroke, or if it's always a gift from God. On the cue ball: the vertical axis, the follow, right English, 3:00, low right, the draw, 6:00, left english, 9:00, high left.

"How old are you?" he asked.

"Ten."

"You need to get an Introduction to Physics textbook. No one in Hopwood county is going to teach you physics at this age. Also you'll need to know something about geometry. Your fool father will say he's good at this game because he thinks in geometry, but he's lying. He never even learned geometry, they didn't go that far in reform school. And this game is about physics, so do that, get a book."

Cassie nodded. She wished she had her notebook.

"And *grow*. You're too short to see what's happening on the table."

"Okay."

"Cassie," Jimmy said, standing at the bar with his cue taken apart and stowed back in the case, "I'm leaving. Put this stuff away and tell Uncle Bud thank you for the lesson."

"You're out of here early," Bud said, crossing his arms across his wide chest. "I thought you'd still be here when the late crowd arrived."

"You were wrong." Jimmy pulled his keys out of his pocket. "Get in the car, Cass."

"You go on, Jimmy. I'll take her home."

"Or I'll call Edwin," Cassie said, shocked as she heard herself say it.

"Get in the car, Cassie."

Bud took a step toward Jimmy. "I've got an idea, how about you head on wherever you were going, which was surely not home where you belong, and I'll take care of getting Cassie back. Sound good?"

The muscles in Jimmy's face tightened and relaxed; Cassie had seen this many times, he did it when he was furious, as lions yawn before they attack. His whole body was tense. But he said, smiling at the end, "Whatever. Save me the trip." He walked over and kissed Cassie on top of her head. "Don't let Bud talk you into playing for money." He strolled out the front door, unlocked now, even by leaving through a door you didn't enter through is very bad luck, Cassie almost said something.

"All right, come here now," Bud said, setting up the three ball in front of a side pocket. "I want you to take this shot a hundred times, I'm going to stand here and count. If you make it fifty times you can come back tomorrow."

It was an easy shot in some ways; she was shooting from the side of the table, and she didn't have to reach. The three was eighteen inches from the pocket at what Bud said was about a thirty-degree angle. But Cassie had seen right away that this was a game in which mysterious forces seemed to be at work, which meant that sometimes things might go well and that was a surprise, and sometimes everything went wrong and that was also a surprise. Bud said there were an infinite number of variables to consider, and Cassie didn't understand what that meant but remembered the phrase so she could ask Belle. He said take the best shot available to you, and if there isn't one, go safe. If you practice a shot many times, you add it to a repertoire until you own the table. He said don't go for the slice beyond ninety degrees, because when you do, you're pushing hard against the spectrum of possible outcomes.

Other people began to trickle in, a middle-aged couple who looked like they'd just woken up and eaten fried eggs. A thin bald man playing alone. Cassie barely registered them. She made the shot sixty-two times, told Bud he could go about his business, then lined the balls up and started all over, and she did that right up until Edwin Meyer touched her on the arm and told her it was time to go home.

They got in Edwin's car, a clean, modest Dodge that smelled like nothing but an unfolded map, and headed home. Edwin was younger than Jimmy but had started school at four and skipped two grades, so they ended up in the same class. Unlike Uncle Bud's, Edwin's life had diverged early from Jimmy's, when Poppy wanted Jimmy to work at the hardware store and he refused. Edwin took the after-school job and stayed right there, no ladder to move up, just more responsibility to take on, longer hours to work, until Poppy decided to retire and sell, and Edwin bought the place. He'd been at Public Hardware twenty years now, Cassie guessed, and he was so much entwined with the building and the smell of nails in wooden bins, the creaking of the old floor, that if the store didn't exist, Edwin wouldn't, either. He'd go thinner and thinner until finally he couldn't be seen, couldn't be remembered.

Cassie forgot him all the time. Laura said he felt responsibility for them all, as if, when he purchased Poppy's business he also purchased his failings; Jimmy was clearly a failing. Someone, Edwin was fond of saying, had to keep everything in working order. He had no family of his own.

"Are you—you were there a long time—all right?" Edwin was wearing the clothes he favored for work: polyester trousers in a horrible shade of tan or green and a seersucker dress shirt from Sears. His thin dark hair lay flat against his head, Laura said he had a Lovely Face. Laura called him Sweet Reason. Cassie told Belle one night she thought Edwin loved Laura, and that's why he was always calling on them for Chinese checkers and hot tea, but Belle said Cassie was wrong. She said he came for other reasons, and he was Pure.

"I'm fine, yeah."

"A pool hall," Edwin said, shaking his head. "I would have been in all kinds of trouble if I'd been caught in a pool hall at your age."

Cassie looked out the window. Roseville was closing the shutters and rolling up the streets, as Jimmy would say. "What kind of music is this?"

Edwin turned the volume up. "It's a polka. A German polka. My parents were German, you know, very firm. Firm, hardworking people."

"Okay."

"This is my favorite kind of music, although I don't ordinarily say so. My parents had a Victrola, a real one, and a collection of seventy-eights. Big records. They used to put on a polka record on Saturday nights, just like tonight, and we would dance, it's very joyful music, as you can hear."

"Okay."

"And my father became a different man. All week long he"—Edwin paused, drove—" counted the grains of salt we were allowed to put on our potatoes. He counted for my mother so she wouldn't cheat. So Saturdays were great. For me."

They drove out to the edge of town, turned on 300 West, headed for the King's Crossing. "Do you know anything about bicycle chains?" Cassie asked, embarrassed.

"I surely do. I'm thinking about your bike, what sort of chain you need." He thought. "It's too old and slow and meant for a boy," he said, as he turned the car around and headed back to the hardware store.

"Not if it's a bother," Cassie said.

"We'll take care of it." Edwin leaned in toward the steering wheel, smiled. "A project."

They finished late. Cassie rode the bike down to the crossroads and back, and told Edwin it felt like new.

"I don't think it was ever new, Cassie."

"It's better, though." She thanked him, and he tipped an imaginary hat and got in his car and drove away, the faint strains of a German polka following him.

The house was quiet: Cassie found Belle at the table, reading her book and making notes. Her reports were so exhaustive, Laura said, that no one would ever need to read the things themselves. Belle drained a book.

Laura was standing at the kitchen sink, staring out into the dark yard where the finches fed, as if it were daylight and as if there were finches. The dinner dishes were done, and Cassie realized she hadn't eaten. She fixed a peanut-butter sandwich, poured herself a glass of milk, and sat down on the floor next to her mother, leaning up against the cabinet door. Behind the door were cleaning solvents and toilet-bowl chemicals and various ammonias and bleaches, some still bearing the neon-green MR. YUCK! stickers from years before. Poppy had put the stickers on.

"Look how dirty your hands are," Laura said, "up against that perfectly white bread."

Cassie looked. "Yep."

"It's sort of pretty, isn't it, the contrast."

Belle made a sound from the table, a small disgusted explosion.

"Is that— Are your fingers *blue*?" Laura's innocent, beleaguered tone. "Were you playing pool?"

Cassie shrugged, looked away from Laura, whom she could feel continuing to stare at her for some seconds. Then there was the snap of the cigarette case opening, and the grinding of the wheel on the lighter, and Laura had looked back out the window, Cassie knew. Leaning against the cabinet door reminded her of a dream she'd had lately, a Replacement Dream, she was thinking of calling it. The Original Dream had been of flying way up in the air, above rooftops and treetops; once she had seen the details of a weathervane on top of an old barn. Once she had crash-landed in a pond and scared herself so badly she'd jumped out of bed. She had those dreams for a long time, she just spread her arms and fell forward (or backward, on one memorable occasion) and let the wind take her, nothing to it. And then she had a dream in which flying required a code word, and Cassie didn't have it. The only way she could get it was to turn her head and look over her left shoulder as a flying horse crossed the path of the moon, and somehow she managed it, and then she was up in the air and the feeling in her gut was stronger than when she was just sailing over barns like Peter Pan. That went on a while, the searching for the code or the key; once it was in a refrigerator in a dark basement, and the refrigerator was filled with vials of something. But the Original Dream was completely gone, Cassie could sense it, because now she was dreaming that she had to enter a windowless room of her own house, or at least she was told repeatedly it was her own house, and kneel in front of what might be a filing cabinet or a kitchen cabinet just like this one, open the door, and roll into it backward as if she were doing a backward somersault, and then she was propelled into what the Other People in the dream called flying, except where was the sky, where was the air? She seemed to remain in the cabinet with this strange, tossed-about, sick feeling in her gut that was like the flying feeling, only much stronger. And no flying.

Laura cleared her throat, said, "I know you're the only one who remembers, Cassie, besides me, and that's what's wrong with you."

Cassie put her milk glass down slowly and rested the sandwich on top of the glass and wiped her mouth with the back of her hand. Belle's pencil stopped for a moment, then continued.

"He was so sweet," Laura said, "he was the sweetest, funniest man. I was engaged to someone else, you know, at home, before I came here."

Cassie didn't move, but of course she knew, she'd known for years.

"*He* had money. He had old family money, which doesn't mean anything here, there's no such thing. And I had my whole life planned out, how things would be after I'd married him, what our children would be named and where I'd sit in church and what my relationship to his mother would be, his brothers. And all that money, like Christmas every day. I even knew which chair on the veranda would be mine during the carnival season. I didn't know, I was nineteen years old, I didn't know that the heart can make grave mistakes and that who you end up married to is largely a matter of accident and then you're stuck with it forever, and I know there are people who are not stuck forever and I envy them. They have something, there's a switch in them or a special gene, I don't understand it. But from the very beginning with your father, I felt that every decision we made, every move we made, was wrapped in a kind of holy light, no doubt because I had been driven mad by Catholic school and I felt guilty for the things I'd done with him which are not the issue and I'm not going to mention them. Two weeks, that was how long we had together. And then he left New Orleans in a stolen truck with a pool table in the back. And I. Cassie. If you ever engage in something you perceive or misperceive as holy, you will not let it go and you will not defile it. And so I packed one suitcase and jumped on a bus and followed him here, it took twenty-six hours, and all that time I was feverish with fear and it seemed such a long time but in fact was nothing. Because time is relative, isn't it, Belle, and now I've been sick with following him for thirteen years and that bus trip passed in the blink of an eye."

Cassie turned her head and looked at she, the tight posture Belle had developed from sitting so long at the table with a pencil in her hand, her head tilted to the right. Belle glanced up, and the look she gave her sister was complicated, it seemed part cold anger and part fish on a hook. If someone else were here, Poppy or Edwin, Laura would stop. But Cassie couldn't make her stop.

"And when I got here, you know. But what I want to tell you is something I've been remembering all day today, it was something that happened after all the drama—well, all the initial drama— had cleared up, and Jimmy and I went to the justice of the peace and got married, I cried all through the ceremony, I didn't even know why I was crying." Laura stared at the yard as if the answer were there somehow, a scene she'd missed in an old tale. "I bet a lot of women would say the same, if they were honest. We were married at the courthouse in Hopwood by a little man who looked just like Elvis would have if he'd lived to be eighty, and if he'd somehow gotten shrunk by a ray gun. And this little judge or clerk or whatever he was couldn't read our names, he called us Larry and Sally. And when he said Do you Larry, your dad said so officiously, *I Do*, and I was laughing and crying at the same time, and we were married under those names. We might not be legally married for all I know. And we went to a motel at the edge of Hopwood and spent one night there and I know the whole idea of your parents' wedding night must be psychologically shocking, but in truth we spent the whole night laughing, Jimmy detailing his many exploits to me, remember we didn't know each other. And then the next morning he said he had to go take care of a few things and he left me there, and I slept awhile, and then walked around the parking lot, and watched the cars on the highway, and the whole day passed. There wasn't a telephone in the room and I didn't know where to call anyway, and that's when it started, I was sitting on the curb in the parking lot and I started saying to myself, *I married him*, *I* married *him*, *I married* him, and I knew I couldn't call my mother because she'd said I was *dead to her*. I'd left her to clean up the mess of my broken engagement, and remember she still had to work for his family, and all of her hopes

for the future had been tied up in my marrying him. And Jimmy
didn't come back all that day or that night, and then I got really
scared, because I didn't know if he'd paid for the room or if I was
going to get kicked out and I didn't have any money, not a dime,
and I was from the South and the people in the Midwest are so
cold, they're so judgmental and superior, they act as if we aren't
all human making human mistakes, but in fact *they* are human
and you are something lower in the hierarchy and you disgust
them. I'm exaggerating but if you knew how people in Louisiana
would react to an abandoned pregnant bride as opposed to how
people in Indiana would you'd see I'm not far off the mark. I
walked around in a daze saying I married him, I married him, and
I had no money and no food. I finally took the change Jimmy left
on the dresser, and got something out of a vending machine. But
the more important thing is that I didn't call my mother or Buena
Vista because it was already too late, no one could help me, I had
crossed over. All I could do was wait for him and hope he would
return and save me, because no one could do it but him. There's
probably a name for this illness, I don't know, I had entered some
other atmosphere. I married him. And he showed up the next day
and of course I cried and hit him and screamed and threw things,
and then he gathered me up and we came here to Poppy's house,
and Belle was born and I knew he was still seeing Barbara, everyone knew it and he didn't really try to hide it, and then you were
born, Cassie, and he was still seeing her, and there was a single
time I might have left him but it passed. Everything before that
time and everything after it was the same and it is still the same, I
want you to understand this, because later you're going to look
back I'm afraid and think I had no pride or I was filled with self-
hatred, that's probably all true but it isn't the whole story."

Laura lit another cigarette and blew the smoke out through her nose, and Cassie looked down at the blue chalk on her fingertips. She scrubbed her hands against her jeans, but it was embedded in her nails and even in the whorls of her fingerprints and wouldn't come off.

"I stayed and I stay, Cassie, because of that holy light. To this very day I pass the grocery store where he and I went for a cold root beer the day I first got here, the day I got off the bus, and even though he told me he was engaged to someone else, I look at that grocery store and see the holy light. The courthouse in Hopwood is holy, the little wizened Elvis clerk is one of the saints. And after you girls were born, you can't imagine how that increased. Everything you wore, every piece of furniture you touched, it's all sacred, this house and yard where you took your first steps, even—I swear this is true—the faucets in the bathtub, because I turned them on and off so many times giving you baths, and he gave you baths, those are our faucets and they're filled with holy light. Do you see what I'm saying, I could leave him, I could leave this house and try to find a way to start again but there is no place to go because I took my vows and what is done can't be undone. I can't very well take you away from Poppy, he has nothing else left, and so I'd have to stay in Roseville and Roseville is sacred because my marriage and my children are sacred, and so I'd be living in the shadow of my own life and every day seeing the light in the grocery store and in a park bench where I sat with him once and in the gas station where we stopped to get gas on a family trip to Clifty Falls when you were babies; it's tender, this feeling I'm talking about, it's a feeling you can't put any pressure on because it hurts too much. If I could go back to the time I had the strength to leave I would, I'd do it and accept the consequences, but I can't go back."

The clock ticked in the sudden silence, Belle's pencil scratched out a description or a question or a revelation.

"I'm trying to say it really really irritates me, Cassie, the way you favor him and wait for him and suffer his cruelties, but I understand it perfectly well. I do. If he said to me any day, any hour, that he was coming home, I'd let him come, I'd welcome him home, and so there might be days ahead, they might have already happened, when I act like I hate you because of him, but in fact it's the other way around."

Cassie stood, stretched her legs. They'd fallen asleep, sitting on the hard floor. She threw the rest of her sandwich away, then stepped in front of Laura and washed out her milk glass, placing it carefully on the towel. "Good-night," she said, to no one in particular.

"'Night," Belle said.

"Good-night, sweetheart," Laura said, without looking at her.

In her bed, Cassie lay on her back and looked out the west-facing window; she thought she would never sleep. Her shoulders ached and she wondered if maybe she should get up and try to remember some of the things Uncle Bud had said so she would write them down, but it was no use. They were tangled up now in Laura's story. When Laura was growing up, Cassie knew, she'd had a religion, she'd gone to Catholic school, and her whole life had been Catholic. Cassie had found a cigar box in the attic years before, filled with cards, prayer cards and funeral cards, Laura must have collected them when she was a girl. There were pictures of Mary, shepherds, guardian angels guiding children over a rickety bridge. And some of Jesus. Cassie had stolen one of him, for reasons she didn't understand. He was looking out, looking at her, and his robes were wide open and the inside of his chest exposed. Belle found it in Cassie's drawer one afternoon, putting laundry away, and had carried it into the kitchen, saying, "Look what I found: the Radioactive Heart of Jesus." Belle had laughed, she had no use for Catholicism, thinking the Greeks far superior. And Laura had laughed for reasons of her own. But Cassie had snatched the card away and, unable to remember why she'd wanted it at all, buried it in the backyard in a sandwich bag.

Laura had had all those cards and a rosary and a lace cap she wore in church—Cassie couldn't quite put a structure on what she was thinking—but her daughters had done without. Jimmy had the gods he believed in and no others, and no one could put a name to them or quite work out their powers; sometimes they were kind and sometimes they kicked his ass, is what Jimmy said. But Laura. She had traveled a long distance, a long, long way. Cassie stretched out her legs and raised her arms above her head, corner pockets, then lowered her arms like a snow angel: side rails. And when Laura found herself alone in that motel room, no mother father sister Christ crucified or Blessed Virgin Mary, she had been . . . Cassie raised and lowered her arms, she felt like the bed was rocking her . . . Laura hadn't been completely alone, had she? Belle had been there, just a seed. But Laura hadn't mentioned that, and Belle, too, had kept her peace. Cassie slept.

In the morning she got up very early and went downstairs, trying hard not to wake anyone. She made lunch, left a note on the kitchen table, got her bike out of the garage, and tested the chain. It was still good. She rode down the King's Crossing to 300 West, turned right, and headed in to Roseville, then through town to Railroad Street. At Uncle Bud's she parked her bicycle in the shade and sat down on the rear steps and waited for him to come and open the back door. She took an apple and a sandwich out of her backpack, along with a chocolate milk; she finished them before the sun was fully up. All that day she waited, and when Uncle Bud arrived at three o'clock, she asked him if he'd be willing to give her a set of keys. She told him she was a person he could trust.

THE FLOOD, 1985

◈

*C*assie had gathered up Laura's library books from around the house and matched them against the receipt she'd been given when she checked them out. They were all present and accounted for. She put them in the truck. Belle had given her the grocery list, and she'd put that in her back pocket and gone to Uncle Bud's to practice for three hours, then over to his ramshackle house on a back street in Roseville. He needed help hanging the kitchen cabinets he'd gotten at an auction. By late afternoon she was headed out of town toward the library in Hopwood.

In the library parking lot she'd gone through the books, removing Laura's bookmarks, the scraps of paper on which she sometimes made notes, and had come across a whole piece of paper folded in half. This:

> 1. *We dream of rational creatures transcending*
>   *the stain. Gauze and feathertip,*

the spill of clean scent like a trumpet bell,
a bargain in the confectioner's market.

In truth they judge and bruise.

2. *Rather than kick it we tried to lift the dead*
   horse. He stood for a moment and we prayed
   he would fall away from us. I remember the place
   on his belly where the fur was rubbed thin
   and how when he landed his head hit last
   and the remaining air in his lungs rutted the grass.

O, for a falconer's voice,
To lure this tassel-gentle back again!

It had been handwritten by Laura, with no date and no title, on a light green sheet torn from a stenographer's pad with the orphaned scraps of paper clinging to the top. Cassie had never held with leaving such scraps, and now, reading the poem, or whatever it was—an idea, a group of sentences—she plucked them off one by one and dropped them on the floor of the truck. Laura and Belle talked about poetry all the time, but Cassie had no particular feelings about it. There was a way in which the obscuring of communication was painful, but the opposite was also true. She had no interest in anyone presenting her with the bleak, unvarnished truth. If Belle were here, Cassie thought, she would try to figure it out a word at a time, and she'd stick with it until she could make some judgment. Belle would take this tack in part because she had nothing better to do, and because the process of analysis struck her as pleasurable. Cassie shook her head at the notion. Belle enjoyed analysis, with the result that she was back at the house with Laura; and Cassie, at sixteen, was the only person in the house with a driver's license and a vehicle, and the beginnings of tendinitis in her right elbow. She rubbed her elbow, then went inside the library to face the kindness of the librarians. The librarians were always kind.

She had memorized the poem, or whatever it was, and was repeating it to herself as she turned on to 732 East, the Percy Creek Pike. It was a long straight road all the way to the reservoir, and she would travel it for miles, so she sped up. Who were *they* who judged and bruised? Which rational creatures could transcend the stain, and the stain of what? And when had Laura ever been on a horse? And when had she seen a horse fall? Cassie passed the squat cinder-block building out of which a man with a wooden leg (which he kept displayed at all times; he actually rolled up his pant leg to do so) used to sell produce in the summer. The building had been unused for years. Next to the front door, in emphatic black lettering, someone had painted NO CAR WASHING!, as if that were the world's gravest temptation. Then there was nothing on either side of the road, just trees and fields. Cassie squinted. Far in the distance she could see something in the middle of the road. Heat shimmered upward. Beware the mee-rahj, as Jimmy used to say; a lot of the world looks like one thing but is really something else. When she was fourteen, she and Bud had traveled to Georgia for a big game, a serious money game, with the man who was at that time unbeatable, Lewis Lee. Cassie had played him all night in a cowboy bar (no cowboys in evidence), her fortunes rising and falling, until finally Lewis pulled it out and remained unbeatable, and Cassie and Bud turned around and headed home. She had been driving for hours in the dead of night when she saw a deer standing in the middle of the road (had it been a horse?), standing only a few feet away, standing and staring in that impassive way of the massive thing. Cassie had slammed on the brakes and thrown Bud, even wearing a seat belt, so far forward he had bruised his sternum and been mad at her for a week. She kept asking, Should I have hit it? And he would say, There was *No Damn Deer*, and she would say, Yes, but should I have hit it?

She slowed. The thing in the middle of the road was about the size of a three-year-old boy and was picking at the stringy remains of something, raising and lowering its head. It was mostly in her lane. A turkey buzzard. She was getting closer to it, and she would be damned if she would swerve. She thought she'd go ahead and speed up, she'd go ahead and get thick into events with this bird. She didn't care what they did or how foul they were, they could ravage all the carcasses of her county. But they weren't going to boss her around in terms of driving. She was twenty feet from the bird and it didn't move, and she was ten feet from it, a hot day and both her windows down, and just as she moved over—she did move at the last minute—the buzzard decided to take flight, and took flight. It spread its wings like an enormous black kite, and as Cassie passed it, the wind moving through the cab of the truck pulled the bird in through her window. For a single moment its lizard-skinned claws, its breast and face, were on her, one claw caught her forearm and tore it. She slammed on her brakes, and the bird tumbled out. It took flight with an awkward turn and then a terrible, fluid ease.

Cassie parked the truck at the side of the road and got out, doubling over in the heat. That, Cassie decided, was what a nightmare would smell like; the unbelievably dense odor of decay, layer after layer, no end to it. Her forearm was bleeding, and she could still smell the bird on her clothes, and in her hair. She gasped, kept her head down. Beneath her the pavement shimmered.

"Where are the groceries?" Belle asked.

"I didn't get to the grocery store," Cassie said from the mudroom, taking off her work boots, her jeans.

"Why not? Oh my God, what is that smell, don't even think you're coming in here. What happened, what is that smell? Where are the groceries?"

"Get me some clean clothes, Belle."

"You smell like. Not a morgue, not a cemetery, not a funeral home. None of those places smell. A slaughterhouse, no, I don't know. A war crime. That's what you smell like." Belle picked at a scab on the back of her hand, under which there was an imaginary blackberry thorn that she had been trying to remove for a couple of years. She was wearing Laura's shoes; every time she took a step, her feet slid out.

Cassie remembered the poem in the pocket of her jeans, removed it, and put the jeans in the washing machine. "I could use some clean clothes here, Belle."

"Did you, have you, did you *roll* in something?"

"And a towel. I'll shower in the basement."

"Please don't go down there, Cassie, those stairs don't have any backs on them, and I don't like the way that bare bulb is, the way that bulb is. And I remember that shower, it's just a nozzle sticking out of the wall, and you just stand there in the middle of the room, no stall or anything, there could be all sorts of, I think you should come on in."

"In my room, Belle, clean clothes and underwear, a towel."

"What is that, what's on your arm? What happened to your arm?"

"I had a run-in with a buzzard."

"Oh God. You're going to get septus, septu-something, I can't remember the rest, like a cat scratch, how did it happen, a buzzard? Did you say a buzzard, like a vulture, you mean?" For a long time Belle's hair had been blond, but lately it had turned toward brown and was dry, she tucked it compulsively behind her ears. She was thin, thinner than Laura, her grocery lists always said: yogurt, celery, ice. Laura added: cigarettes, butane fluid, corn flakes. One of the scabs on Belle's upper arm was bleeding, and a piece of toilet paper was stuck to it.

"It was squatting in the road like a three-year-old boy."

Belle swallowed, picked now at her left arm. "A three-year-old boy?"

"Or a midget dressed all in black."

Belle said nothing, looked away.

"It was picking at the strings of a rabbit."

"A rabbit?"

"I passed it too close with my windows down, I thought it would fly away before I reached it."

"So you were in a bit of a contest. With the vulture."

"Sort of."

"And you lost."

"It would appear." Cassie stood in the mudroom in her boxer shorts and sports bra, her arm throbbing. She remembered the grocery list, retrieved it from the jeans. Put them back in the washer.

"Should I get Laura?"

"No, you should get the things I asked for, along with some iodine and a bandage. I need to get this washed out and medicine on it."

"Should I call Poppy or Edwin Meyer?"

"No. You should think about the iodine, it's in the upstairs bathroom, and a bandage, and some clothes and a towel for me."

Belle nodded, then looked down and studied one of the imaginary thorns under her skin. "A little boy, you say? Or a dwarf?" She would write these phrases, Belle would, on slips of paper and save them.

"That's right. I'll shower, then go to the grocery store, then I'm going to Emmy's. And bring me my cowboy boots, they're next to my bedroom door. The ones with the two holes over the left ankle."

"Two holes?"

"The snake bite. Where the snake bit me."

Her sister stood still a moment, blankly. Then said, "You've had a great fright."

Cassie took a deep breath. "Belle."

At Emmy's house, hanging on the wall in the family room behind the big television, was a plaque that showed a man's dress shoes and said THE GREATEST GIFT A MAN CAN GIVE HIS CHILDREN IS TO LOVE THEIR MOTHER. Emmy's mother favored pastel-colored scented candles, never lit. In Emmy's kitchen was wall-to-wall indoor-outdoor carpeting in blue, and the walls were painted light blue with a wallpaper border of blue ribbons; the furniture was heavy early American. A corner hutch displayed dishes and glassware, including plates Emmy and her younger brother, Jeremy, had painted in a ceramics class at Vacation Bible School. The round kitchen table shone with a thick varnish, and in the center sat a wooden lazy Susan that held salt and pepper shakers shaped like windmills, a plastic bottle of ketchup, and a basket of peach-colored silk flowers. These things, the windmills, the ketchup, and the peach flowers, had been there as long as Cassie could remember. An infinite number of props are necessary to shore up a serene family life, that's what Laura would have said, and once Emmy's parents, Mike and Diana, had gathered those props, they didn't change them. They didn't even move them.

"Heavenly Father," Mike began, "we thank you for this meal spread before us. We thank you for our health, and for our loved ones, for giving us the fruits of the spirit and the blessings of Your Love. Please help us use this food to the nourishment of our bodies so that we are better able to perform your work, in the name of your son, Jesus Christ, Amen."

Also on the table was a bowl of canned peas that had perhaps been in the can too long. They had gone sort of gray. A plate stacked with slices of white bread just out of the loaf, a tub of margarine, five glasses of milk, dehydrated Parmesan cheese. A serving bowl was filled to overflowing with spaghetti in a hamburger sauce, and beside each plate was a steak knife, because Mike and Diana had taught their children to carve their spaghetti into one-inch strips before eating it.

"Cassie, your mom's okay?" Diana asked, serving the spaghetti.

"Fine. Thanks."

"And your sister?"

"Also fine."

"Her last summer at home." Diana gave a sad smile. "Emmy, pass this to your brother. You'll miss her, Cassie."

Had it been a question? One never knew with Diana, in the same way one never knew whether she was content in her life or had moved so far to one edge of the Despair Continuum, as Laura called it, that she appeared to be content. Cassie was tempted to say something like Miss Her? What does that mean, Miss Her? The bread at Emmy's was always too soft to withstand the spreading of the cold margarine, so Mike and Diana had taught their children to fold the piece of bread in half, with margarine in the middle, and eat it that way.

"I won't miss Emmy when she goes to college," Jeremy said. At fourteen he was so insufferable that Emmy had taken to calling him Greasy Little Monkey, and even he didn't dispute the name. "I'll never miss her ever, not a day of my life."

"I'm sure you don't mean that," Diana said, carving her pasta.

"I do! I hate her! She's—"

"You know you love each other."

"I don't love her! I hate everything—"

"That's enough." Mike gave Jeremy a warning glance, then went back to eating. Jeremy blinked back tears, his face red, all of his acne agitated and glowing. Cassie thought Jeremy might be less pimpled if he were allowed to say how much he hated Emmy. She could hear Laura's voice asking blandly, *So you hate your sister? That's fine.*

"Belle's valedictorian speech was really something, wasn't it, Cassie," Diana continued. "I wish I'd taken a dictionary with me to the graduation."

Emmy, who had so far stayed quiet, took a deep breath and sat back in her chair.

"Now, Emmy, don't get huffy, I was trying to say how impressed I was."

"No you weren't, you were—"

"Put a plug in it, Emmy." Mike wiped his mouth with his napkin, went back to eating.

Cassie took a few bites of her spaghetti. Diana put sugar in her tomato sauce, Cassie didn't know anyone else who did that. She took a drink of milk; at Emmy's house they drank whole milk, at Cassie's house skim.

"She's leaving for IU in the fall?"

"Excuse me?" Cassie asked, setting her glass down.

"Belle's leaving for IU in the fall. To study what."

Emmy took another deep breath, Cassie cleared her throat. "Classics. Classical culture, Greek and Roman literature. Latin, I think."

"All those things!" Diana had a skin ailment that had caused the pigment around her eyes to die, so she had the opposite of dark circles.

"Mom."

"They're mostly the same thing, I think," Cassie said.

"I see." Diana gave her the smile again. Her sleeveless blouse was white with small red polka dots and a wide collar. "Well."

"Mom."

"Can it, Emmy." Mike never made eye contact with anyone. He sold cars at a Ford dealership on the edge of Roseville and spent all his spare time mowing his lawn. Cassie wondered if he looked directly at his customers. He severed his spaghetti, shoveled it in his mouth.

"Emmy will maybe never go to college, will you, Emmy, because you can't pass algebra, even though I've already passed algebra and by the time I'm your age I'll be taking trig and calculus and by the time I'm your age you'll be a fat housewife."

Jeremy seemed to be riding the rails of something; Cassie felt like congratulating him, except he was red-faced and his lips seemed to periodically get caught on his braces, and he still looked like he was about to cry.

"Shut up, you little— Just shut up," Emmy said, her jaw clenched. She moved as if she might hit him, and Mike didn't say anything but rose out of his chair and hovered slightly above the table, his hands in fists at his sides.

Diana ate a bite of peas. "You'll give your mom and sister my best, I hope, and tell Belle we're all real proud of her. She certainly is one of Roseville's finest."

Emmy stood up. "We're leaving."

"Where are you going?" Mike asked, the threat thick in his voice.

"To Wal-Mart, Dad. And then probably to McDonald's for ice cream."

"Why do you need to go to Wal-Mart every night, Emmy?" Diana asked.

"If I see you in the McDonald's parking lot," Mike said, shoving his napkin under his plate, "with that group that loiters there, I'll take your car away."

"I'm well aware of that."

"Is that an attitude?"

"You know it's an attitude!" Jeremy sputtered. "What else does she have, she hasn't got brains or a personality!"

"Thanks for dinner, Mom."

"You didn't eat much."

"Yes," Cassie said, "thank you."

Diana smiled. "Anytime. Come back anytime."

*   *   *

They stepped outside into a fair summer evening, a couple hours left of daylight, Cassie patted the short stone statue of Jesus in the flower bed, as she always did, for luck. Emmy tipped her head back, spread her arms, said, "A beautiful night. A perfect night for killing one's parents. You drive first." She tossed Cassie the keys to her used Ford station wagon. "I'm not nervous, I'm getting way better about that. I still don't want to parallel-park. And I don't want to pass anybody. I don't understand why passing is so all-fire important. But I'm not nervous, I just want to change my clothes."

Cassie slipped into the driver's seat and started the car, which always gave a death rattle but never actually died. Emmy reached into the backseat for a pair of shorts and a pink tank top with spaghetti straps and began changing in the front seat as Cassie wound them through and out of Emmy's subdivision.

"What would old Mr. Lange make of this, I wonder," Emmy asked, shirtless, as they drove past a white colonial on the corner, "or Mrs. Griffin, the widda-woman. They'd love it, probably, you know in the sixties? in places like this development? people used to have sex all over the place with everybody, I'm telling ya. Something about keys in a bowl."

"Key parties."

"Exactly, key parties. You just know my mom and dad and Mr. Lange were all up in each other's business before we were born." She laughed. "Poor Mom. Are these shorts too tight, I'm sucking my gut in, I can't really breathe, are they too tight? Why won't you look?"

Cassie approached a Village Pantry, turned in. "They're tight enough, I bet."

"What are you doing?"

"You need gas."

"I've got plenty of gas, look at that, there's probably, is that a fourth or an eighth?"

"Neither one."

"Well, it's still plenty, let's go."

Cassie pulled up to the pump, put in ten dollars' worth of gas, paid the skinny woman behind the counter who'd been there for years, smoking and looking like a chicken, a smoking chicken, then got back in the car, where Emmy was applying orange-scented lip gloss, and eyeliner to the inside of her bottom eyelid.

"Cassie, you about filled my tank up. I don't have any money."

"I don't need your money."

"Yeah, well, that's true. You know my mom was all raggin' on Belle because she couldn't say what she really wanted to."

"Which was what."

"'So, Cassie, I hear you're quite the billiards player. The apple doesn't fall far from the tree, does it. You've turned out exactly like your dad, haven't you. A charming man, as I understand it.'" Emmy's imitation of Diana was perfect. "'Is this, now, is billiards going to be the way you—'"

"Emmy."

Emmy looked at her.

"I don't give a shit about what your mom thinks of me."

"I know."

"No offense."

"None taken." Emmy looked out the window.

Cassie turned on to the highway, headed out of town.

The house had been in bankruptcy for a year, and there didn't seem much of a chance that anyone would buy it *today*, Puck was fond of saying when Emmy fretted about them getting caught. Someone might eventually buy it, but not *today*. It was a gruesome little place on a floodplain; a gruesome house, that is, but anyone could see why the people who owned the land would be tempted to build there. The lane leading back to it was a quarter mile long, a straight lane traveling down a hill and into what looked to be a thirty-acre bowl surrounded by old hardwoods. You couldn't see the house or anyone visiting it from the road, and from the house there seemed to be no other world. When Cassie and Emmy arrived, there were already four or five pickup trucks backed around the big fire ring they'd built as a group, the fire was just getting started. Somebody was playing a Lynyrd Skynyrd tape in his truck—this was the usual fare, along with the Stones, Little Feat, Grand Funk Railroad. Cassie parked the car and Emmy hopped out barefoot because Brian was there and she was compelled by the baroque and unyielding urges of mating, according to Laura.

Cassie walked around the perimeter of the house. It looked the same as it had last week, an ugly, ugly dwelling. It was a cube made of cinder-blocks trimmed with cheap pine painted to look like California redwood; one corner of it was windows that looked into what had been the living room. The flimsy screen door would no longer latch, and after the house flooded, the storm door wouldn't close, either. Cassie stepped inside. Something here never ceased to be interesting: the fishy, moldy smell, or the brick floor unevenly laid, the freestanding corner fireplace wrapped in a metal bell like a woman's skirt. There must have been a rug on the floor, and maybe bookcases. Probably not bookcases. The couch would have sat here, facing a television. Life, Laura would have said, faced the television. But not at her house. It had been allowed when Cassie and Belle were little, but it had since become Forbidden, and had been given away. Casssie didn't walk into the kitchen. There was a gap where the refrigerator had been that glared like a missing tooth, and the cabinet doors had swelled and now hung open on their hinges. But here, in the living room, she could see again the interesting thing—The Line—all around the room and only six inches from the ceiling, where the water had stopped. The Waterline. This room, this house, had been completely submerged. There were moments when the elements converged in such a way that this ridiculous little cube, badly planned and poorly constructed, had taken on the majesty of a sunken ship, and everything inside, the silverware and the coffee cups, the floating end tables, became poignant.

"Where is Miss Cassie?" she heard Puck call. "Where is yon Cassandra? Get away from the stinky house, maiden! Be not obsessed with the stinky house!"

Or this could be one spot, one tale, in a town that voted to flood itself. Perhaps the government had said they would no longer rebuild, no longer declare a state of emergency, your bad planning does not constitute, etc., and the only option the cinderblock people had was to sell. Cassie had had dreams of houses: she had a long series of dreams in which she drove along roads she recognized, a grid, and arrived finally at her house—*her* house—and there was so much to be done to repair it. The inside was filled with old furniture, debris, clothes left lying as if the Rapture had come and the righteous didn't even get to keep their pink dresses and coveralls.

"Cassandra! Put down your tape measure! The cause is lost!"

She walked into the hallway, and there was The Line. The bedrooms were also cubes, the visual representation of inner desperation, Laura would have said. In Cassie's dream house, the front door had three stained-glass panels: on the left was a perfect rendering of a small and twisted tree. In the middle was a boy kneeling in prayer, looking up at the sky. On the right was the sky itself, deep blue, a moon, a star. And the staircase in the parlor was dangerous and wide, and led up into pure darkness, and every night she could work on only one room. So she had started at the beginning, in the parlor, its mountain of debris, the hulking old piano. She had worked all night, hauling things out to the truck and studying the damage to the hardwood floors, and before morning she had taken a sledgehammer to the disintegrating walls and discovered that the plaster was mixed with horsehair, and in her dream the hair waved through the walls like seaweed.

"I know you're in there, Cassandra! You must come out and join America's beautiful people!"

Mornings she felt as if she'd never slept at all, and every night she thought it was surely over, she'd never see the house again, but somehow she returned. She completed the whole ground floor, she did things she'd never attempt in real life, and all alone. The tools she needed were always within reach. Then she moved ahead, into the darkness upstairs, and everything changed again. She was confronted with nostalgia, the discomfort of studying someone else's family photographs, trunks filled with memorabilia and rotting letters, fur coats, a contraption that might have been a birdcage and which Cassie was loath to study, a nest made of daily leavings. She had dealt with it gently, kept what she could keep, discarded the most intimate artifacts of the lost life, and she had turned the upstairs into one large room made of light, the room she would truly, standing here awake, live in if she could choose.

"I'm worried about what Brian Whittaker will attempt with our Emmy! I fear his intentions are less than honorable! He's afraid of you! Please come out!"

One night, the final night, she had driven the now familiar roads out to the house and pulled into the driveway, and there was the wide front porch painted dark blue, and there was the front door with the boy in prayer, but when she turned the doorknob, it was locked. The back door, too, was locked, and all the windows, and Cassie with no key. And she knew it didn't bear thinking about, how she had felt in the dream and the questions that had plagued her all the next day. Awake, asleep, the line was so thin, she looked everywhere. She didn't have the key, hadn't seen it, wouldn't know it if she found it. But over the weeks they'd been coming here, to the sad little cinder-block on the beautiful land, Cassie had begun to develop a theory: in truth she'd been standing on a precipice all along. Somewhere in the tangled garden behind her dream house, once when she'd explored it surrounded by lazy bees, once when she'd traveled as far as the boneyard, she had dropped it. She'd dropped the key, and it had fallen into the water at the edge of the world, it had fallen past the place where light can penetrate, past the steeple of the sunken Methodist church; it had slid down the curved metal roof and floated on a current completely out of town. It had ended up here, at this ugly house, a site so deep only the blind fish could survive, and a blind fish had swallowed it.

She stepped out the front door just as Bobby Puck was about to call for her again.

"There you are," he said, his spreading smile. He handed her a pint of Southern Comfort, and she took a long drink. "Cassie, we want to watch you *dance*."

* * *

They all smelled smoky, they had eaten and danced. Cassie was not drunk but not entirely sober when she realized Emmy and Brian and Emmy's car were all missing. And where was Bobby Puck? Cassie could hear him somewhere at the edge of the flooded bowl; there was a stand of trees there, surrounding swampy land. This season Puck was claiming Satan lived there. He said, That is Satan's house, and everyone around the fire said, Okey-doke, Bob. And then he would wander over to confer with Satan, who was, he claimed (as many before him had), merely misunderstood. Ready to patch things up with his Brother. *A fallen angel, Cassie, just imagine, there is no idea more intoxicating than that.* Most of these summer nights, Cassie liked to reach the point where she wasn't precisely steady on her feet. Then she stopped. By morning she was fine, or relatively so, and she could practice two or three hours and still work.

"You can go with us."

Cassie turned. Clay and Gary were standing next to Gary's truck, the two were always together. She went over and slipped in on the driver's side; the vinyl was still warm from the day's sun. Gary got in after her, he was a giant, shambling man in an old T-shirt from a Dead show, the sleeves cut off, and overalls. His long hair was down, his beard was full. He was only in his mid-twenties but seemed much older. Cassie imagined him lying down, a bearskin rug. Clay had long red hair tied back in a loose ponytail, a big red beard, more a Viking than a bear. He worked with his father on the family farm east of Roseville. His marijuana crop was legendary for its potency and consistency; he specialized in a Hawaiian variant called Orange, so named for the orange buds, heavy and sticky with resin.

They pulled away from the house and down the lane lined with locust trees so old they would eventually begin to die and no one would be able to prevent it. Honey locusts, too, the kinder of the species.

"You're a pool player, huh?" Clay asked, smoking a cigarette with his elbow out the window.

"Yep."

"It's early, you want to go shoot a few games? That okay with you, Gary?"

Gary shrugged. "Fine with me."

"I'll play you for money. Otherwise, take me on home."

Clay laughed. "Play you for money, huh, Spark-plug? Those the rules?"

"Otherwise, take me home."

Gary drove silently.

"Gary's not competitive," Clay said, blowing smoke out the window. "He says of our baser nature, *just like cheetahs on the veldt.*"

Cassie looked straight ahead, thinking of the house. "Whatever."

Most of the tables were busy at Uncle Bud's. Cassie got three beers out of the refrigerator; Bud was washing glasses in the sink behind the bar. He couldn't abide men with beards, or any other characteristic that made them appear escaped from a cave, but he didn't say anything. Clay had been there before and was widely known. How known he may have been to Bud was not Cassie's business, or any interest of hers. They each chose a house cue, then Cassie unlocked the glass room and turned on the light. She asked Clay if he wanted a handicap and he smiled and said no. She said they could play as a team, two against one, but no trick shots on this table.

"Straight, 9-ball, 8? Which one do you want to play?"

Clay said he'd only ever played 8-ball, and would ten dollars a game be too much? Cassie said that would be fine. They lagged for the break, which Cassie took, and as she was racking the balls, she realized that in the truck she'd had a warm feeling for the two men, a sort of camaraderie, and it was gone. The best course of action, she decided, would be to kick their asses and take their money, and they could make it up around the campfire some other night.

She shot so hard on the break that her feet came up off the floor, and the crack of the balls caused Gary to jump. She sank a solid and a stripe and could choose which to take by the layout of the table. She chose highs, moving around the table quickly, sinking the eleven on a slice so thin Clay moaned and slapped his head. When only the eight was left, Clay whispered to Gary that she couldn't make it. The cue was on the center spot and the eight was an inch or so from the side rail. The two ball was between the eight and the pocket. Cassie used her cue to sight the angle to the opposite pocket, called it, and banked it with a medium shot. Clay took a ten-dollar bill out of his pocket and handed it to her; she asked if they'd like to play another.

On the next break Cassie pocketed the one and the nine. She could have made a long shot on the three—if the stakes had been higher, she would have taken it—but took a safety instead. A part of her wanted the two men to enter the game. Clay let Gary shoot first for their team, and a lot was revealed about him, first by his shot, which was bored and imprecise, and later by his choice of songs on the jukebox. "Box of Rain"; "Don't Think Twice, It's All Right"; "Walkin' After Midnight." Cassie guessed he had problems with authority that he disguised with laid-back affability.

The two men blew every shot Cassie gave them, although Clay played better than she would have guessed. After ten games Cassie had taken a hundred dollars from them, and she decided that was enough. Gary, who hadn't said much all night, asked if they'd like to go back to his house for nightcaps. There was something between the two men that made Cassie think they had a nightcap together on a regular basis. Dependence, commitment. She could vaguely hear Belle's voice, describing the love between men in ancient Greece—not the merely sexual but a love believed to be higher than any other, even that of a mother and a child. Warriors, of a sort.

Gary lived in a plain, small house in an old neighborhood in Hopwood.

"It's quiet," Cassie said as he unlocked his door.

"Lots of old people."

"Old people don't make a lot of noise," Clay said.

Inside, two large tapestries hung from the ceiling. One was Indian and depicted two lovers next to a river. The other was a medieval banquet scene swirling with images; men and women, dogs and dishes, musical instruments. A red carpet covered the floor. There were more tapestries on the wall, and lots of places to sit, pillows and a small couch, a futon in the corner. In the center of the room was a low octagonal table, old dark wood Cassie couldn't name, with lighter inlays forming a six-pointed star. The table held a brass lamp and an elaborate pipe.

"Have a seat," Gary said, gesturing toward the pillows. Clay had already settled in: he lit incense from a shoe box full of different scents; he took rolling papers and a bag of dope out of a drawer in the table. The large new television was a shock amid the tapestries—the television and VCR, the Swiss stereo, the small speakers tucked into the corners of the ceiling. Gary put in five CDs and poured them all orange juice. The orange juice would taste brilliant and clean after the bitter taste of the joint. Cassie suspected he was also the sort of man who would turn the heat up too high in the winter, just to enjoy the feeling of stepping out into the snow. A lot of people Cassie knew needed to feel the extremes of available sensations.

Clay told her that Gary worked with him on the farm, had for ten years. "Strong as an ox," he said.

In the background a thin, unnerving voice tunneled through the conversation and reached Cassie. *More than this, you know there's nothing.*

"You're a helluva pool player," Clay said, shaking his head. "You spanked us."

"Thanks."

"My dad always says a horse runs faster against a faster opponent. I'd love to see you play somebody good."

"Your dad's a shithead," Gary said, from far away. Cassie turned; he was right next to her. "His dad's a shithead."

"So you said."

"Aw, he's all right," Clay said, coughing." "Old man, is all."

"A fascist is all. Zieg Heil is all." Gary sat up, rubbed one eye. "Dude? Don't get me started."

That song ended and another began, and Cassie didn't know this one, either. The dope was hard, waving and cresting, sometimes so violently Cassie was sure something terrible was about to happen. She could sense it but couldn't locate it, a dark shape at the edge of her vision. She closed her eyes. "Oh, listen to this, I could die when she sings this chorus," Gary said as the woman's voice soared above them, *Heathcliff, it's me, it's Cathy, I've come home*. When Cassie opened her eyes again, feeling queasy, everything was so close to her, the room, the colors, the incense, the song so gorgeous it was like a spur against bone. Gary was looking at her, his eyes arctic. For a moment Cassie thought she could sense the edge of her own tendencies, the beginning of her pirate days, their eventual end, she could not articulate this. She picked up a large pillow from the floor, said, "Leave me be for a while," and went outside and lay down in the bed of Gary's truck. She could see plots of sky through the trees; there were lots of stars. Belle and Laura and Cassie all hated that the stars were named, and changed the designations on those rare occasions they were all looking at the sky at once. Laura might say, "Look at that group over there, the one that looks like Marleybone's Back Leg," or Belle would say, "God, Cassie, pay attention, I'm talking about Poppy's Pipe, the pipe-shaped cluster." Cassie could see nothing worth naming in these sections, even stoned. She closed her eyes; the night air on her face was like a live thing. Imagine being blind, she thought, all the amazing pleasures still right there. Blind. She remembered, suddenly, a night years ago, she must have been seven or eight, when she had dreamed she was in school, making a log cabin out of pipe cleaners, and her vision began to fade. It faded a piece at a time. First she couldn't see the cabin, and then she couldn't see her teacher, and then her own hands disappeared. When she woke up in her dark bedroom, she thought it was true and stumbled out of bed with her eyes closed, because to open them would be to confirm the bare facts, then crept down the hallway to her parents' room, touching the walls along the way. She walked first into the linen closet, then backed out, hitting her face on the door. The doorknob to her parents' room was cold, and when she stepped inside, she was doubly certain she was blind because all of her other senses were heightened. She could hear her mom's shallow breathing, her dad's quicker, raspier breaths. She could smell their clothes, their tobacco, the oil from the Yoruba priestess; each scent was discrete, and Cassie could pull one away from another like rose petals, all the way down to the tight, familiar core. This was not how she thought of it at the time but was how it had to be rendered now, by a stoned person. She reached the edge of the bed and felt for her father's feet, then for his bony knees. She climbed up on the bed and lay down next to him. He smelled like her dad, no doubt about it, but to make sure, Cassie leaned over his chest and put both hands on his face, tracing the shape of his brow, his low, straight hairline, his short, straight nose. Under her fingers, his lips, which had been parted, abruptly closed. Jimmy's chin was strong, and stubbly with a day's growth of beard. He had a single dimple in his left cheek, mostly unnoticeable; one of his ears had a bump on the ridge. She had gently rubbed the fringe of his eyelashes, the soft, puffy skin under his eyes. On his right cheek he had three scars: three straight lines each about an inch long, running from under his cheekbone to the edge of his mouth. He would never say how he had gotten them.

"Cassie, can I ask?" he had said, his voice low.

"I've gone blind."

"Ah," he said, as if that often happened to sleeping people. "Want a root beer?"

In the bed of the truck Cassie dozed, flew higher, came down.

"Lot of lights on at your house," Gary said, pulling in to her driveway. And there were, especially for one o'clock in the morning. Laura and Belle weren't in the habit of waiting up if they were tired, and when they were awake, they stayed in the kitchen, at the back of the house. Edwin's car was there, too. Gary had barely slowed the truck before Cassie was out and running toward the porch. She stopped midway, then turned around and ran back. "Thank you," she said.

Gary nodded. "My pleasure."

She ran past the glass cases with Buena Vista's figurines, she ran through the living room where one of Belle's old radio-drama cassettes was playing. Cassie vaguely heard, *And then he turned the corner and discovered . . . !* The actor's voice was deep and tinged with hysteria. Belle and Laura both loved that sort of thing. In the kitchen all the lights were on, even the one over the stove. Belle and Laura were at the table with Edwin and Poppy, surrounded by cold tea cups and the butt ends of a hundred of Laura's cigarettes.

"Is he dead?" Cassie asked, breathless.

Belle made a *pffft* sound and rolled her eyes.

"Sweetheart," Laura said, "sit down."

Cassie sat down next to her mother. Poppy was holding one of his old red handkerchiefs, the kind some of her friends rolled up and tied around their foreheads, as if she were in the original cast of *Hair*. Poppy's eyes were swollen, he sniffed repeatedly, and one of his suspenders had fallen down.

"Cassie," Edwin said, leaning toward her from across the table. "I've had a disturbing phone call from your father, and also from the sheriff."

Cassie swallowed.

"Six months ago your father changed his legal residence to Barbara Thompson's house, her mobile home, you know where I mean."

The room was silent.

"Today he filed for divorce from your mother, and additionally, he filed other motions with the court."

Cassie looked at Laura, whose face betrayed nothing.

"He is seeking to emancipate you and Belle, to have you declared emancipated, and also to sever all parental obligations and rights. He wants to have you removed from the health-insurance policy he's carried for years through Farm Bureau. He is filing a lawsuit to accomplish these things."

Poppy gave a sob and covered his face with his handkerchief.

"Your grandfather feels very ashamed." Laura reached over and squeezed Poppy's shoulder, which she had probably done dozens of times over the course of the evening, and which was an indication of the gravity of the matter at hand. Laura didn't touch; she wasn't touched.

Cassie could barely breathe. She sat up very straight and took in as much oxygen as she could, then blew it out slowly, like a woman in labor.

"If you don't fight these proceedings, Cassie," Edwin continued, "Jimmy and Barbara won't prosecute you for willful destruction of property. They claim you stood outside Barbara's trailer, one week ago today, while they were inside, and threw large rocks, breaking three windows and leaving thirteen very noticeable dents in the trailer's aluminum siding."

"Fourteen," Cassie said.

"Fourteen, then," Edwin said, nodding. "They must have missed one. Jimmy also claims that when Barbara emerged from the trailer to stop you, and she has admitted to carrying a cast-iron frying pan into the argument, you delivered a single blow to her face, breaking both her nose and her eyeglasses. They won't press assault charges, either."

Poppy sobbed. His dogs whined at the door. Belle said, "Barbara Thompson is a white-trash cow."

Laura said, "Belle, you're not helping."

"I wish Cassie had killed her. Cassie could have killed her if she wanted to, I've seen her working out in the backyard with that punching bag, I've seen how hard she can kick, why didn't you kill her, Cassie, while you had the chance? And also, Edwin Meyer, and I won't say this again, tell Jimmy that I would be honored to be free of the disgrace of being his daughter, I would have jumped at the chance any time in the past eighteen years."

"Belle," Laura said.

"Cassie, your father also wants you to return his pool cue to him, which he says you are unlawfully holding."

"She won that cue fair and square!" Poppy shouted, his face a trembling mess. "I know she did, Bud told me, and everybody in Roseville heard about it, she whooped him! He didn't have to bet that cue, he could have stopped!"

Cassie placed her hands flat on the table's scarred surface. "I'll agree to anything he wants, but he can't have the cue back."

Edwin nodded. "I told him that's what you'd say. Cassie, we can fight this if you want. I'll help you."

She smiled at Edwin, at Poppy, her mother and sister, something gave way in her chest, she could actually feel it, she shook her head *no*. Fight what? What was there to fight?

She sat on the porch rocking, with Poppy's two remaining dogs. Roger had died of a seizure two years before. He had been fine one moment and gone the next. Cassie was no longer high or a little drunk, nothing. Steady on her feet. Laura went to bed, Belle went to bed, Edwin and Poppy had been washing the dishes when Cassie left the kitchen.

"Cass? Can we join you out here?" Poppy said from the doorway.

"Sure you can."

Edwin and Poppy came out, took chairs, rocked awhile without saying anything.

"I'm worried," Cassie began, "about Belle going to Bloomington."

"Well, yes," Edwin said.

"I don't want to hear anything about Belle!" Poppy said, his voice still shaky. "People are odd, they've always been odd!"

"Pop, I didn't mean—"

"What about old Luke Foster who didn't believe the right side of his body belonged to him?" he cried, now taking up gestures.

"He was kicked in the head by a horse," Edwin replied.

"What about that young fella who wore a muskrat skull around his neck? Charlie Something?"

"Charlie Something is in prison, Poppy."

"Your very own grandmother Buena Vista! looked to weigh two hundred pounds when she died, but when they took off her dress in the hospital, she weren't but skin and bones! She'd been carrying most of her belongings in bags tied around her middle with bailing twine, afraid the government would try to take her daddy's signet ring!"

Cassie had to admit it was all true. Poppy was silent a moment.

"And what about that woman Virginia Ludebecker, drives by in her old Cadillac. She didn't want to keep working at Holzinger's, so she gave up food but for German chocolate cake, and now she's got diabetes, sores all over her body, lives on disability."

"Cassie, I called the dean of students," Edwin said, directing his comments away from Poppy. "I explained the situation, and they're putting her in a single dorm room. She won't have to eat anywhere there's upholstery, and they'll make sure there's nothing blue in her room. I called Health Services, too, and they'll monitor her medication and keep salve on her arms."

"I, myself!" Poppy said, pointing at his chest, "am afraid of the dentist and have been known to pull my own teeth out with pliers. I would never swim in the ocean, even though folks do it every day, and I won't step into a place that ever held a goat."

"I'm worried is all," Cassie said.

"I know." Edwin rocked a moment. "I think she needs to go, I think she should at least try."

"I bury my fingernails after I cut 'em off," Poppy said.

"I wish this hadn't happened right before she's supposed to leave."

"Me, too. I'm so sorry, Cassie."

"They'll take her away! You're going to do or say something, and they'll take Belle away!" Her grandfather had begun to cry again.

"Lord above, Poppy, I'm not selling Tara."

Edwin patted Poppy on the knee, and he calmed down. Marleybone lay his head in Poppy's lap. The three rocked awhile longer; the hour grew very late. The black dog shook.

Part Two

A PRIVATE LANGUAGE

SAMHAIN, 1987

*A*t eight in the evening Cassie carried in the mail. It had surely been there all day, but Laura would never bring it in, left to her own devices. They got coupons for pizza, a Have You Seen This Child?, the electric bill, a letter from Belle. The sky was fully dark, but no wind. Cassie could see her breath. She studied the bare trees against the sky; this was her favorite time of year, a lull between two punishing seasons.

She carried the mail in to Laura, who was in the living room writing. The room was dim outside the circle of light from the reading lamp; Cassie didn't know what Laura wrote, had written all these years. Ten, eleven notebooks were stacked next to her rocking chair. Who would dare read them? Cassie handed all the mail but the electric bill to Laura.

"Ah," Laura said, tilting her head to see through the bottom of her reading glasses. "I see our Belle is one step closer to a degree in Letter Writing."

They owed the electric company $126.37. Cassie took out her

wallet and slipped $130 into the envelope. She would pay the bills in Hopwood tomorrow, the phone, the propane, her truck insurance.

"Belle says—hmm, let me find something we don't already know—we know she's in a different dorm. Oh, here: she got an A on her paper entitled 'Treacherous Women at the Crossroads: Aspects of Hecate in the Delta Blues.'"

Cassie nodded. "A good one."

"Indeed. She says to tell you thank you for the letter and the explanation; you helped her pass the physics test."

To get in three hours of practice in the morning and take the job putting up siding in Haddington, Cassie would have to leave the house at four in the morning. And then after work she'd pay the bills.

"What was the problem?" Laura asked.

"Excuse me?"

"What didn't Belle understand?"

"Oh. She had to write a three-page paper on how physics can be applied to a practical problem. Just conceptually. She didn't have to do any math."

"She couldn't think of anything?"

"You know Belle. She panicked." Cassie had forgotten to put on a belt. "Have you seen my knife?"

Laura glanced at the coffee table, the couch, the floor. "Not today. What did you tell her?"

Cassie slipped her hand down between the couch cushions. "I told her to look up the formula Thomas Jefferson used to design a plow." The knife wasn't there. "Maybe it's in the truck."

Laura went back to reading the letter. Belle wrote almost every day. She had settled on an area for her senior project:

women in antiquity, with an emphasis on ritual. At home over her spring break, she'd been reading a book called *Goddesses, Whores, Wives, and Slaves*.

"Do you need anything before I go?" Cassie asked.

Laura folded the letter, ran her finger along the crease. "No, thank you, sweetheart."

"Want the stereo on? You could maybe pick up Mama Jazz out of Chillicothe."

"That's okay. You're going out?"

Cassie nodded. "Puck and Emmy."

"Will you trick-or-treat?"

"I'm a little old to start." Cassie leaned back into the couch; the room felt like warm twilight. "Do I need to go to Bloomington? Is she worse?"

Laura lit a cigarette, blew the smoke up toward the lamp light. "I'll let you know. Edwin saw her two weeks ago on his way back from Cincinnati, described her as 'thriving.'"

But things could change quickly; Belle might suddenly become afraid of telephone poles or the feeling of grass beneath her feet. It could happen overnight. Cassie didn't say this.

"She's halfway through," Laura said. "Just two years to go."

They sat in silence. Laura smoked, Cassie let her head fall back against the couch. She wanted to say to Laura, *Please*, explain to me how you withstand this diminishing. Their house had become dense with absences. Buena Vista in her casket—Cassie could still see her so clearly, with her thin white hair combed out against the satin pillow. Poppy had put on her reading glasses because they made her look dignified. And there was a moment when Buena's toothbrush went missing from the bathroom, and her denture cream, the special comb she used because she was tender-headed.

Then Jimmy, his breath mints, his razor, his dancing glide through the kitchen on the way to the refrigerator. He'd grown up in this house. Gone. Belle. Cassie massaged her temples. And now, of all things, Juanita, the black dog. An inoperable tumor had grown into her jaw. Cassie had taken her that morning to be put down, then brought her back and buried her behind Poppy's trailer, next to Roger. Poppy was inconsolable and wouldn't leave the Airstream. Only Marleybone remained, a dog as tough as whit leather, but old himself, and there was nothing Cassie could do. Nothing would slow down the arrow shot through their lives. "I should change clothes and head on," Cassie said, standing.

Laura looked up over the top of her glasses, smiled at Cassie. "Be careful. There are haints abroad tonight."

The odometer in Emmy's battered station wagon was ticking toward two hundred thousand miles. As often happens, the car was kept and driven for no other reason than the goal of reaching an arbitrary number. Cassie sat in the backseat, behind Puck on the passenger's side. She could see the road through a hole in the floorboard, a hole that had begun when Emmy spilled a quart of Clorox on the carpet; the rough tan carpeting had first faded, then faded away, as had the floor itself. From the remains, Cassie guessed the floor had been either made of plywood or covered in plywood, a no-good situation. The asphalt was first charcoal gray and bumpy, then lighter and smooth as they drove faster, and finally a colorless blur. In the front Emmy and Puck smoked the joint Emmy found in her ashtray.

"Where are we going first?" Cassie asked. They were flying down an old back road, the Laramie Pike. Most drivers became greatly cautious when stoned, but Emmy sped up; it was one of her joys. They passed a crumbling family cemetery, unnamed, and the house of the veterinarian, Jay Thomas, who specialized in large animals. His own quarter horses grazed in the flat five acres next to his ranch house. They, too, were just a blur, but Cassie loved them, loved all horses. Jimmy had taught her as a child to spit on her thumb and press it to her elbow when they passed the snow-white mare who lived next to a tumble-down farmhouse between Roseville and Jonah. He said, *Wish*. She wished and wished on that horse. She wished *for* that horse, for her own dog, for the school to burn down, for hard rains and hot chocolate with tiny marshmallows, for a real Jeep she could drive whenever she wanted. Some of Cassie's desires were vague and unexpressed. Trains that blew the blues from their whistles; effigies in the trees around her house. Flight, a time machine, medicine that would make her older and taller and bound with muscle. Like all children, she wished that life might be better for her mother, that the world and all its inhabitants would change, and change again.

"Where are we going first, Emmy?" On her right was the barn where the high school built floats for the summer parade—closed up now, dark.

"You already asked that," Emmy said, rolling down her window, blowing out smoke.

"Did you answer?"

"Not yet."

They passed the Lampwell house, a disaster in the making. Ernie Lampwell hadn't had a job since he came home from Vietnam, had lived all the intervening years on government disability and his take from bathtub LSD. He used a recipe from *The Anarchist Cookbook*. Someone was bound to die, maybe already had. It was hard to keep track of people out here. And there were guns in the house, Ernie was loaded for bear, as Jimmy would have said. Cassie turned away. There was no future in looking at Ernie's house, in the mood she was in.

"Puck's looking for Dante," Emmy said, in answer to the long-ago question.

"Where?" Cassie leaned forward.

"Dante is so gone," Emmy said, flipping her ashes out the window.

"He's not entirely gone." Puck sat like a Buddha, his arms resting on his thighs. "He's around some. I heard he might be out in that trailer at the Conway place."

So that was where they went first, Halloween night. A squatter's trailer at the edge of a cow pond thick with slime and mosquito eggs. A path from the pond led straight to the barn where the livestock was kept when the Conways still owned the place. Cassie had been to parties in the barn; she'd found a cat's skull there, and had stood in the shadows cast by kerosene lamps, listening to the boasts of boys who were lean and hard, and smelled like the interior of trucks. Their hair was perpetually flattened from seed caps; they kissed so hard they split the lips of relatively innocent girls, and later turned them into ruined brides. Their mouths and their minds were black holes. Nothing with those boys lasted long, not tenderness or conversation or a bruise. In later life, after their particular brand of rage had ceased to be interesting, or after they had flown drunk through the windshield of a car, they took up religion and found pleasure in smaller ways, like kicking their sons for firing the losing shot in a county basketball game. Cassie knew just where they were going.

*   *   *

"This trailer is crooked." Cassie stood in a patch of scrubby grass, tilting her head and righting it again.

"I believe their methods of procurement were honest, all things considered," Puck said, hitching up his pants and settling them under his belly. "I believe Misty and Leroy saw it was empty and simply took up residence."

"She isn't making a moral judgment about the trailer, doofus. Where's my lighter? Puck, do you have my lighter?"

"This trailer isn't sitting on a level foundation."

"I don't have your lighter."

"Puck, if you have my lighter, give it to me. That's my favorite. I got it for free from a Marlboro man, and it seems to have an infinite supply of fluid."

"Do you understand," Cassie said, kneeling down and trying to see under the trailer, "what will happen in a high wind, I'm not even talking about a tornado?"

"Why would I steal your lighter?"

"Because your life is a constant quest for fire. You scam for lighters all the time, don't act like I don't know you."

"Is there even anybody here?" Cassie asked, looking at the dark windows of the trailer.

"Misty and them don't have a car, so I'm thinking in the affirmative."

"I'm getting a flashlight out of the car. Don't go in there yet." Cassie popped open the door to the wagon and felt around among the debris in the back: Styrofoam cups, underwear, a spare tire, a jack, a toolbox, a brown paper bag filled with rejected cassette tapes, paperback books, and finally the handle of the strong flashlight she'd insisted Emmy carry. The batteries were fine, and the beam was wide, although the light lost definition at the outer edge. Cassie thought of something she'd read; Einstein, she thought. She walked back toward the trailer, what was it? When you widen the circumference of the light, you widen the darkness outside it.

"Take out what's in your pockets and let me look," Emmy was saying. "Cassie, bring that flashlight and give Puck the once-over."

Cassie walked around the edge of the trailer, but she had been right. It wasn't even on concrete blocks. Behind it she saw a cage made of chicken wire, maybe twelve feet square, and a makeshift doghouse. She approached it carefully. One of the preferred props of the squatter set was a vicious dog, for all the obvious reasons. There was no sound from the pen, so she shone her light inside the doghouse door. Two eyes reflected flat green, and Cassie took a step backward. But there was no growling, no threat, so she walked closer. The dog stuck its head out, right into the light, then stepped fully out with a stretch.

"Jesus," Cassie said, kneeling down. It appeared that Leroy and Misty had gotten themselves a pregnant coyote. The pen was poorly constructed—strong enough for a domestic dog but not nearly so for any wild thing. Cassie had heard tales from friends who had tried to tame coyotes, or raise hybrid wolves, that the dogs could escape from any enclosure. They could watch a person open a complicated latch one time and repeat it themselves.

"Where oh where is the mistress of the torch?" she heard Puck call. The dog's ears straightened, and she turned her head in the direction of the car. Cassie's blue-jean jacket, old and washed soft, a streak of mahogany stain on the left pocket, wasn't warm enough, even with a cardigan underneath. She felt her teeth begin to chatter. The situation with the dog was bad, it was cruel and wrong to keep a pregnant dog locked in a tiny pen outside in the cold, and whatever happened when the pups were born would be even worse. They would die of some wasting disease, and the mother, who looked wild but surely wasn't, would grieve herself senseless and eventually die, too. Or Leroy and Misty would disappear in the night and never think of the dog again, pups or no pups; it was the way they lived. They didn't know how to change. The night was young; the trailer was dark. Puck was looking for Dante. Cassie didn't move. After a while Emmy came around the corner of the trailer, and the dog ducked back into the doghouse.

"Would you mind?' Emmy asked, allowing her cigarette to dangle from her bottom lip like someone she was not. She didn't know she was not, but Cassie did.

"Yeah," Cassie said, "okay." And she walked away from the dog, who let her go without a sound.

The screen door on the trailer was sprung and hung open—all the evidence anyone would have needed that the place was out of plumb. Puck knocked on the thin metal storm door, then tried turning the handle, but it was locked. He knocked again.

"Hang on!" someone shouted from inside. "I'm coming!"

Leroy opened the door, buttoning his jeans. He wasn't wearing a shirt, and Cassie noticed that he was thinner than the last time she'd seen him; his narrow chest was even more caved, his neck seemed longer. He was a tall man with curly brown hair, and his eyes were close-set over his hooked nose. Altogether he was sweet-looking, gentle and nonthreatening, a Harpo living rough. Emmy took the flashlight and shone it on her own face, then Puck's and Cassie's.

"Hey!" Leroy said, scratching his head. "A bunch of people I like!" He pulled them in one at a time. "I like you," he said, kissing Emmy on the cheek.

"I like you, too," she said, patting his back.

"And I like you, Cassie."

"I like you, Leroy."

"And I like you, Puck."

"You bet, Leroy," Puck said, embarrassed. "Where's Miss Misty?"

"She's here, she's sleeping. Mist," he called, "wake up."

"I'm awake, Leroy, I can hear you fine."

Leroy flipped a light switch, and the room came to life. The light was harsh and the room was cold and humid. Misty was prone on a queen-size mattress on the floor.

"You've got lights," Puck said, looking around. "How'd you manage that?"

Leroy shrugged. "Friend owed me a favor, came over and tapped in to that main line. Said he could give me phone service, too, but I was, like, who do I want to talk to?"

"That's the truth," Puck said, who loved his telephone.

"Man, everybody I know is hooked up in their possessions, slaved just about to their car payment and all. Ain't for me. I'm taking it easy."

Emmy walked over and knelt down next to Misty, speaking softly, while Cassie continued to stand in the doorway, studying the situation. Leroy and Misty were eighteen, they'd left home years before, and Cassie had seen all the places they'd lived. This was the worst. They'd started out in an old tenement in Jonah, living off the social security Misty got for her real dad being dead. There was something beautiful about that building, as if even the worst of intentions could grow subtle with age. They'd had an old sofa covered in red velvet, and a dining room table and chairs Leroy had stolen from a restaurant going out of business, and a proper bed in their bedroom. Misty's childhood dresser, something she'd inherited from the Buells. There were teddy-bear decals on the side, leeched of color, and her collection of school lunch boxes lined up along the floor: Strawberry Shortcake, the Care Bears, Scooby-Doo. That apartment hadn't lasted long, a few months, maybe. They were evicted when the property manager discovered fifteen people sleeping there, and Misty and Leroy had been going down ever since. Nothing was left from that first hopeful place, at least as far as Cassie could see. The sofa was gone, the table and chairs. If the lunch boxes had survived, they were nowhere in sight.

Everywhere Cassie looked, trash was tangled up in clothes and dirty blankets. There were flattened cereal boxes, spoons stuck inside plastic bowls, used Kleenex, dirty socks. And normal dirt, dead leaves stuck to the bottom of a pair of sneakers, mud, ants. Old magazines. The smell was complicated: bodies and sleep, love, smoke, grease and mice. Puck and Leroy were talking, but Cassie couldn't hear what they were saying. She was thinking of Belle away at school, the way she carried privacy with her when she walked around campus, the way even her letters seemed to be written in a private dead language. The attention to detail that made her a good scholar, her patience, her relentlessness—Belle would faint just seeing this.

"I'm looking for Dante," Puck said.

Misty sat up and ran her fingers through her hair. She stretched. She was pregnant, more than halfway there, from the look of things. She was wearing a faded maternity T-shirt that featured Garfield clutching a blanket and his teddy bear, Pookie, and sucking his thumb. Misty's breasts were swollen; Cassie had to look away.

"He's not here, man," Leroy said, pushing trash out of the way with his bare foot. "Here, have a seat. Take the best chair, you're my guest." He settled back on the mattress with Misty.

"You know where he is? Seen him lately?"

"He was here," Leroy said, looking thoughtful. "But he's not now."

Puck cleared his throat and carefully lowered his bulk to the space on the floor. "When was he here?"

"Hmmm." Leroy looked up at the ceiling. "Couldn't tell ya. You know, Mist?"

Misty yawned. A strand of her stringy hair got caught in her mouth. "What day is it today?"

"It's Halloween," Emmy said.

"Wow. *Whooooo,*" Misty made a ghost noise, then yawned again. "Wow, that late."

Cassie leaned against the wall. The light switch had no face-plate. She glanced up at the ceiling, the suspended acoustical tiles in which a cheap globe was mounted. The tiles around the light were darker, a tan fading into white. "Leroy, what kind of bulb do you have in that overhead, do you know? It seems kind of bright."

Leroy laughed. "Cassie, man, you crack me. You ask the weird-est questions. So who brought what?"

Emmy reached in her jacket pocket. "I've got a doobie or twelve. Ooh! And there's my lighter."

"Apologize to me. Apologize swiftly, Emmeline." Puck pointed a thick finger at her.

"I won't," she answered, unrolling the bag. "You didn't steal this one, but you stole a hundred others."

"You bring any food with you?" Misty asked.

"I need to find Dante, Leroy, I get the feeling he's in these parts somewhere."

"Dante's a free spirit, dude. He's cool."

"I'm partial to Tater Tots these days, seems like I can only eat Tater Tots and cold cereal."

"I've got a message for him from LeeLee."

"That his older sister? They have the same daddy?"

"I don't know his paternity. His mother has cancer all through her. She's on morphine, he needs to know."

"Mmmm," Misty said, laying her head in Leroy's lap. "Morphine and Tater Tots."

"Dante loves his mother," Emmy said, lighting a joint.

"He loves everyone."

"You got any music in here?" Emmy squeaked out the sentence around the smoke.

"Nawhh. I can sing, though."

"French fries will do when I can't get ahold of some Tots. Fried potatoes is what I'm talking about."

"What about that dog out back?" Cassie asked.

"Woof! Woof!"

"That's Nomad, she just wandered up one day." Leroy rubbed his fingertips over his chest.

"She pregnant?"

"I reckon. Puppies! I love puppies. It's going to be fun to have those little fellas around."

"Will you keep them in that pen all winter?"

"I'm thinking we'll let them stay in here with us until they get big enough, and then we'll let them go. Be free! Freedom for all living things!"

Something skittered in the kitchen, knocking over a bag of trash. An empty Pepsi can rolled through the doorway. In the kitchen they put the trash in a bag, in the living room they threw it around. Emmy passed the joint to Misty, who took a giant hit off it. She and Leroy belonged to a group, mostly boys, who called themselves the Army for Hemp Liberation, as if hemp were being held in a dingy prison in a third-world country. Leroy and Misty already had one baby, but nobody seemed to know where it was.

Cassie considered the darkness in the kitchen, the skittering, Tater Tots baking in a blackened oven. "I'm gonna go get some snacks," she said, feeling in her back pocket for her wallet.

"Whoo-hoo! Snacks!"

"Here's my keys, Cass." Emmy pulled the ring from her jacket pocket and tossed it.

"Halloween snacks!"

"Oh, that's right," Emmy said, already stoned. "It's Halloween."

Cassie had her hand on the doorknob when Puck said, "Hey, Cassandra." She turned and looked back at him.

"*Boo.*"

The Ford ran rough. There seemed to be a problem with the fuel filter, the air filter, and the plugs. Cassie drove into Jonah and went to a strip on a side street. At the Pizza King she ordered four large pizzas with everything—the Royal Feast—trying to imagine how much a group of stoned people could eat. A lot. While the pizzas were being made, she drove down to a convenience store and bought what she could there: white bread and bologna, a gallon of milk, a gallon of orange juice, eggs, cheese, four liters of Coke, and a bag of candy corn. They didn't have vegetables, but there were some apples and bananas, so she bought those and a box of chewable vitamins. She also bought three cans of wet dog food with pull-off lids, a bag of dry food, a gallon of bottled water, and sixty-watt lightbulbs. She filled Emmy's car with gas, then picked up the pizzas and drove back.

Before she carried the groceries into the trailer, she went back to the dog pen with the food and water. Someone—she couldn't imagine it was Leroy—had devised a gate of two-by-fours and chicken wire that closed with a hook and a ring. Cassie stepped inside, but the dog stayed in her doghouse. All three cans of wet food went into a corner of an old rusted cake pan, then Cassie emptied half the bag of dry, filling the rest of the pan. She found a metal bowl, completely dry, and poured the bottled water into it, then stepped outside the gate and watched the dog, a shadow among shadows, slink from the doghouse and eat the wet food desperately. She ate some of the dry, then drank water until she began to cough. Cassie opened the gate wider, as wide as it would go, headed toward the car. When she looked up again, the dog was gone. Cassie took the groceries into the trailer.

"I'm driving," Cassie said, still in custody of the keys.

"You bet you're driving," Emmy said, standing like a soldier outside the car. "I can't even make my knees move."

"Are those your real knees?" Puck asked, pointing at them. "Or are those your Lee Press-On legs?" He and Emmy collapsed on the ground, panting with dry-mouthed laughter.

"Ho," Emmy said, wiping her eyes and struggling to her feet.

Puck sat down heavily in the passenger's seat. "I ate, Jesus Lord, like a lot. Was anyone watching me? I can literally feel my gallbladder at work."

"Where are we going?" Cassie asked.

"You know what I hate?" Emmy asked from the backseat, where she was trying in vain to locate a seat belt. "Awareness of my tongue."

"Where to now?" Cassie asked, pulling out on to the dark country road.

"Puck, have you ever been so stoned you started to pee and then couldn't remember whether you were in a bathroom or, like, sitting on the couch?"

"I pee standing up, Emmy, it's an anatomy issue. So I can look around and gather whether I'm in a parlor or whatnot."

"Where do you want to go now, Puck?"

"One thing I hate is feeling like a great deal of time has passed and then discovering it's been, oh, four minutes. Try listening to a Led Zeppelin song stoned sometime, you'll see what I mean."

"Ooooh, you know what I hate—"

"Could someone please tell me where we're going?"

"West, dearest."

"We're already headed west."

"How convenient, then."

"Puck," Cassie said, trying hard to remember the days she'd been on the interesting side of this conversation, "I need a destination."

"Well, I'm thinking you'll take exception to the destination."

"You still have to tell me."

"Cassandra, master of the craft—"

"You know her name's not Cassandra, right? Do you have my lighter?"

"Cassandra, I wish to visit the abandoned, what shall we call it, the institution that formerly served the mad, broken, and neglected of our fair county."

The old state hospital was tucked away in what passed for a valley in rural Indiana, back a long lane; the spread of buildings had been condemned. It was possible Dante was there; it was possible that Puck's reasons for searching so fervently for a person whose way of life was *missing* were not what he had stated.

"I'm worried about your car, Emmy."

"I know. But my dad will give me five thousand dollars toward a new one if this one makes it two hundred thousand miles."

Puck had rolled his window down a few inches and was sticking his nose out like a retriever.

"Why are we really looking for Dante?" Emmy asked. "Why are we not at some party, safe and warm?"

Puck rolled the window back up, then tilted his head back against the seat and closed his eyes. "We're looking for him because he is a beautiful child."

Cassie glanced at Puck, but he didn't say more.

"Do you have my lighter? Cassie, could you put on some music, for the love of God? Is this a holiday or not?"

Cassie pushed the tape in, and Robert Smith began to sing; she could see him in her mind, as she was certain Puck and Emmy were seeing him. A man in shadow, his eyes ringed black as crow, red lipstick smeared across his mouth. *Oh oh oh I want to change it all*, he sang, and Puck and Emmy sang with him. *Oh oh oh I want to change.*

* * *

Puck kicked the rear tire of Emmy's car, not like a man who intended to buy it, then stomped on the ground. Kicked the tire again. "Two hundred thousand miles my ass, Emmy. We could have been in my Camaro, the gorgeous Camaro my dear widowed mother bought for me, but no. We always have to ride in this piece of—"

"Puck," Cassie said, from under the hood, "that's enough."

"I didn't do it on purpose, doofus."

"Still, my shrink says—"

"You don't have a shrink, you have a social worker."

"—my shrink says I need to express myself. Shall we fire up another one against the chill?"

"Emmy, have you had problems with the piston rings? Because look, the radiator isn't leaking, but there's smoke, like maybe from the engine—are you burning a lot of oil? Have you had the catalytic converter replaced?"

"I don't know all that, don't ask me, here—here, Puck, light this, I just want to look at something inside." Emmy opened the driver's door and sat down. "Okay," she called out, "the lights still work, so it isn't the battery, and damn! I have six thousand miles to go. Damn." Emmy slammed the door, stomped her tennis shoe on the ground, then kicked a tire.

Puck blew out a stream of smoke. "How far are we from the hospital, Cassandra?"

Cassie looked around, then down the road. "Two miles? Maybe three."

"We should push ahead, troops, don't you agree, Miss Emmy? Shouldn't we see this through to the end?"

"Fine with me," Emmy answered, hopping up and down. "I'm game either way, but I'm freezing."

Game. In truth Emmy had made her choice long ago, toward becoming the girl of her parent's dreams. She'd done it by picking Brian—her boyfriend since the tenth grade, with his myriad and subtle restraints, the way he controlled her every move, even from a distance—and by leaving earlier in the fall for the nearest state college, the one her parents chose. She was studying to be a middle-school teacher, as her parents had demanded, rather than majoring in journalism, as she'd wanted. Tonight everything Emmy was doing was for show: the leather biker jacket she'd orphaned in her closet, but had taken out for this occasion. The quarter bag of dope she'd scored, surely the last time that would ever happen. Even now the hopping, the coolness of saying she'd be willing to walk in the pitch darkness into an abandoned asylum in search of Dante, all were designed to suggest to Puck and Cassie that her story wasn't over. Puck was the real thing; he would lead the stroll into a minefield, he *wanted* to go to the old hospital. He wanted to chase the beautiful child across the freezing landscape of Halloween night.

Cassie lifted the hood off the metal arm supporting it, put the arm down, and dropped the hood from its height. The dense explosion as it landed echoed out across the fields. "All right, then. But we take the first ride offered to us, no matter who it is, right, Emmy?"

Emmy shrugged, casual. "Sounds good."

"Ahhh!" Puck passed the joint to Emmy, then raised his arms in the air. "By the pricking of my thumbs—"

"Dude," Cassie said. "Enough."

"Here, we'll need this, too." Emmy pulled a pint of Southern Comfort out of her back pocket. "It's getting colder."

They passed a pig farm squatting on a hillside and began to speak of pigs, an unfortunate topic. The house, under the waning moon, looked like the sort of place Grandpa Jones from *Hee Haw* would pick on his banjo as a bunch of barely dressed white trash-girls sang backup.

"That used to be Cassie's dream house when she was little, wasn't it, Cass," Emmy said.

"Shut up, Emmy."

"Oh dear," Puck said, taking a deep breath. "It is aromatic. I've never taken you much for a hayseed, Cassandra."

"I like farms."

"Has a single car passed us *yet*?" Puck asked, looking around as if in disbelief.

Cassie had worked, when nothing else was available, on farms all over the county, sometimes for a day or two, and she'd done work she hated and wished to forget: bailing hay, detassling corn, not demeaning or cruel work, but abysmally hard. She'd done things she loved: rounding cattle on horseback, delivering lambs; even building fence had a certain joy, although it nearly broke her back. She had ridden all day in an air-conditioned combine, listening to country music, and that had been good, had left her butt sore and her head clear. But there was something that arrived in the end, a kind of information you gathered working on a farm. Every day was a plundering; ripping food from the earth and life out of animals.

"What time is it?" Puck asked, stopping to feel for his watch.

Emmy pushed a button on the side of her watch, and the face lit up. "It's eleven-oh-two, or thereabouts."

Puck gave a stomp, which caused his heavy belly to ripple. "I have gone and missed trick-or-treat again. This is many years in a row now."

Emmy set off walking again but made a soft humming sound. "Candy. Candy. Candy."

Puck joined her in the chant: "Can-dy, can-dy, can-dy." Cassie heard the van coming up behind them before the others but didn't turn to meet the headlights. She walked straight ahead, scuffing her boots against the gravel of the shoulder. The heavy flashlight was tucked inside her jacket, and the Southern Comfort was curved securely in her pocket. Those who would stop, stopped. Rides were predetermined, like points on a compass: if you started out at A, C was set in motion. The van had been driving toward them a long time. Cassie had felt it, or the air it displaced, all the way back before the day began.

It was a white van, extra long and with no windows in the side or back. If it had been black, Cassie would have thought it belonged to a funeral-home fleet. It was probably used to deliver something, just not the newly dead. It drove past them slowly, then pulled over a hundred feet in front of them.

"This may very well mean candy," Puck said, winking at Cassie.

She walked up to the driver's window as he was rolling it down. He was a thin man in his late forties with dark hair going gray and an aggressive salt-and-pepper mustache. Cassie thought she'd been in line behind him at the grocery store. Him or someone like him, a man who bought only three things: cigarettes, ammonia, and honey buns. He blew a stream of smoke at his windshield, smiled at her.

"Where you headed?"

"Where are you headed, kind sir?" Puck asked from somewhere behind Cassie.

"Where are *you* headed?" the driver asked again, looking directly at Cassie.

"We're going to the old state hospital," she said.

"Climb in on the other side, I'll take you there."

When the three stranded travelers reached the passenger's side, they were surprised to find a man holding the door open for them. Cassie glanced at him but said thanks as she slipped over the passenger's seat and into the back of the van. He was handsome and cold, with pale blue eyes that seemed to have migrated up from Appalachia and the body of a high school wrestler: dense through the shoulders and small-waisted. Puck made an ooomph as he joined Cassie in the back, and Emmy slipped in silently.

The floor was uncovered, corrugated. There were indistinguishable items pushed against the walls, maybe televisions or microwaves, and a ladder hanging from two hooks. Emmy found a stack of motorcycle helmets and put one on, then handed two over to Puck and Cassie.

"May I wear one of your helmets, sir?"

The driver offered a vague wave. "Knock yourself out."

"Oh, I can't seem to fit— Emmy, hand me another, this one is too small. Don't fear, sir! I'm not suggesting that your helmets aren't big enough, it's simply that I am quite large through the cranium."

The cold-eyed passenger found something in the glove box,

then climbed in and closed the door. Cassie sat on her helmet and leaned against one of the metal walls, slowly reaching for the knife she carried on her belt. No belt, no knife. She wrapped her arms around her knees and considered the odds. If the passenger was armed, they were doomed. If it came down to fists and feet, Cassie would be alone with her flashlight, as Emmy and Puck would do nothing but scream and dance around like nine-year-old girls. She leaned over and whispered to Emmy, "Until we're out of the van and the situation is clear, keep your helmet on."

Emmy nodded like a spaceman, then leaned over and said the same to Puck, who gave Cassie a sage wink. His helmet was propped atop his head, the straps dangling around his face.

The driver pulled out on to Old 7 slowly, as if afraid his cargo might be disturbed, then accelerated gently, so that their passage over the first of the heart-thrilling hills passed without incident. Cassie was still trying to read the passenger's profile (which was chiseled, square-chinned) by the dim light of the dashboard when Emmy screamed and bonked her helmet against the van wall.

"Furry! Something furry touched my hand!" She tried to get up, and fell sideways. "Fur!"

The driver laughed. "Calm down, it's just a rabbit."

Cassie looked at Puck, who smiled. "There's a rabbit back here?"

"More than one."

Cassie reached into her jacket and pulled out the flashlight, shining it on the floor of the van. At least six rabbits, a black and white one, a solid black, a beautiful deep brown, and others in combination, were hopping around freely.

Puck laughed aloud. "Isn't this unexpected?"

The floor of the van was marked by large brown spots—rust or blood. If the passenger had a knife, they continued to be screwed. If he had a blackjack, nunchucks, Chinese fighting sticks, anything like that, they stood a chance. Cassie played it out in numerous ways in her mind: one behind her, the other in front, with a gun, with a knife, with nothing but menace and the unusual strength of the crazy. She repeated to herself the mantra that calmed her, walking out of a pool hall to her truck or down a darkened street: nose, throat, instep, solar plexus, groin. A man's testicles can be removed from his body with eight pounds of pressure, and he will bleed to death in under a minute. A car key delivered swiftly to an eye will stop most assailants. An average man will panic if you sink your teeth into his tongue, but only if you mean it, only if you're willing to bite it off and go on with your life. Walking out of a pool hall, however, she carried a cue in a hard case, and sometimes a .22 pistol in an ankle holster, and it was easier to be sanguine.

"What do you make of the bunnies, Emmy?" Puck asked.

"I think they're making me higher," she answered, pressed against the side of the van. "Also everything sounds flat inside this helmet."

"I like them," Puck said. "Oh, look, I caught one. It's heavy and, my goodness, very warm. Imagine if we could gather them all up into a blanket. A rabbit blanket."

"Imagine," Emmy said, "lying under the rabbit blanket with morphine and candy."

The driver used his turn signal on the empty road, then turned right on to the stretch of utter darkness that would lead them to the darker blackness of the old hospital. Cassie considered his use of the turn signal. It could be ironic. He could be saying, I am a law-abiding citizen, with the glint in his eye that marked the onset of a heinous crime. It could be unconscious, the reflex of a careful driver. Now that she knew they were there, Cassie could smell the rabbits strongly, but above or below them, little else. Gasoline, as if in a closed container. Something like a hot transistor. Puck and Emmy. But no alcohol on the driver or the passenger; no jittery junkie smell; nothing like the sharp chemical leak that came from the skin of a meth addict.

The lane they were on was rough, mined with holes, unattended by any bureaucracy. The van sank a few inches, came back up. Emmy bumped her metallic helmet against the side of the van four or five times in a row. The springs sang; rabbits skittered and hid behind the mystery boxes.

"Man oh man," the driver said, flipping from his high beams to his low, trying to determine the best course of action. "What do you want back here? Why would you come back here?"

"Thank you for asking," Puck said, coming to attention. "We are searching for someone, a friend called Dante."

"I know Dante," the passenger said, and his voice was surprising, breathy and boyish.

"You *do*?"

"We went to school together before."

"My heavens," Puck said. "A surprise to meet you. I'm Puck, by the way, and who would you be?" The van hit a hole, and Puck lost control of his rabbit.

"Jeff," the passenger said, turning around in his seat and shaking Puck's hand.

"And this is Cassie, this one with the flashlight, and over there is Emmy, she's a college gal, and oops, she's, maybe she's asleep."

"Nice to meet you. This here's Wally, he used to be my stepdad."

"Hello, Wally who used to be my stepdad."

"Howdy," Wally said without taking his eyes from the road.

Howdy was always ironic, except when it became a habit. And then it was the speaker's entire life that descended into irony, and later into self-parody. Cassie studied Wally's face in profile but couldn't tell where he stood.

They passed the first of the institutional buildings, built in the late 1940s, and situated under a row of hundred-year-old maple trees. It had served as the office of the director and the counselors and was the part of the sprawling camp most often shown in the newspaper and in television reports. All the buildings were variations on a theme: the large lake cottage, covered in cedar-shake shingles painted green, with screened porches. There was a humane vision, Cassie thought, in the construction and in the location. The land was beautiful, lonesome, on a knoll overlooking a strip of forest a mile long and hundreds of acres wide. In the summer the inmates would have found themselves above a green canopy; in the fall they would have seen the drama of hardwoods in the weakening midwestern sun. The county had closed the place a few years before, after an intrepid newspaper reporter went undercover as an orderly and audiotaped an old man being beaten for wetting his bed. The reporter had gone on to disclose the names of dozens of people who had died by accidental drowning since the 1950s, most of them mentally retarded and suffering from seizures. And many more dead from unknown causes.

They drove past the medical facility, a squat block rectangle that could serve in any historical atrocity. Wally turned right again, following the gravel lane along the edge of the knoll.

"There's light back here," he said, "behind that last house."

Cassie leaned forward between Wally and Jeff as the van slowly made its way deeper into the compound. They passed the residence of the former director; a swing set, mostly dismantled, sat mute at the edge of the yard. then a building on the left, larger, longer than the other cottages. Something flashed white in a window, but Cassie couldn't have said what it was.

"Looks like a fire back there," Wally said. He parked in the drive next to the last building, and he and Jeff got out, quietly.

Cassie sat back and touched Emmy on the shoulder. "Em, we're here." She shone the flashlight above her friend's sleeping face.

Emmy opened her eyes and stretched out an arm; her eyes were swollen and bloodshot, and she seemed disoriented. "Yikes. Sleeping in a helmet isn't half bad." She sat up and adjusted her jacket. "I'm dying of thirst, I'm dying, seriously."

Puck was feeling around on the floor for his rabbit, but it had gone missing. "Here, alien girl. Don't drink it all." He handed her a plastic bottle of Mountain Dew from his jacket pocket.

By the light of the fire Cassie could see Wally and Jeff peering behind the empty house, then conferring. She got out of the van and walked toward them, cold again, surprised by the air.

"There's nobody here," Wally said, looking around him, "but that fire is pretty big."

"They're here," Cassie said.

Puck stepped out of the van and thrust his stomach forward, causing his helmet straps to swing to and fro, then marched toward the fire. "What is this?" he shouted. His voice rang out across the silent valley below. "A fire with no one tending it? Have our educational institutions been entirely remiss in teaching fire safety?"

Shapes began to emerge, one at a time, and approach the fire. A girl—maybe it was a girl, a person in a skirt, anyway—crept out from under a black tarp at the edge of the cottage, a boy from behind a tree. A screen door on the cottage creaked open, and three more people came out.

"Puck!"

"Hey, dude!"

"Where you been, man? We've missed you!"

Puck threw his arms around each of them in turn. They squatted by the fire.

"These friends of yours?" Wally asked Cassie, tipping his head toward the scene.

"Not so much."

"But you know them."

"Some."

"But this . . . Puck? He's your friend?"

Cassie nodded. "We go way back."

Wally was wearing faded blue jeans and an old sheep-lined leather jacket. Standing this close to him, Cassie could smell the leather and hear it creak when he moved. She relaxed. Jimmy had worn a flight jacket; she remembered hiding in the closet and breathing it in when he was gone.

"You looking for a boyfriend?" Wally asked, raising his eyebrows not quite lasciviously.

"Nope."

"Already got one?"

"Nope."

"You gay?"

"You tryin' to piss me off?"

Wally shook his head and reached inside his jacket, pulling out a pack of filterless Camels. A book of matches was tucked inside the cellophane. "Smoke?"

"No thanks." Cassie took Emmy's bottle of Southern Comfort from her back pocket. "Drink?"

They stood that way awhile, Wally and Jeff passing the bottle back and forth, Cassie watching the fire. Jeff didn't smoke, didn't speak, wasn't wearing a coat, just a thick hooded sweatshirt with a school logo on the front, something Cassie couldn't quite make out. A Trojan, a Viking.

Emmy wandered up, and the firelight reflected off her silver helmet in flashes. "Somebody stop me next time," she said, rubbing her eyes.

Cassie watched Puck with his ragtag army. She wondered what they thought of his living in the immaculate ranch house in the deathly subdivision off the highway. His middle-aged and overweight mother was generous in her grief; she had been waylaid by widowhood, and now Puck had, in addition to his midnight-blue Camaro, a snowmobile, an expensive stereo system, a wardrobe that changed constantly to accommodate his ever expanding girth. He had gadgets: handheld video games and walkie-talkies, TVs and VCRs, a motorbike he was too fat to ride. His mom had finished the basement in his honor and filled it with shiny electronics and a wide, sturdy bed. He had his own bathroom down there, his own phone line. But these children, as he liked to say, were his chosen people.

He was talking with the girl who called herself Anastasia, and the boy, Romeo. Both of them were slight and dirty, dressed in layers of vintage black clothing and combat boots laced tight against thin legs. It was the new look—for Indiana, anyway—the bat cave death look. Peter Murphy was worshiped here (if you loved Bauhuas, you were too old), and the Cure, Siouxsie and the Banshees, Nick Cave; all the thin and wasted boys and girls who might have been junkies but at least had mastered the fashion. These were children who believed—at fifteen, sixteen, seventeen—that they were falling from a great height, and that what would save them was love and drama. They saw the planet they hurtled toward as having a breakaway skin, like the warm swimming pool of a rock star. Cassie and Puck had talked about it many times since Emmy left for college, Cassie shaking her head against their doom, Puck gleeful.

"He not here," Romeo was saying, "he in love. He leave with that mean spider-looking girl, call herself Maleficent. She harsh on him *night* and *day*, tell him to leave her alone, go get her some jelly beans."

Puck rubbed his chin thoughtfully, looked up at Cassie, who was listening. "I fear," he said, "I know not of this Maleficent. Do you know her, Cassandra?"

Cassie shook her head.

"She new," Romeo said, taking Anastasia's hand. "From California, where she used to write songs on a guitar and own a cat call Tragedy. I haven't seen no cat with her."

"Well, then," Puck said, standing up and brushing off his thighs, "I am ready to celebrate Halloween without distraction."

They gathered around the fire and finished Emmy's bottle, and then someone produced some dark rum and they drank that, too, Cassie watching. When the fire began to wane, someone would duck into a cottage and steal another piece of abandoned furniture and toss it on. Old desk chairs burn a long time, a child's desk a long time, too. Someone had located a spool of copper wire that they broke off a foot at a time and tossed into the fire to watch the flames burn darker blue.

We found a box of bones, Cassie heard someone say. *A big box, it was in a locked closet in the hospital building. There were long bones, like from your thigh, and little tiny ones like a hand or a finger. But no heads.*

"Does anybody have any food?" Anastasia asked, swaying. She was so small, Cassie noticed, tucked inside her layers of clothes like a two-word note in an envelope.

A sigh rose up, *food.* She could do it again, Cassie could face it again, maybe, taking Wally's van and driving in to Jonah and loading up.

"I do," Wally said, heading toward the van.

A cheer: hooray for . . . what's his name again?

"Wallace," Puck answered, who sought always to restore dignity.

Cassie's eyes scanned the gathering, landing on first one sleepy face and then another, but no Emmy. Emmy had taken her helmet head and was gone. Cassie turned and looked behind her, moved slowly toward the trees. No one. She was walking to the van, taking careful steps on the uneven ground, when she saw Wally coming back with two rabbits, the black and white and the dark brown, and from his belt there hung a skinning knife, sixteen inches long from the look of it. He was holding the rabbits by the scruff of the neck, and they seemed relaxed, not kicking or fighting. She watched him go without a word. Every day was open season on rabbits. They had trained themselves, as a species, to die of heart attacks when necessary, a clever adaptation if every day meant death. Laura called this Evolution Knows Best. Would the people around the fire watch the killing and eating of the rabbits? They were not brutes themselves; they were gossamer, trapped in their culture, bound by its conventions.

Cassie's flashlight beam illuminated the side of the white van; it squatted at the edge of the grass, cold and silent. It looked like a photograph, admissible evidence. She called Emmy's name softly, in case she was sleeping and didn't want to be disturbed, and heard a soft sound in reply, like someone dreaming, coming from the screened porch of the cottage. Keeping the beam low to the ground, Cassie walked toward it. At the hedge she raised the light and saw Jeff's back, rising and falling, a ship at sea, and then Emmy's hands flat and delicate on him, her voice murmuring like water. Even with the flashlight beam, even with Wally capturing rabbits, they were unaware. They were alone.

Under a tree a little way up the lane, Cassie found Emmy's helmet. She sat down on it, rested her head on her knees. Emmy would at some point remember or realize that Cassie had seen her, she would recall the breeze of light passing over Jeff's back and know who had stood there. Emmy's marriage to Brian had already been ordained: by her secret domesticity, her wish for legitimacy, her wish to stand inside a blameless life and cast a stone against the world. Cassie was the world. She closed her eyes, thought of Diana, with her pointed collars and questions. And Brian, in engineering school at Purdue, his amiable scorn for everything Emmy had left behind.

At some point she realized that all talk around the fire had ceased. She stood and walked back toward Puck, smelling, for the first time, a current of the lives the bat-cave children were living. They might not keep their teeth, they might be spreading disease. In a year there would be a group of babies given interesting names, and a few months later their parents would part. Little poets in the making, a bumper crop.

But for now, Cassie saw, there were two rabbits on a spit, quite competently skinned and skewered, and everyone was quiet. Puck's hands were in his pockets and his helmet was gone. The smell of meat began to rise into the trees, and the smoke hung there like a banner proclaiming the holiday, a welcome to all who were hungry and heavy-laden.

Wally dropped them off one at a time. Cassie, last who lived farthest away, was last. As she got out of the van, saying thank you, she asked, "Where were you going when you stopped for us?"

Wally shrugged and said, "The video store."

Edwin and Poppy had been there for tea and Chinese checkers earlier in the evening, and there were, little sugar-dusted cookies with jam in the center on a plate on the table, and a bowl of apples. Cassie was suddenly ravenous, but there was a stiffness in her mother's gestures that wouldn't allow her to eat. Laura moved to the sink, carrying cups and saucers, then emptied her ashtray and put it in the sink with the dishes. The water she ran looked scalding, a cloud of steam rising into her eyes. Cassie sat on the counter and waited for her mother's swift glance, well aware of what Laura might have seen: the grass-stained blue jeans worn sheer in the butt and the knees; the cowboy boots clocked down at the heel; the black Harley-Davidson T-shirt under a brown cardigan that had belonged to Jimmy. Laura, thin and sharp, still wearing the cashmere sweater sets and peg-legged pants of her youth, her dark brown bob going white in a stripe above her forehead, was an elegant woman for these parts.

"Is that your costume?" Laura asked, and Cassie didn't know how to answer. She shrugged.

"Well, when you look in the mirror, do you recognize yourself?"

Cassie nodded, unsure if she was telling the truth.

"Do you feel you celebrated the holiday appropriately?" Laura put the cookies in a tin, slid it into a cabinet.

Cassie thought about what had happened at the very end of the night, after they'd left the state hospital. She traced the words on her palm. "I don't know. I don't know what's appropriate."

Laura finished the dishes and reached for her leather cigarette case, unsnapping the tarnished gold top and shaking out a single cigarette expertly. Out of the front pocket she pulled the thin lighter Cassie had won in a long game at fourteen. She always tilted her head to the right when lighting a cigarette, as if she had become accustomed to keeping her hair out of a high flame.

"Well, let's see," Laura said, blowing smoke at the yellowed kitchen ceiling. "It's the summer's end, correct? and the day of the dead. As I understand, the, how should we say it, the *seam* between this world and the Other is very thin, and it's easy to cross over. We're between the autumnal equinox and the winter solstice, a time of slaughter in some countries."

"Then yes," Cassie said, rubbing her eyes. "I did everything correctly."

"Of course you did," Laura said, "smart girl."

Cassie tucked a strand of Laura's hair behind her ear, studied the gold earrings Laura wore almost every day, a gold ball connected to a thin seashell, the gold gone rose with time.

"Did you consider the dead?" Laura asked.

Cassie thought a moment. "I think they considered me."

Laura laughed, took a long draw on her cigarette. "I spent some time thinking of your father."

"Jimmy's dead?"

"Tonight he is. He's dead to me."

This was an answer Cassie understood; grief is grief. Only last winter she had awakened the morning after a winter storm and found the whole of their property, all seven acres, covered in a thick, undisturbed whiteness. The early sunshine on the expanse caused her eyes to ache. Instinctively, she had looked for the place her father, arising earlier than anyone else, would have distressed the walk between the back porch and Poppy's trailer, going over in the predawn hours for a hand of cards and a cup of chicory coffee. But there was nothing.

"And how was he, in your thoughts of him?"

"He was a villain, a rogue, and a coward."

"Was he wearing Poppy's ring, the one he stole, or had he hocked it?"

Laura gave a rueful smile. "You have to ask?" She let water run over her cigarette, mixed herself a drink. "Tomorrow is All Saints' Day at home. It's a strange feeling, to be one place in your heart and another in your life. I'm always there, in New Orleans, in my mind. I think it's a feeling you'll never know, Cassie."

They sat down at the table, Laura with a gin gimlet in a frosted glass, Cassie with a beer.

They had been driving down Old 7, Cassie in the passenger seat, Puck in the back chasing rabbits, Emmy somewhere even farther back with Jeff, a fact about which no one spoke. Wally's high beams were on, and they saw a man walking along the shoulder of the road far ahead, and something wasn't right. This was the story Cassie thought she might tell Laura, if the time came.

"Do you know," Laura said, tracing the lip of her glass with her fingertip, "that we live our lives and trade our days for lies invented thousands of years ago, Cassie? I've been thinking about this all day. We no longer recall or question the source. The lies are that we must attend school, we must excel, we must take our place in the factory line applying, I don't know, plastic to the tips of shoelaces, or slicing the throats of chickens. We used to rise early to collect food, and go to bed early in preparation for the next day, but now we do it because we're told to by banks and accountants and the government. I'm not paranoid; I know reality is a tide that forms out of a collective agreement, right?"

Cassie nodded, looked down at her beer bottle. Laura's eyes were hot, gleaming.

"I've accepted it, all of it, Cassie, but there is one lie that troubles me every day, it makes—it's making me *angry*—I pray for a revolution, a manifesto, violence in the streets, I'd take to the streets and let the police spray me with tear gas and attack me with dogs and choke me with nightsticks, anything, but no one will join me. You'd join me, I suppose, for any cause, am I right?"

Cassie nodded.

"It's marriage, family, home, sentimentality, continuity, these are the lies that eat women like a machine." Laura smacked the tabletop with her open palm, then smiled. "A Woman-Chipper, can you imagine how that would sell? Everyone, anywhere on the political spectrum, would want one. Republicans? Oh my God! Line up black welfare mothers and crackheads, the ex-wives of senators who want the house in Aspen, Jane Fonda, lesbians, feminists—pop 'em in the Chipper! And then ask Andrea Dworkin to face those silent, furious, fundamentalist homeschooling moms, and Phyllis Schlafly, and those crazies—Chip 'em! And the televangelists! Well, they'd probably put almost all women in the hot seat, wouldn't they, I mean, first they'd probably have sex with them, and then: fire up the Chipper!"

They had seen a man walking along the shoulder of the road, and something wasn't right. His pants were light green, and his shirt? or his jacket? was white.

"It starts with an invading army, Cassie." Laura walked to the counter and mixed herself another drink. "A new movement, a cult of death, and the lie is forced upon women like a rape, and within a few generations the women are the perpetuators, daughter to daughter. I taught you by example, after being taught by my mother, who was taught, etcetera. It's like this: do you know that once I had a friend, one friend? a woman who lived down the road, in the years after I first moved here, you girls were small. I learned from that, I never mingled again." Laura had been reading *The Chalice and the Blade*, carrying it with her from room to room.

His shirt or jacket had been white, and his arms seemed to be behind his back, and too long. His arms were hanging loose and too long. Laura was going to tell the story of Shirley, who Cassie had seen last week at the grocery store, and who spoke warmly and asked after her mother.

"She could be kind, Shirley, and so funny, and sort of rigid, smart but rigid, her ultimate faith was in her own sanity and rightness, even though she'd never gone to college, didn't read extensively, I don't know where she thought her authority came from.

That's a sort of confidence some people have, some don't, Shirley looked inside herself and saw two categories, right (herself), and wrong (everyone else), and she wasn't afraid to lay out your crimes and failings. Her husband suffered the brunt of it, but I didn't feel any sympathy for him then and I don't now, because he was participating in the lie with the same fervor she was, and my feeling was, well, good luck, fella. For a while I passed muster, mostly because I was quiet and pregnant. Pregnancy is good, pregnancy gives you carte blanche in Lie Land. There is no better, more beautiful woman than a pregnant one, because she's immobilized, she's weakened and frightened and must turn every moment to her mate, who tucks her inside the wagon, wraps her in bear hide, and goes out to kill in her name."

The man's arms were hanging loose and too long. Wally had slowed down, leaned forward. Cassie had leaned forward, squinted. As they got closer, they could see the man's hair, black, standing up in matted clumps. His cheeks were hollow, his eyes were dark, and his white jacket was a straitjacket, his feet were bare. This was the moment Cassie kept seeing in her mind, the moment he came clear.

"And Shirley and I got on famously, we made light of our humiliations, the swollen places, the leaking, we couldn't sleep, we had to pee all the time," Laura laughed, lit a cigarette, "we were short of breath, we felt faint, we were fat, we threw up, we had hemorrhoids, we were exposed to medical students and sadistic nurses. Pregnancy and then breast-feeding made us too stupid—it makes you too stupid, Cassie—to read or to talk about much of anything at all, and then when you were three and Belle was five, I decided to leave your father, and Shirley was the first person I went to."

Cassie rubbed her forehead. How could she ever explain to Laura that hearing this story still caused a shimmer in her belly, she was *still* afraid that Jimmy would leave and she'd lose her family even so long after he'd left and she'd lost?

"And basically, Shirley looked around frantically and said, Where's the Chipper? She said I couldn't destroy my home, that my children were more important than I was, that I had made my commitment and I had to keep it. I said, Where is this commitment, hand it to me, I'll tear it up. I felt like she was saying I had to honor her double-dog dare. There was no thought to the fact that we were bankrupt, that I was borrowing money from Poppy for groceries, that he and Buena Vista had given up and done without to take care of us, that I couldn't say a word to Jimmy because he simply left, he said he had to go, and left. I saw what was happening, that our life was on the downward spiral and would only get worse and worse until we were penniless and living in a shelter, or until someone was in jail. Or we would hang on and hang on and wake up old. Things would get worse, and we would get old."

His white jacket was a straitjacket and his feet were bare. Cassie gasped, they had just passed him when police cars came flying over the hills, and the man heard the sirens and saw the lights and turned in to the cornfield next to him and began to run across the stubble, a scuttling sort of run that caused the arms of the straitjacket to dance like two drunken men.

"Shirley called me selfish," Laura said, taking a drink, "she said I was sick, that I would cause permanent damage to my children, I couldn't accept that with your births I had been replaced and my needs no longer mattered. She said Jimmy was a good man, a kind and loving and generous man, funny, she said, Does he ever hit you? And of course I said no, because he was, yes, sweet as a ripe peach. I said Hitting isn't the point. She said Does he yell at you, yell at the kids, break things, kick the dog? I said No he doesn't do anything at all like that, he has a girlfriend, he's irresponsible and not a grown man, he doesn't live in relation to me at all, he won't pay bills, he won't hold down a job, he doesn't take care of the house or keep the cars running, I am living in an advanced state of entropy, and soon I will wake up and everything will be falling down, lost, broken, repossessed, I'll be insane and the children will be feral, and I want to move on and take care of us myself without the black hole of his needs. *I want to go home.*"

Cassie stood up from the table, rinsed out her beer bottle, set it down quietly on the kitchen counter. She stared out the kitchen window at the yard, at the bird feeder where the finches would be, if it were morning and if there were finches.

"I didn't say this," Laura continued, "I didn't say the bottom line, which was that I wanted to go to college, I wanted to study something hard and beautiful, like philosophy or astronomy or art history or literature. And Shirley not only said no, I don't support you, you aren't my friend, she persecuted me, she sent me hate mail, she talked about me to everyone in town, she told your teachers, year after year, that I was mentally ill, and when *Jimmy* finally left *us*, she said I'd driven him away."

Laura paused, and Cassie listened to the kitchen clock tick. In the Airstream bathroom a light came on briefly, then went off.

"I haven't seen or heard from Shirley in years; I did hear she takes care of her husband's elderly mother full-time and has gotten quite fat. This is America in a nutshell, I think, Puritan America, capitalist, land-owning, the State has an interest in the life of every person from infancy on, because we'll all be taxpayers.

We're driven by biology to reproduce, that's a truth no one can argue with, and then perhaps we're driven by biology to move on, to reproduce with someone else or cease, but the State, the Church, can't allow that fundamental fact to rule our lives, because the bureaucracy couldn't withstand it. Couldn't withstand the freedom. And so I wanted to end my marriage, and some people said I couldn't because of the Hebrew God. And I said, I don't know this God anymore, he makes no sense to me, that isn't my life or my world. And others would say I couldn't because of Jesus Christ, a dead man, and I would say, What are you talking about, this Jesus? I lost him years ago. I have no idea what you're saying," Laura waved a cigarette in the air, "it's like telling me I can't change my life because the Jabberwock says no, or the elves, or someone's late uncle Marvin. And finally poor Poppy and Buena Vista pulled out the stops and said, You can't leave because it will destroy the children, the experts all say so. I looked around, my children already destroyed, and I didn't see a single expert peering into my house, not one. I was here alone night and day, nothing but my library job a few hours a week and the books I read, nothing to convince me there was even a world beyond my sight. And when that didn't work, your grandma cried, this was her son, after all, and said, Look at your jackets hanging side by side on the hook next to the door, his and yours and the little girls', look at these plates you got as a wedding gift—"

Cassie closed her eyes, swallowed.

"—wouldn't they break your heart later? He knows what you like in your coffee, you have albums of photographs, there is half of him in your children, this is *your life*. I tell you, sweetheart, people will say such things, they will say anything to keep you at odds with your own human liberty. I said Buena Vista, I love you, but those are jackets, plates, it's just coffee, I can make my own. Those are photographs, little deaths, they are not my life. I said to her, Can you imagine if I were living in Paris and said to someone, anyone, my neighbor, my only begotten life is being seized from me second by second, can you imagine what she'd say? She'd say, Darling! Take a lover! Get out of here, take your girls and move to Italy, get a job, how silly you are! But here everyone says, *What about your pots and pans?* And what was I to do, I finally grew so weak from argument, and being alone so much made me think I was crazy, and so I stayed, just like everyone else. Cassie."

He turned in to the cornfield and began to run across the stubble, a scuttling sort of run that caused the arms of the straitjacket to dance like two drunken men. He ran behind the old power station, into the black woods behind, and the police cars skidded to a stop on the dusty shoulder, raising up clouds. Wally had driven on; the man didn't stand a chance.

"Cassie, look at me. My point is that women live the lie from birth on, and then one day they realize that it's too late for them, they're too old to write a book or solve a difficult problem in math, they'll never learn to sing or play the piano, they showed such promise early on. So they run to the priests, their voices take on a hysterical edge, like the one mine has right now, and the priest tells them they have lived righteously and their reward will be in heaven, and he could certainly use someone in the kitchen for the potluck Sunday night."

Laura carried her empty glass over to the sink and stepped in front of Cassie to rinse it out.

"I'm going to see Belle tomorrow," Cassie said, watching Laura's reflection in the window over the sink.

"Oh, she'll appreciate that." Laura looked up, dried her hands. "I found your knife, by the way."

"I didn't need it after all."

Laura turned and faced her. "When I was growing up, women weren't made like you, so hard and strong."

Cassie breathed in her mother's smell, the same as ever: mothballs on the sweater, cigarettes and cloves. "I could say the same. There's no one left like you, either."

ALL SAINTS

*B*elle lived in one place in Cassie's imagination and another in the world. She should have been, Cassie thought, in the cell of a visionary nun: rough whitewashed walls, the stark crucifix above the single bed, a mattress stuffed with horsehair and resting on ropes. Soup and bread twice a day, which Belle would refuse. Only there, in that depth of silence and austerity, could her work truly be done. Whatever that work was. Cassie was no longer sure, and it was something she missed: first the book reports, then the complicated Olympian family trees. By the time Belle left for college, she could recite what seemed to be hundreds of myths, along with the variants of different historians. Last summer, the summer after her freshman year, she'd added a kind of interpretation to the mix, and now her papers and her conversation felt to Cassie like a walk on a long road in overhead sun. She wasn't sure where the road started or where they were to arrive. She still sometimes studied a diagram Belle had drawn for her one night at the kitchen table, in an attempt to explain the aspects of the god Hermes. Hermes, it said: the son of Zeus and the nymph Maia, daughter of Atlas and one of the Pleiades. Stole Apollo's cattle, killed a tortoise, made the first musical instrument, the lyre. (Belle had written: lyre, i.e., liar. Cassie asked, Do you mean he didn't steal the cattle?) God of shepherds, measurements, poetry, travel, athletes, and thieves. Cassie was following along fine, but then Belle moved on to the *psyche*, the way Hermes reveals himself in the colors green and silver, in tricks and robbery, escorting us from one realm to another, through liminal states. She said the archetypes were *autonomous*. Cassie asked, Where are they then? And Belle said they were wherever they wanted to be. All this to explain why Hermes was the key to understanding a favorite short story of Laura and Belle, Sarah Orne Jewett's "A White Heron." Cassie had read it, thought it was what it appeared to be, a story about a little girl who loved the woods, loved nature, and had to decide whether to betray the location of the rare and beautiful bird to a hunter. But no. It turned out to be a coming-of-age story, and the bird was actually an aspect of the girl's psyche, and would she betray her *Self* to the man, who was himself an image of something else, on and on Belle went until Cassie didn't like the story so much. And what about Hermes, after all? Well, the story was thick with green and silver, and there He was, waiting to trick the girl into adulthood.

Cassie had tucked the diagram and the copy of the story Belle had given her into her desk drawer, with the thought that maybe it had been a trial of her patience. But a few nights later she'd had a dream that she was driving her truck through the streets of Roseville and everyone was gone, the end had come. She was wondering: had it been a plague, a sudden flash of light? when down the street a troll-like figure appeared, coal black with green hair, wearing a flannel shirt and red pants, almost like a monkey dressed in Poppy's clothes, and he was hopping madly, dancing. He gave a shimmy to every step. He stopped and knocked on the door of a house, and Cassie had thought, *No*, a thought like quicksilver, and as soon as the door opened and the face of a frightened woman appeared, the little man had jumped up and down like Rumpelstiltskin, and the woman vanished. Cassie closed her eyes in fear, and when she opened them again, the monkey man was gone. She reached for the gearshift and looked in her rearview mirror and up he popped! an elated, sinister face wrinkled like a raisin. Cassie jumped awake, got completely out of bed. She paced to clear her head, then sat down to record the details in her notebook, and that was when she'd seen it: a shrewd trickster figure, taking people from life to death, his face still present at the very moment Cassie went from being asleep to awake. His green hair. She'd never told Belle that she had gotten it, maybe, understood a little that what Belle had given her life to was a magical art. Belle said that deep in the hearts and minds of all people were secrets, like a safe filled with treasure, and there were combinations known to some, and Belle was one. She said it, and within days the safe in Cassie had opened. But she wouldn't tell Belle; she'd put it in the safe instead, like a letter opened and read and tucked away.

In Cassie's mind, Belle lived in a room suitable to her work and her temperament, but in fact she lived in a dormitory built of concrete and shared with girls Cassie would as soon kick as look at. She climbed the stairs to the second floor, aware, as she always was when visiting her sister, of the requirements of housing transients. This building was like an enormous dog pound: everything was bolted to the floor and made of materials that could be sprayed down with a hose. Belle's room was at the end of a hallway, a single. No living, unrelated person could accommodate Belle's frank limitations. Cassie passed doors cluttered with pictures cut from magazines, collages that meant nothing to her; they all seemed to be advertisements. The smell in the hallway was dense and disheartening: cologne and hair spray over unwashed laundry and old shoes. There seemed to be a film of such products over everything. The floor was sticky, the lights in the hallway were dim. Loud music from one room was competing with a soap opera from another. It was here that Belle wrote her precise sentences and puzzled over the traces of what time left for us to decipher.

On her door Belle had left a note: *C., I'll be back from class at 1:30. The key is under the hood of my car. Nothing on the table is secret or private. B.* Cassie looked around. The key wasn't on the floor. She walked over to the window, and there it lay in plain sight, on the sill above a radiator clanking and hissing against the November cold. People will look long and hard for what they can't see right in front of them, Laura said.

The door to Belle's room was heavy and scarred. But inside she'd done her best to fulfill Cassie's wishes for her. The twin bed was made up with a plain white coverlet alleged to have survived the Civil War, left to her by Buena Vista, a subject on which Hoosiers were famously neutral. The only decoration was a single phrase, framed in black and hanging above the large window:

> . . . easy is the descent to Avernus: night and day
> the door of gloomy Dis stands open; but to recall
> thy steps and pass out to the upper air, this is the
> task, this is the toll!

> —*Virgil*, Aeneid *VI, 126–129*

Between the built-in dresser and the wall was a metal rod, functioning as a closet, and Belle's few blouses, a single dress, and three pairs of pants hung there. On the shelves above the dresser, where other girls probably kept photographs of friends and trinkets from home, Belle had only books. Running from wall to wall under the window, ten feet long and three feet wide, was a wooden desk, no drawers. Just an enormous surface, and all of Belle was there.

Cassie closed the door, and most of the sound from the hallway disappeared; only a residual thumping in the floor remained. She slipped off her pack and her coat and laid them on the bed, careful not to disturb the quilt pulled tight. When she'd called Belle this morning and said she'd be leaving around nine, a two-hour drive, Belle hadn't mentioned that she'd be gone until after one. Just like her, Cassie thought. She walked around slowly, not touching anything. Belle's former dorm room had been this ugly but had felt more like sickness. There was less light, and Belle's medications had always been visible on the dresser, along with plastic pitcher of water. The pitcher had come from Buena Vista's hospital room, and Cassie didn't want any part of it. Belle hoarded it, probably had it in here still. In that other dorm there had been girls on either side who tortured Belle, who woke her up in the night to tell her Laura was on the phone in the hallway, who threatened her with antique hats and handbags, knowing that Belle feared threadbare fabrics more than snakes or spiders.

A portable stereo sat in one corner of the desk, and a box of radio dramas Cassie hadn't seen before. She wondered where Belle had gotten them. There was a grainy reproduction of a painting. Cassie leaned forward and read the title: *Saturn Devouring His Son* by Goya. Horrible. She recognized some of the names among the stacks of books on the desk. Ovid, Hesiod, Homer, Apuleius, Aeschylus, Aristophanes. James Hillman's *The Dream and the Underworld*, which Belle had carried around her last year at home and quoted from until Cassie threatened her life. "Let us say vesperal" was one of her favorites. Cassie shook her head, remembering. The IBM Selectric typewriter Uncle Bud had given Belle as a graduation gift was silent and cold; Cassie lifted a corner of it: heavy. Belle was working hard on something, from the look of her desk. The wooden bowl she kept her image phrases in was brimming with slips of paper, and there were six or seven arranged in a sentence next to the typewriter. Cassie hesitated to look at it. A tarot card was lying faceup next to the bowl. The air in the room was thick and still; even the thumping from the floor had ceased. Cassie leaned over and studied the card: an old man, hunchbacked, walking over a dry landscape, carrying a sickle and an hourglass. On a piece of paper below the card, Belle had written:

> *Dominus Necessitatis*
> Suit: Swords
> > Element: Air
>
> *Tempus, rerum edax.* (See Ovid, Met., xv 234–6)
> *Omnia fert Aetas, aminum quoque.* (Virgil, Ecloga 51)
>
> Deities: Cronos, Saturn
> Dice: 2+6 = Virtue + Offspring (water)
> > 5+1 = Time + First (fire)
> Lambda, Lachos (fate), Leukophrus (white eyebrows)

Cassie's left hand hovered above the card, but she didn't pick it up. She moved on to a book lying open, and this written in the margin of page 36: "Nigredo—alchemy, the pain of assimilating shadow characteristics. *Parental complex*. Kore. The *via regia*." There were stacks of photocopied articles from various encyclopedias and periodicals, all neatly stapled in the upper left-hand corner. From the first page of each, Cassie could see the story emerging. It was the Greek creation myth, she guessed, Chaos, then Gaia (Earth), who gave birth to Uranus (Sky). Uranus slept with his mother, apparently, and she gave birth to the Hecatoncheires, the Cyclopes, and the Titans. But Uranus hated all his children and cast most into the Underworld. No surprise there, Cassie thought. Belle had drawn, on a sheet of pale green paper, a sun with a face and the hands of a clock; she was no artist, but there was something in the face that interested Cassie.

Gaia was angered by Uranus and called upon one of the sons, Cronos, to punish his father. Or so said Hesiod in the *Theogony* on page 165. Cronos rose up and castrated Uranus, and many were born from his severed genitals, including, Belle had carefully noted, Aphrodite. Cassie sat down in Belle's desk chair and picked up the thread. Cronos was the next ruler and swallowed his children so they wouldn't destroy him as he had destroyed his father. But one child, Zeus, was spirited by his mother to the nymphs to raise, and Cronos was given a stone to swallow.

Cassie looked out the window at the bare branches of the trees. Swallowing children, swallowing stones. There was a lot more to go through, but she thought she could see where Belle was heading. Cassie tapped her fingertips on the arm of the chair, tried to imagine Belle explaining the law of cause and effect, something so simple, to a visitor from another planet. Belle, who didn't understand the application of most practical principles, and who, even though she'd lived in the same house as Cassie,

same parents, had probably never seen one colored ball strike another.

There was a stack of paper next to the typewriter: Cassie took
a few sheets and chose a mechanical pencil from the cup on the
windowsill. Belle seemed to be collecting them; there were ten or
twelve, all with pastel barrels and unused erasers. The room was
warm, and the view from the window was actually nicer than
Cassie would have expected: meandering lanes around an open
grassy space. The lanes intersected periodically and led off into
other directions. Belle had said in a letter a few weeks ago that she
could walk as far as the library, but beyond it was a field of resistance that hit her like wind. Cassie drew the rectangle of a table on
the top sheet of paper, and the Chinese characters from the hanging red lamp. She had practiced the characters many times but
still found the act awkward. Belle had found someone at the university to translate their meaning: *Bird in Flight, Wish Me Luck*.
She began a letter to Belle, or something like a letter. Cassie didn't
know how far the library was, but she hoped for all their sakes
that it was miles and miles away.

I couldn't have known, Cassie began, that Jimmy would show up
there that night. In the year after he left home for good, there
were a few furtive phone calls made from gas stations or rest
stops. He told Cassie he wanted to come home, but Barbara
wouldn't let him. One call had been in the middle of the night,
and Jimmy was drunk, said he had gassed up the Lincoln and was
heading to New Orleans, did Cassie want to go. She did; she gathered a few things, wrote a note to Laura, and waited on the porch
the rest of the night. He never showed.

Once he'd actually come by the house (but wouldn't come in) and left a bag for Cassie. Inside she'd found three hundred dollars in rolled quarters.

"What in the world?" Belle said.

Laura leaned over, looked inside. "Hmm. He must have ambushed a vending machine."

What did he mean, what did he want? Laura said she thought Jimmy was probably torn. A simple thing. Or else he honestly didn't want his children but didn't want anyone to say he couldn't have them. He was like a child himself, Laura said, who ran away from Barbara, then went home when it got dark. He'd been scarce all over Cassie's life that year, even when she fought it and fought him. Uncle Bud had the locks changed, and Laura did the same, so Cassie wasn't expecting him to show up that night, she wrote, then realized she was repeating herself and erased it. Belle never erased.

She had played against Bud awhile and cleaned his clock, as Jimmy would have said, then was shooting alone. The place was busy—it was a Saturday night, and this was what Cassie wrote for Belle: *Saturday night, busy, I was alone in the room with the table. A song by Alabama was playing on the jukebox.* (Cassie had done her best to get Uncle Bud to add two or three or even *one* album she could tolerate. She had nearly sold him on Etta James, but in the end he fell back on the old argument, which was that patrons in a pool hall are by and large nostalgic and want to recall sitting on a porch swing with Grandma.) She didn't see him come in; her back was to the door. There were some bluff greetings, louder talk. What finally made her turn around was the change in atmosphere. She turned around and he was at the bar, surrounded by cronies he had long since abandoned, men who still thought him a hero for exploits a quarter of a century gone. His black leather cue case rested against his leg.

Cassie's breath quickened, and she could hear her heartbeat. Jimmy still evoked elation and dread—she wanted to run to him before he got away, and she wanted to run past him and have it over with. Behind the bar Uncle Bud stood with his arms crossed. He glanced at Cassie, and she lowered her cue and rested it on top of her boot. She suspected, and Bud probably did, too, that Jimmy and Barbara had had a fight, and he was here to prove something. Uncle Bud shook his head, took a deep breath; he hated drama, his look said. Jimmy said something to him with a laugh, fellow feeling, and Bud didn't move; finally, he turned and got Jimmy a beer from the cooler.

Cassie studied her father. He was wearing a pale pink shirt so finely woven that the fabric looked shiny, with gray slacks and the black wing tips he'd had for years. She wrote these details for Belle because they both knew the shoes, for a while had been forced to shine them on Sunday mornings, as if Jimmy were on his way to a church that prized such care. Cassie loved doing it, Belle was made so angry by the task that she sometimes broke out in hives. That night Cassie was still wearing the clothes from her weekend job, painter's pants on which she'd wiped the residue from twenty different colors, a John Deere T-shirt, one of Poppy's old flannel button-downs. Jimmy drank his beer, talked to his friends, made his way slowly back to the glassed-in room that held his dearest conquest. He looked like a model for a certain kind of father; Cassie looked like a vagrant. When his eyes met hers, he let his gaze flicker over her face, and she knew why he was there.

"Cass?" he said, coming through the door.

"Hey."

"How's my girl?" He kissed the side of her head. "You're dusty."

"Drywall," Cassie said, running her hand over the grit on the back of her neck.

"Well, don't get it on my table." Jimmy put his beer on the shelf and began unzipping his cue case.

"Okay."

"You've worked yourself up a good game, I hear."

Cassie shrugged, looked back at Bud, who remained behind the bar, watching her. He would stop this if she asked.

"Your mom's okay? Bella?"

Cassie shrugged again; he was wrong to ask. She noticed then that his hand shook as he tried to screw in the butt of his cue, a gesture she'd seen him make a thousand times. It was possible he was drunk; with Jimmy it was hard to tell. He gave nothing away in his gait, the whites of his eyes, his speech. He simply grew more malignant around the edges, and then he was gone.

Cassie leaned back in Belle's desk chair, stretched out her fingers. It had been two years since she'd seen Jimmy, and two years since Belle left home, and in that time she'd written more than in all her years of school. Neither she nor Laura liked to talk on the telephone; Belle didn't, either, really, so they wrote and wrote. It didn't come naturally to Cassie and she didn't enjoy it and it made her fingers ache. But Laura said it would come in handy if Cassie were ever arrested and forced to write a jailhouse confession. Cassie said they could *break* her fingers, she'd never confess to anything, and Laura nodded.

* * *

Jimmy racked the balls without bothering to ask Cassie if she was done with her game, and then he pulled a roll of money from his pocket. "You want to show your old dad what you're made of?" Smiling.

Maybe she imagined it, or maybe it happened internally, but the whole establishment grew unusually quiet. Then Bud leaned his head in the doorway. "Cassie? Talk to you a minute?"

She walked with Bud behind the bar as Jimmy used her cue to break and to take his practice shots.

"How much do you have on you?" he asked.

"One-fifty. My paycheck."

"All right, look." Bud kept his eye on the room where Jimmy was playing alone. "There's five, six hundred in the till, two or three thousand in the safe. Use it all."

"Okay."

"Lose it, let him bury himself. He's not carrying that much. You drop below, say, four thousand, we'll talk options. Lose the lag."

"Okay."

"Don't play this hotheaded. You go in and beat him every game, he'll make an excuse and walk. Or worse, he'll beat you. You—"

"He's not going to beat me."

"You bring Laura into this, Belle, Poppy, he'll beat you."

"He's not going to beat me."

Bud leaned in close, tapped her chest with his finger. "You bring your history into this, he'll beat you. Because you feel it and he doesn't."

"You best back that finger up."

Bud gripped his temples. "See? This is what I mean about you, you are your own worst—"

"Cassie?" Jimmy stepped away from the table. "Bud trying to talk you out of a friendly wager?" He shook his head. "Far as I can tell, he doesn't own you yet."

Cassie looked Bud hard in the eye. "No," she said. "He doesn't." But just before she walked away from Bud, she offered him Jimmy's half-wink, and he opened the till. Then she turned to the table where her father waited, a slight man with a swing in his step. She was going to give him what he wanted: she was going to play like a girl. And then she was going to kick his ass.

To her sister she wrote: *Bud backed me.*

Cassie put the pencil down, turned her attention back to the desk. There were articles on chaos theory, fractal geometry, astrology. A small book-length collection of French surrealist parlor games. An introduction to Sufism. An article from a group called Solarplexus, which promised to lead the reader to an alchemical paradise at the edge of the sun. Nearly at the bottom, the sort of thing Cassie thought she might find: a blurry photocopy of an article on billiards and the law of reflection. At the top Belle had written, *A ball in motion on a pool table behaves like a light ray reflecting off a mirror.*

Cassie sighed. This was just like Belle. *In truth,* Cassie wrote in the margin, *the velocity at which the ball strikes the rubber rail determines the angle of reflection. The law applies only if the ball is moving slowly. A ball in motion on a pool table behaves like a ball in motion on a pool table.* But the accuracy of the physical hypothesis wasn't what interested Belle, and Cassie knew it. What interested Belle was the mirror.

* * *

Jimmy called fifty bucks a game, and Cassie chose 9-ball. There were some things she'd let float in the interest of the outcome, and a couple things she wanted made clear from the outset. Through the first game Jimmy kept up a steady stream of talk, all vaguely hostile, as Cassie said nothing. She'd seen him do it at home, knew it threw some men off. It was a miracle Jimmy still had all his organs, the way he sharked. She lost the first game, the second. Jimmy drank, became giddy with victory. She lost barely, and only at the last possible second, on thin slices and long shots, letting Jimmy think she was playing at the edge of her skill. After the third game she took a bathroom break and picked up the money Bud had left for her there, along with a note: Lose one more, then come back for two. Then double the bid. In the bathroom Cassie flushed the note, tucked the money in her pocket. There was money in this, she'd realized. Jimmy's roll was all hundred dollar bills. He'd either mortgaged something of Barbara's or had a handsome accident. Either way there was plenty in it for her, for Laura and Poppy and Bud. But she already knew, though she wasn't ready to say it yet, that she didn't care much about the money. She wanted something else of his, and it was simply a matter of pushing him to lose it.

Jimmy claimed the cue was an original Balabushka, which was no doubt Jimmy talking. George Balabushka had been dead for twelve years, and if Jimmy weren't lying, the cue was worth twenty-five thousand dollars. It still had the original ferrule and finish, the original Irish linen wrap, Balabushka's signature burned into the butt. She didn't believe, and Bud didn't, either, that even Jimmy would use it if it were authentic. But they'd both held it, Cassie only once, and they agreed that there was something unusual in the balance. It seemed to have its own heat, more like a fast horse or a gun. The cue was the last artifact in Jimmy's possession of that fateful night in New Orleans, and Cassie thought maybe some things should be restored as a set. The table, the lamp, the cue. Whatever else he'd stolen and hadn't advertised.

"There she is," Jimmy said as Cassie walked back out into the hall. "You're a good sport. This is a tough lesson, I know. Don't take it too hard." He smiled his crooked smile at her. His shoulders, the line of his chest under his pink shirt, made Cassie want to cry.

"I'll try not to."

She won two games, dropped the third, let herself look desperate. She was exhausted from working all day and from straining against her inclinations all evening. A small and silent crowd gathered as the night wore on, and the phone rang repeatedly, but Bud ignored it. "A hundred a game," she said as Jimmy racked the balls.

"You're on," he answered, without even glancing her way.

To her sister she wrote: I raised the stakes.

Barbara arrived around midnight, and threats were issued. A friend of Bud's from the sheriff's department sat outside in his car, keeping her at bay. At two in the morning Bud locked the doors. Jimmy was down thirty-seven hundred and out of cash.

"This is unacceptable, Cassie," he said, lighting a cigarette with shaking hands. His pink shirt was unbuttoned, his T-shirt drenched with sweat. "You and that sumbitch Bud set something up and scoured me, and you'll pay for it."

Cassie rocked her head back and forth, trying to loosen the

muscles in her neck. Her left shoulder felt like someone was frying bacon on it. "So quit," she said.

Jimmy took two steps toward her, then shouted in her face, "I
can't quit!" Bud jumped up from the stool in the doorway, but
Jimmy ignored him. "You know I can't quit, that money is *hers*,"
he said, gesturing toward the parking lot, "and if I leave here without it, she'll not only kick me out of the house, she'll have her
goon squad of relatives kill me, they will *kill me*, Cassie, is that
what you want?" He ran his fingers through his hair. He looked
sick, feverish.

"How is this Cassie's fault? Huh? You came in here blowing,
you lost the money."

"She hustled me, and you helped her. She just happened to be
carrying around that kind of money?" The veins in Jimmy's neck
stood out, and a vein in his forehead throbbed.

Cassie remembered that moment in particular and wrote to
Belle that she had felt clearheaded but distanced from her body.
She heard what Jimmy was saying, that if she beat him, he would
Literally Die, and Cassie would be responsible for it. She didn't
doubt what he said; Barbara Thompson came from a long line of
puppy-drowning rednecks who target-practiced with a twelve-
gauge in the woods behind a trailer park filled with children.

"You know what I think?" Bud was in Jimmy's face, and even
though his voice was raised, Cassie could hear a hum coming
from the hanging light. Below the argument was such a silence. "I
think you're a chickenshit failure who got himself—"

"*What* did you say to me? What did you say?"

"You heard me, you—"

"Hold on a minute," Cassie said, raising her hands. "Bud, stop."
She turned to her father. "It sounds like you're in a bind."

"Cassie," Bud said, "don't do this. He pulled this on your mother for fifteen years—"

"No," Cassie said, "it's okay." She looked at Jimmy, whose face was flooded with relief.

"I knew it, I knew I could count on you."

"Here's how I see it. You need to leave here with your original stake, and maybe even a couple hundred extra to sweeten it at home?"

Jimmy nodded.

"So how about this?" Cassie began racking the balls. "One game. If you win, you leave with four thousand even. If I win, you can still have the money, but you lose the cue." She lifted the rack and hung it on a hook. Both men stared at her, astonished, and no one spoke. Cassie could nearly hear Jimmy's mind at work, the full constraints, the bind he was in pressing against him. He'd never make it out past Bud, he could never move fast enough to hurt her. She realized that her clarity was temporary, that something was struggling underneath it; over and over she imagined Jimmy charging at her, and saw herself pulling the knife out of its sheath on her belt; she saw herself pulling it so fast she went through Poppy's shirt and nicked her own side. Bud was staring at her and blinking slowly, like a predator in overhead sun.

"You're saying"—Jimmy held his forehead—"that if I beat you I leave with all my money, but if I lose, you're taking the Balabushka? You're out of your mind."

"Okay," Cassie said, yawning. "I'm going home then, I'm beat." Bud yawned, too.

"Wait! Wait, what's plan B?"

Cassie shook her head. "I'm sorry, that's my only plan. Otherwise, I'm taking this money home to Laura." She headed toward the door.

"Jesus!" Jimmy laughed, letting his head fall back. "You're going to take everything away from me, if not you and Laura, then Bud. You're a bunch of *cannibals*." He wiped his eyes, laughed again, then stood very still.

Cassie looked at Bud, at Jimmy, at the floor. For a moment she couldn't swallow. She cleared her throat and said, "Take it or leave it."

He took it, Cassie wrote, and I broke and cleared the table without him ever taking a shot or saying a word. After I sank the 9, Bud went to the safe and got more money, and we counted it all out until he had four thousand. Jimmy took the cue apart slowly and carefully, and wiped it down, then put it in the case and handed it to me, but he never met my eye. Bud let him out the front door, then locked it behind him, and we watched him give the deputy a salute. Then he got in Barbara's old Mustang and she peeled away. You know he must have been out of sorts to leave the Lincoln there. For a while I couldn't take the stick out of the case. I couldn't even look at it. But in time that feeling went away, although I never saw Jimmy again.

She straightened the pages, attached a paper clip, and slipped the letter underneath the essay on chaos theory. She stood and straightened her back, crossed her arms and looked out the window. A clear November day, and colder than it looked. Girls came and went in the rooms around her, laughing loudly and slamming doors. From this angle, stared at long enough, the walkways leading up to and away from Belle's dormitory looked like streambeds, tributaries meeting and diverging on the way to some greater body. Cassie stood that way twenty minutes or so, looked down at the clock. One-thirty-six. She watched for a thin girl braced against the cold, head bent and moving with great purpose. Cassie waited for her sister.

Part Three

◈

RATTLESNAKE KITE

CATTAILS, 1999

◈

At two in the morning Cassie was still sitting alone at the scarred kitchen table. She remembered these hours after Poppy's death, too, the way her mind struggled against the information and wouldn't let her sleep; the strange doubling of consciousness that lasted for months. She might be driving or measuring a piece of hardwood for flooring, and she *would* be driving but also telling herself that Poppy was gone. Pulling the tape measure out, marking the board, measuring it again, Poppy is gone, until he was in every gesture and every breath. There seemed to be no other way to allow him to die.

Laura would have said that at two in the morning the soul was less moored to the body than at any other time, and could fly free, and Cassie felt that, too, the vague awareness of a door not yet open. But a door that could be opened. And staying or going was the question at hand. On the table were Laura's journals, a stack of letters bound with a bright blue ribbon, scraps of paper torn from envelopes and message pads. The yellow lined notebook in which Cassie and Belle and Laura had been leaving messages for one another. And two plane tickets. She gathered up the scraps of paper—on each was printed a few words, a phrase, in Belle's block handwriting—and lined them up randomly in front of her. *A man walks down the street / to be pregnant in a dream / In the chthonic realm everyone is wealthy / Like the ghost of pure spirit / Followed by a gray dog / and everything is cheap / the tyranny of the door frame / is to be pregnant with* **something.** She read it, rearranged it, Belle's method of sense-making made no sense at all to Cassie.

She tipped her head back and closed her eyes. Her fingertips were cold, and she pressed them against her eyelids like a compress, letting the chill through. The act felt medicinal but was not. She had been awake almost seventy-two hours and would not rest until she had decided what to do about the plane tickets; she could go, or she could leave them somewhere in the house; no one would blame her either way.

The letter Laura had left in her jewelry box already looked worn, as if years had pulled something from it and put something different back in. Cassie had seen it for the first time only four days ago; since then, the letter, typed on the heavyweight cotton bond Laura favored for correspondence, had been taken from the envelope, unfolded, pored over, refolded, and tucked away more than a dozen times. It was dated March 21, a little more than a year before, the day Laura was told she had lung cancer, and decided, after what surely had been only a few agonizing hours spent alone and without counsel, to forgo treatment. The letter, addressed to Cassie and Belle, was intended as a justification.

Play The Odds, Never Do Anything On Principle: these were the two pieces of advice Cassie had received from Jimmy like an Old Testament blessing. They had filtered through to his wife as well, because Laura cited her chances of surviving the treatment of her cancer in a way that suggested anyone who held the hand would have folded. Laura saw no good end. "I would have cared for you if the situation were reversed," she wrote, "I would have seen you through to the end. But to bargain for my life at your expense is untenable." She also gave the reasons for her secrecy; the day, she wrote, that Buena Vista had been diagnosed with breast cancer, she had ceased to be Laura's mother-in-law, the grandmother to Laura's children, and had become instead the Dying Thing. "All that last year I read her life in reverse. When I thought of her as a young woman, when I thought of her in the kitchen rolling out pie crust, the picture in my mind of her at Christmas the year we gave her the photograph of all her loved ones gathered in a studio, in that ghastly light, I saw a woman who was always about to die. You will do the same, I suspect, now that I am dead, but at least you haven't done it for the past year or six months, however long. At least we lived normally. When you said good-bye before leaving the house, you did it because you chose to, not because you were measuring out your affection against my death. When you sat talking with me late into the night in the kitchen, you were not coerced by our limited time. I withheld the information for no reason but this, and I doubt I even need to ask your forgiveness. I think you, Cassie, are especially prone to such silences, and will respect mine."

Cassie looked up at the clock. It was two-twenty-seven, and she felt closer to a decision than she had for the last two days (The Way To Decide Is To Decide, Jimmy's voice rang in her head), and because she was close to something, she went ahead and read the next section again, even though the pain it caused her had begun to seem formal. "And frankly," it began, "I see no reason to fight to stay in this world. I could lie and say it's poverty or the abuse of children or the destruction of the planet that makes me want to go ahead and die, or I could blame it on your father, which heaven knows I have done before and is closer to the truth. The truth is that I don't want to spend another day with the cat, Miss Mittens. That's for starters. I get up in the morning and she's waiting right in front of my door to be fed. And so I open the can and feed her that smelly wet cat food, and she eats it, and then I pick up the bowl and cover it, because if I leave it on the floor it draws ants and probably worse things. And then Miss Mittens wants to go outside, and so I open the door and let her out, and go to wash out the cat-food can, and while I'm in the kitchen I hear her meowing at the door or tearing at the welcome mat, demanding to be let in. So I let her in, and she comes straight into the kitchen wailing for her food, so I take the foil off and set it down, and we begin the process again. I do this all day. I ask myself, Should I kill the cat? and the answer is no, I can't. But Miss Mittens never stops, except sometimes to nap, and not when I wish she would. If she is outside she wants in, and vice versa. If she is eating she wishes to cease eating and go outside, etc. If I set the food outside, she becomes confused and even more frantic and it draws bigger animals. And what I can read only as her deep dissatisfaction seems to me to be both projection and apt metaphor, and this knowledge is terrible, and life with Miss Mittens is no way for a grown woman to live. I ask myself, What does the cat want? And the answer seems to be, For the food to stay on the floor, and for a world with no doors. Surfaces, obstructions, thresholds. They pain Miss Mittens, and they pain me. The world was too much for me before I knew I was dying. But to face it with no hair or fingernails, with bleeding lips and diarrhea, to go blind as Buena Vista did and then die anyway, sweet Jesus, as she used to say. No thank you.

"And another thing is: Belle, like you, I used to believe that everything I saw had a secret in it, that it was a portal to an unseen world. I remember one afternoon during tornado season, this was many years ago. You girls were very small, in elementary school, and I was working at the library in Jonah, and a man came in and said there was a tornado warning for our county. (The man was Donnie White, by the way, who had a crush on me and I considered having an affair with him but didn't, don't worry that I'll confess it later. I was always faithful to your father, even for the last twenty years, it's no wonder I have cancer.) I dropped the rubber stamp I was holding, grabbed my purse and ran out the door, I could think only that you would be frightened, that I had to get to you. When you were little, and I think this is true of almost every mother of young children, I was less afraid that one of you would die than that we wouldn't all be together. I jumped in the old Jeep—do you remember that Jeep, the one I bought from the man at the grain elevator? Jimmy sold it? and began the forty-five-minute drive like a woman possessed. I listened to the radio all the way, even though I couldn't understand what I was hearing. What did the broadcaster mean when he said the funnel cloud was twelve miles west/southwest of Haddington? How was I to know which way was west when the sky was green and I have a terrible sense of direction? I tried to picture Haddington, the grid of streets, and to determine what lay west of it, but I couldn't see anything in my head. I was driving down a straight country road, the one that man lives on who flies the model airplanes. The fields around me were perfectly flat. No corn was up yet. And there in a field, right next to me, a herd of deer was running under that unnatural sky, eight, twelve deer. They seemed to be running as fast as I was driving, sometimes leaping, and I know they were running for their lives, but I swear to me it looked like joy. Just then a transformer on an electrical pole in front of me exploded in a burst of blue, and I felt the explosion more than I heard it, the air seemed to have absorbed the sound. I lost sight of the deer when I came to a crossroads. I stopped at a stop sign (not the thing a woman possessed ordinarily does), and in front of me was a beautiful old farmhouse with a wraparound porch, the relic of an orchard on one side, a flowering hedge in the front. The backyard was enclosed with a black iron fence, and in front of the gate leading into the yard, a cloud was hovering. I don't know how to say this. The air had gone flat and still, and there was a cloud. I don't know what it was made of. And it just hung there, I thought to myself, That cloud is levitating, and in my mind I saw Saint Theresa. Do you see what this is leading to, how the storm and the deer and the cloud became the elements of transport, of ecstasy? Belle, I know that the word transport is somewhat lazy. I was in a car after all, and I was literally moving. Sorry. And then the lightning began to strike, hot bolts of it encircling the horizon, and it was so constant I couldn't tell whether it was coming down from the sky or up from the ground. It looked more like a conductor's baton, up and down, and a black cat leaped out from where it had been hiding behind the flowering hedge and ran toward a break in the lattice under the porch. I drove on, and when I was a mile from your school, I was stopped by police cars blocking the road. They told me I couldn't continue on our road, a tree was down. I backed up, turned around, and approached your school from another angle. Again I was stopped; I couldn't take that road, either. I didn't complain—by that time I felt crazy,

I believed in everything. I tried the third road and made it into the school parking lot, and that was when the sirens started. I remember thinking, What a lot of noise, the sirens and a train coming all at once, and imagine that, living in Indiana all those years and not recognizing what it meant, the sound of a freight train when I was nowhere near tracks. We weren't hit by that tornado, but twenty-six people died in Dennison, which was barely a town to start with and was nothing when the storm was through. Every town has its own disasters. Down on the Gulf we had hurricanes, some places have avalanches or tidal waves, I hope that the disaster you face determines the life you live. Because here, at least as I understood it then, a tornado could pass right above my head or touch down briefly and drive a goat through an oak tree. I saw those things that day, I saw the secret, and there were countless such sights. There were. There aren't anymore. On the bus from New Orleans to Indianapolis, when I ran after your father and never made it home, we were passing through a crossroads in rural Louisiana and I saw a woman walking from her front porch across her yard toward a horse behind a fence, and the horse was walking toward her, too. The woman was middle-aged and heavy, pretty, and she was holding up the corners of an apron filled with apples, and every step she took toward the horse the horse took a step toward her. All I wanted was to stay right there until the two had met, until I witnessed whatever love or hunger pulled them together, but the bus drove on and I landed here, and in all the years since I never got to see that place again. I never saw New Orleans again, or my mother. I never took the two of you, although I swore I would. I imagine that the house on Rendon Street is still standing, that someone has painted it pink and blue, a few blocks from Bayou St. John. Heat, mosquitoes. There is nothing to see here. I have stared at the cattails on the edge of the pond until my eyes burn. I stand on the porch and there is the fencerow across the road, sometimes a hawk circling and dipping, I have worn this place out. Miss Mittens, doorways. Your father, the deer, the woman with the apples. I am tired of flossing, of hand lotion, of the food pyramid. Years before I knew I was ill I had already felt every single morning, rising from bed, that I had to get up and do something about my corpse. Kundera may have been correct, that we fear first our own annihilation and then our own dead body, but I lived the other way around. I am tired of cigarettes. I adore you, take care of each other. I don't know what else to say."

Cassie had read the letter so many times, and there was plenty in there, but Laura Withheld. She was a withholder, that was either her nature or had become so. The larger question, which was how her daughters should go about not living their mother's life, was left unaddressed, and then there were the cigarettes. Laura claimed that when she wasn't smoking a cigarette, she was thinking about doing so, and sometimes while smoking one, she mentally rehearsed lighting the next. While other mothers prepared for snow days by freezing loaves of bread and gallons of milk, Laura stocked up on filtered Camels. In the three days it took Laura to die, Belle had gathered up her mother's possessions and put them in a box, now sitting at the top of the attic stairs, those things that were the clear line between a life being lived and a life vanished. Laura had been, for instance, on page 243 of Randall Jarrell's *No Other Book*, and had underlined, of Marianne Moore, "she has widened the scope of poetry, if poetry, like other organisms, wants to convert into itself everything that is, she has helped it to." Howlin' Wolf's *Cadillac Daddy* had been in the portable CD player in the kitchen, and Belle had left it there; the battered cookbook was off the shelf but not open. In the box at the top of the attic stairs were Laura's hairbrush, toothbrush and special toothpaste for sensitive teeth, a bottle of pills (unmarked), her favorite lipstick shade—Night-Blooming Jasmine. Only the most intimate items went in the box. If they'd tried to erase their mother completely, they would have had to burn the house down. Cassie had returned from the hospital with Laura's glasses and seashell earrings, as well as her wedding ring, which Laura had been wearing on a chain around her neck. A puzzle, the ring. But nothing pained Cassie more than the cigarette case, oxblood leather with the gold clasp worn dull, the thin silver lighter; Laura was bound to the case the way other people were to a watch or a religious medal. The hole in the air left by her death was here, in the kitchen, staring out the window at the finches darting to and from the feeder, her arms crossed over her chest, the cigarette case clutched in her left hand, a burning cigarette in the right. She was a woman who led with her hipbones, thin and tall and restless; she complained of her wavy black hair going gray in the center of her forehead, of her thin lips, her bottom teeth she called crooked as a dog's hind leg. But for Cassie, Laura's face was the human face, well constructed, orderly, staring out the window homesick and aggrieved.

Laura's last attempt at quitting smoking had been years before, when she drove to Jonah to consult a hypnotist. The man, Marshall Something, Cassie couldn't remember, had been overweight and top-heavy, a mouth-breather with a beard. A terrible thing, her mother reported later, to face the circle of his panting mouth in the midst of all that fur. His fat pink lips. Marshall sat down and told Laura what he was going to do. The primary focus of his therapy, he said, was aversion, and many women had reported successful weight loss after he hypnotically suggested that they see highly caloric foods covered with maggots. This would also work with people who were attempting vegetarianism but still loved the taste of meat. Laura realized that Marshall had mistaken her for some other client and was preparing to hypnotize her into emaciation: Laura, curled like a cat in the corner of an overstuffed chair, an Anne Sexton double, her cold glance.

"Perceptually dead," Laura had pronounced Marshall later, at home. Therapeutically blind or not, he had changed their lives. After explaining that she was not Betty Templeton, his two o'clock, and ergo not in need of his maggots, Laura asked him how successful hypnosis was for smoking cessation.

"It depends," he'd said, resting his hands on his belly; Laura had imitated him, holding her own arms two feet from her waist.

"On what?"

He panted slightly. "On if you're a smoker or not. If you are deeply and truly a smoker, you know it, and nothing will make you quit. If you're a person who smokes and could also not smoke, it will work for you."

Laura had paid him his thirty-five dollars and left without going under; she was a smoker, and she knew what would finally make her quit. Morphine, a sort of drowning, her own final fire. Cassie folded the thick letter and slipped it back into the envelope. Her mother and Belle thought Cassie didn't know the meaning of the doorway, the door frame, the doorknob, they considered it a code. But Cassie knew; Belle had once quoted it in a letter. It was from a Martin Amis novel. "He could never understand what was *in it* for inanimate objects, behaving as they did.

What was *in it* for the doorknob that hooked your jacket pocket as you passed? What was *in it* for the jacket pocket?"

Bleak, funny. And then Cassie had found this, photocopied from a book, unsourced, tucked into Laura's journal:

THE FIFTH DETAIL: RATTLESNAKE KITE

For we have agreed that there are two different ways to come to knowledge: either we set out seeking the intelligence, or the intelligence seeks us. **Sometimes It Is Difficult To Discern Whether To Move Or Stand Still: This Is A Discrepancy.**

We spent many days in concern for edges, as you may recall: the edge of the desk, the door frame, the table, the tips of our fingers, beyond which was Space. What do we see, what do we know? We know that our hand displaces a particular amount of Space: that it occupies: that it ends.

We drove south in a particular midwestern state, and flatness gave way to cliff walls, mostly sheer stone, which rose up around us as we drove down. We began to feel the information seeking us as a repository, and so our openness was heightened; just at the moment we felt patent, we saw a coyote dead at the side of the road and stopped to examine it.

As we have established, **Sudden Death Is A Discrepancy,** *and that information was abundantly present on the face of the dead animal. His feral nature was intact, visually. A high wind shifted his fur. The fur itself was remarkably delicate, and a high wind shifted it like a wheat field. We held our hand above the fur without per se touching it, and felt the movement of the fur in the high wind. The animal's spirit had* *flown; its hide existed as substantially as our own hand hovering above it. This was hard for us to synthesize. Cars passed us at a high rate of speed, and suddenly we saw ourselves as if from a great distance: our bodies kneeling at the side of a highway, above the dead coyote. The edge of the coyote, the edge of our bodies, the rock walls climbing above us into the greater space above. What about the unimaginable edges of the sun, which burned above us? How do we take into account the edges of the burning sun?*

We left the coyote. **The Corpse Is A Discrepancy That Fades Over Time; The Fact Of Death Does Not.** *Farther down the highway, trying to integrate our recently acquired information, we saw something in the air, rising higher and faster than the sheer rock walls rose around us, something rising light and swift. We barely had time to make out its details. It was a red kite in the shape of a rattlesnake. We thought at first that it was yet held by a human hand, perhaps a child's hand (as we ourselves held kites in days past), but it rose with a lightness and speed that suggested a lack of restraint or encumbrance.* **The Rising, Unencumbered Image Is The Soul's Image.** *We again pulled our vehicle to the side of the road; we stood in the blazing heat, we watched the rattlesnake kite float free, carried first on one current of air and then another, we watched it move as if directly toward the edge of the burning midday sun. Finally we saw the kite go up in flames.*

The plane tickets lying on the kitchen table were to New Orleans, one for Cassiopeia Claiborne and the other for Laura Dubuisson Claiborne, leaving April the first. Four days away. They were intended as a surprise; Cassie and Belle were going to make an early Easter basket for Laura, placing the tickets lightly in the crinkly plastic grass behind some Marshmallow Peeps. Cassie had reservations at the Maison Orleans, five days and four nights, and she'd even had matching T-shirts printed up with WWJE on the front, and on the back, WHAT WOULD JESUS EAT? Cassie laughed and shook her head, closed her aching eyes; it had been a surprise, all right. The six thousand dollars she had intended to spend on her mother in New Orleans had instead gone, all but a thousand of it, to Robbie Ballenger for Laura's funeral. He hadn't blinked when Cassie paid him in cash, although he must have been taken aback. Most people in the county didn't pay him at all.

Years ago when Poppy was still alive, Cassie had asked him where he'd hide a bit of cash, household expense money, she'd called it, and he said the last place he'd look if he was a burglar was in the kitty litter, so they'd devised a two-tiered scheme in the litter box, with the money sealed in freezer bags at the bottom, under a separate pan. Miss Mittens hadn't used a litter box in many years, preferring to employ the flower gardens Laura painstakingly planted. Cassie walked out in the mudroom and removed the bag, quickly counting the bills. This was the money Belle knew about and drew from to pay their bills and buy groceries. They were down to just over thirty-eight hundred, and there was no way to know what Laura's hospital bills would be. She'd been a patient for only three days, but Cassie had lost track of whether her mother had health insurance. There was another five thousand under the false bottom of a dresser drawer in Cassie's room, which she reserved for a stake, and another seven thousand wrapped with venison in the freezer. If Cassie went to New Orleans and didn't make it back, the money wasn't much for Belle to live on until she figured out something else. Her food would have to be delivered, someone (undoubtedly Edwin) would have to carry her manuscripts to the post office and pick up her packages. She had a small income from editing, but the only thing that would save her without Cassie was if Belle could be legally declared unable to work and could begin receiving government benefits and Medicare, and who would verify what was wrong with her when Cassie couldn't get Belle to leave the house that someone could verify that she couldn't leave the house? Cassie would do anything, she had already done things she couldn't have predicted to save her family, but it seemed beyond her to do that one, to voluntarily cast herself into the jaws of bureaucracy. No one in the world wanted to save Belle, no one but Cassie, alone now in rural Indiana, and if she placed their lives in the hands of the government they would be beaten as if with whips. Cassie had not ever, in her adult life, paid an income tax, and how to explain that one?

At three-forty Miss Mittens, whose radar was uncanny, began scratching at the back door. Cassie jumped, then realized she'd been dreaming. She opened the back door and scratched the old cat on top of her bony skull; Miss Mittens purred and wound between Cassie's legs as she opened a can of cat food and placed the whole thing on the floor, bypassing the food dish. She looked at the cat, at the floor, at the door, then propped the door open with a boot. As Cassie passed the kitchen table on her way to bed, she gathered up the letter, the journals, the plane tickets, leaving the constructed sentence as it was, so Belle would see it in the morning. She picked up a piece of yellow notebook paper Belle and Laura had been passing around for a few months, on which they debated which historical suicide they'd undo if given the option. Their first choice had changed a number of times, from Sylvia Plath to Dorothy Parker to Cleopatra (back again to Plath), with notes about the song "Gloomy Sunday," until Cassie had picked up the list and written *Elvis Presley.* Next to his name Laura had written, *Yes, that's perfect.* And Belle had engraved with her Eversharp, *He's not actually a suicide.* But later they'd discussed it and agreed: there are lots of ways to kill yourself; it just takes time.

She slept like a person falling down a hole, and woke at ten the next morning. Brutal, cherished Laura was not now and would never be again standing at the kitchen window waiting for her daughters to get up; no coffee made, no smoke hovering in the air like Saint Theresa. Cassie dressed quickly in a thermal shirt, a flannel shirt, jeans, and boots, then headed into the bathroom to wash her face and brush her teeth and hair, surprised to find she still recognized herself.

In the kitchen Belle was sitting at the table, going over a manuscript. The sentence from the night before was nowhere to be seen. "You left the door open last night, and when I got up the house was about seven degrees. The furnace has been running for its life for the past three hours, I made coffee," she said without looking up.

Cassie stopped halfway to the stove, having smelled coffee without fully realizing it. "Thanks."

"Well, thank me after you've had a cup. I was winging it."

The first two cups in the cabinet were Laura's, Fiestaware in pink and green, not the radioactive colors. Cassie moved them aside and took out a battered piece of stoneware, dark brown with a lighter brown rim. They owned a whole set of these dishes, a wedding gift to Laura and Jimmy; they were ugly, and sacred as a relic.

Belle's face this morning was fine-lined, with a faint yellow tint; her eyes were puffy, and the skin around her nose was irritated. For years she had worn Laura's clothes, saying she had no interest in shopping or developing a personal style, but it was harrowing to see her in them now: Laura's green blouse and narrow black pants, her flat black shoes. Belle didn't say, and no one else said, that she didn't buy clothes because she never left the house, would never leave. She had retreated from the Wide World and come back to the kitchen table, and worked there every day, so what were clothes to her? "What's this?" Cassie asked, pointing to the manuscript Belle was correcting.

"It's a chapter of Peggy's dissertation on ancient Athenian festivals. This one concerns the Munichion, which was dedicated to Artemis."

The coffee was too strong—it caused Cassie's tongue to curl—but she drank it anyway. "Good?"

"It depends on how you feel about the sacrifice of she-goats dressed up like young girls. I frankly think it's a good idea. And there were cakes covered with candles: imagine that. But the sentences are bland. I can't help but rewrite it as Roberto Calasso would have." Belle ran her hands, shaking, through her brittle hair, going gray.

"You want something to eat?" Cassie asked.

"I ate already. Are you going to Bud's?"

"In a minute. What did you eat?"

"Toast."

"I don't see a plate."

Belle looked up, staring at Cassie for a moment with no expression. "I ate it over the sink."

Cassie stared back, said nothing.

"Don't think for a moment that you're going to start telling me where and when to eat, I won't have it."

The coffee seemed to be getting thicker as Cassie neared the bottom of the cup. She swirled the dregs around, trying to see the future, but she'd never understood the concept.

"Even Laura never hassled me about eating, I don't know where you get off."

Cassie rinsed out the cup and placed it in the dishwasher, then started making a sandwich to take with her.

"Peggy misplaces modifiers right and left, and within a few months she'll be called *doctor*. Dr. Mosley. I can hardly stand it. And another thing is I could say plenty about how you live your life, but I keep my own counsel, so why don't you do the same."

Cassie took a small carton of orange juice out of the refrigerator, stepped into the mudroom for her backpack and her coat.

"Are you driving into town?" Belle picked at the scabs on her forearm.

"I'll ride my bike."

"Cass, it's cold outside. I nearly froze just picking up the paper this morning, and don't say it's because I've got no insulation, if I hear that one more time."

Cassie pulled on her black wool cap and gloves, opened the closet where she kept her cue. The leather case fit against her back like a quiver of arrows. She searched in her pockets for her sunglasses, then wheeled her bike out of the corner and propped open the back door. Miss Mittens ran in, turned around, ran out again.

Belle walked out onto the porch. "Why don't you go ahead and take your truck?"

The back wheel of the bike bounced down the two cement steps. "Thanks for the coffee, Belle." Cassie strapped her pack onto the back of the bike, pulled her left sock up over her pant leg, and climbed on. Belle sighed and closed the door as Cassie rode away; Miss Mittens clawed at the welcome mat. How were they to know how to live? Who would tell them?

Cassie passed the fencerow on her right, where sometimes a hawk circled, and the pond surrounded by cattails a little farther up. It was too cold to ride the four miles into downtown Roseville. On either side of the road, mobile homes and double-wides sat tucked away in the tree stands farmers left when the land was originally cleared; at night the trailers twinkled like narrow gift boxes, and there were more every year. Large tracts of land went up for sale in five-acre increments, and within a year ten to fifteen mobile homes and their inevitable accessories—plastic flowers and wooden cutouts of overweight women bent over weeding, garden gnomes and small plaster donkeys—dotted what had been a soybean field.

Cassie turned right on 300 West and sped up. The road had been repaved only last summer, so the Indiana winters had not yet destroyed it. She lowered her head and leaned into the miserable air, her legs beginning to come to life after the many motionless days. It was flatly too cold to be riding into town. She reached into her jacket pocket and pulled out a handkerchief; her nose was running, her eyes were streaming tears behind her sunglasses, but the feeling she'd had earlier of her knees being made of old cork was fading. She breathed deeply, rode, thought of herself in motion, as she had when she was a child. Then there had been no limit to how far she could ride, not because she was stronger but because she thought differently. The trees and fields began to give way to businesses dotting the edge of the Price Dairy Road, a used-car dealership, a lawn-mower repair shop. The Granger School was in ruins. The gas station was still there; the florist's shop now held a custom framer. April and May's was still standing, although the sisters themselves were dead. Cassie remembered one of them sitting on the front porch of the house where they had been born and always lived, it might have been April or it might have been May, the way she sat on the front porch wearing a dress and red lipstick. The candy shop was now owned by two gay men who did well there. They had taken the pathos right out of the candy business, as Laura had said. Cassie passed Holzinger's and approached the center of town. The mechanics and body shops that had dotted Railroad Street when she was a girl were gone; even a car wash had been abandoned, its fiberglass walls gradually buckling as volunteer trees grew up too close. It sat in a green pile, covered with last autumn's leaves and young shoots of ivy. Only Uncle Bud's remained on Main Street, with Howdy's hanging on behind it. Cassie unlocked the steel back door, then rolled her bike up the steps. She pulled the string and turned on the light in the storage room, a corner of which was kept clear for her bike. She stowed her jacket and pack, carried her lunch and her cue up front.

Cassie had owned the cue fourteen years and handled it so gently that only the tip had been changed. Uncle Bud had given her the best advice, which was to treat it as if it were an original; no harm done if she was wrong. She screwed the parts together, felt again the brilliance of the balance. Jimmy loved things more because they bore a certain signature or earned him greater respect. If someone had told him that this very cue had been made by someone in Hopwood County in a garage in his spare time, Jimmy would have given it away without a second look. But what her father would have done with the cue, and who he would have lost it to had he not lost it to Cassie, no longer mattered. Because he'd lost it. She racked the balls and practiced for the next three hours.

Uncle Bud opened a Diet 7UP. He had recently been diagnosed with high blood pressure and high sugar, so he'd given up alcohol, caffeine, and regular soda. His life was miserable.

"Didn't see Jimmy at your mom's funeral," he said, pushing an open bag of pretzels toward Cassie.

"Ha."

"Anybody let him know she died?"

"Why would we?" Cassie took a drink of orange juice.

"Well, they were married. They had kids together."

Cassie said nothing, unwrapped her sandwich.

"Just seems like maybe a person would want to know if his ex-wife died."

"Are you *trying* to piss me off?"

"All I'm saying—"

"Seriously, are you trying to piss me off?"

"Cassie, knock it off. Sit back down and eat your sandwich."

She sat down on the bar stool, heart pounding. Bud took a drink. Cassie took a drink.

"What about New Orleans?" he asked.

"What about it?"

"You going?"

"I'm thinking about it."

"What's to think about?" Bud's dark blue T-shirt was stretched taut over his broad shoulders and heavy stomach, and proclaimed, in white letters, FAIR WARNING.

"A lot of things."

"Like? start your next sentence with Like."

"Like are you *trying* to piss me off?"

Bud opened a second bag of pretzels. "Like maybe you don't want to go without your mom, like maybe it would be too painful, maybe you'd feel a little like you were betraying her."

Cassie said nothing, picked at her sandwich.

"Why don't you cut your hair, Cassie? It's so long it gets on the table when you play, it's a distraction."

"It's a distraction to you. Don't tell me to cut my hair."

"I'm just saying."

"Dude, stop crossing me."

"Dude. Listen to you, a grown woman talking like that, you sound like Leroy Buell, for pity's sake. Grow up."

Cassie said nothing.

"I'm also thinking," Bud said, spitting some pretzel salt Cassie's way, "that you have good reasons to go to Louisiana, maybe you recognize them, maybe you don't."

"Yeah? Name one."

Bud rocked back on his heels, then crossed his arms over his chest. His own haircut seemed fresh and raw. "You name one, Cassie. I'm going to stand right here, the door locked, my business not open for business. You name one."

Cassie clenched her fist under the bar, didn't let Bud see it.

"What, what do you want me to say? that I need a little voodoo? I don't."

"Okay."

"Or that I'm planning to run away and not do right by Belle? I won't."

"I believe you."

"I want just one thing," Cassie said, "no, two." Her whole body ached with the effort required not to hit Bud, she didn't understand why he hadn't been killed before now. "I want to see where she lived. And I want to meet Jackson LaFollette, the man she almost married."

"Ah, Christ." Bud shook his head, looked to the ceiling for mercy.

"What? What's wrong with that?" Cassie appealed to him, palms up on the bar.

"You can go and do that, Cass, you can see where she lived and what she missed and wanted to go back to. But that other thing is bullshit."

"Why, how? Tell me why?"

Bud gave her a tight smile, tilted his head, this was his look of love and contempt. "Because, *dude*: The Worst Thing That Can Happen To You."

The unassailable law: Is That You Will Find What You Seek. Cassie's hands relaxed, the muscles in her shoulders unwound, she took a bite of her sandwich, swallowed. "I know."

Bud stared at her.

"I know," she said.

He walked away, unlocked the front door, turned on the neon sign that said Open.

*　*　*

"Oh, we are going to Emmy's house," Puck sang, a meandering tune, "I'm usually not welcome at Emmy's house. What will we find at Emmy's house? God. Only. Knows."

"Roll your window down if you want to smoke."

"It's cold."

"I don't care." In truth, they knew exactly what they would find at Emmy's house. Puck knew so well he'd begun a graphic novel about her life called "Saucy Little Broadcaster," after Emmy's old dream of reading the evening news on television. Emmy had not seen the novel, didn't know it existed. It was quite long, and every time Puck and Cassie saw Emmy, he added another chapter. He called it his Life's Work.

"Do you think Brian would kick me out if I kissed Emmy on the lips?"

Cassie struggled with the truck in the first two gears; it had hung on a long time. She was hoping to get it to two hundred thousand miles so she could present it to Emmy's dad.

"Do you think Brian would kick me out if I kissed Bart or Dylan on the lips?"

In third gear the truck usually caught on and was fine. Not always. Patience was required.

"Do you think Brian would kick me out of the house if I kissed their furniture or, like, their spatulas and whatnot?"

Billy Poe was her mechanic; he called the acceleration problem a head scratcher. He literally scratched his head when faced with it.

"Oh, their married towels! their toothbrushes! the way their sink is always clotted with blue toothpaste! their married bed, Cassie, do you see where I'm going with this?"

"I do."

"I DO! she said." Puck leaned over and kissed Cassie on the cheek, he'd been drinking. "My hero."

Emmy yelled *Come in*, she was standing in the kitchen holding her married spatula, she yelled at the boys to stop running, but they ignored her. She said If you're going to run, at least take those popsicle sticks out of your mouth, if you fall they'll go right down your throats.

Puck and Cassie took off their jackets and draped them over a chair. All of the furniture was new, from a department store in Jonah, it all matched. Dark blue with small red flowers. Dylan, who was five, ran down the hallway through the kitchen, through the dining room connected to the living room, into the living room and up onto the couch. His Popsicle stick was in his mouth. He wore no shirt or pants, just little-boy underwear patterned with trucks. Dylan was the one Cassie liked. He looked her in the eye. "Hello," he said.

"Hello," Cassie said.

"I wonder if you remember about the Pokémon."

Puck covered his eyes with his hand. "Precious Savior," he prayed, "I beg you, not this."

"I do remember," Cassie said.

Dylan rubbed his wet Popsicle stick against the wall like a pencil. "Who's your favorite Pokémon?" In the spring Emmy shaved the boys' heads, said it was easier to keep them clean. Dylan looked like a tiny prisoner.

"Butterfree."

"Mine is that—that ghost Pokémon, what's he called?"

"I don't know," Cassie said. "What is he called?"

"You tell me."

"I don't know," Cassie said, "you tell me."

Puck whispered, "Do you think Brian would kick me out of the house if I licked their walls?"

"Do you know what Butterfree ebolves into?"

"No."

"Don't you like Squirtle?" Dylan put his left hand down into his underwear, took it out again. "Do you know what Squirtle ebolves into?"

Emmy yelled, "Dinner's almost ready, Dylan, leave them alone."

In the kitchen Emmy hugged them both, apologized for her bad haircut, for her weight, for the clutter in her kitchen, for Dylan, who refused to wear clothes. Bart slunk through the room pulling a suitcase on wheels. He was the one Cassie didn't like. At seven he already walked as if into a windstorm, his head down, a nervous scuttle. He was worried about everything, trusted nothing and no one. What was in the suitcase was A Secret, but Emmy looked all the time. It was nothing, she said, a broken microscope, a book about dinosaurs. A lot of rocks, a model airplane missing a wing. In Puck's novel, the suitcase was filled with nuclear waste.

"Brian will be back in a minute, Cassie get yourself a beer, Puck I'm afraid if I offer you a beer I'll be Enabling you."

"Oh," Puck said, eyes wide, "I wouldn't dream of allowing you that personal compromise."

On the counter next to the stove was a crock filled with light blue plastic utensils, but in Puck's novel they were in all the colors of the rainbow. Bart came through the kitchen again, wearing a short-sleeved shirt buttoned all the way up to his throat and a pair of shorts hiked nearly to his chest. Cassie could see him plainly as an adult—if no one killed him in junior high—walking across a college campus, furtive, clutching his thesis to his chest. Dylan ran through with an action figure, then Bart, then Dylan again, there were only two of them, but they had the ability to swarm.

"Kids!" Emmy shouted, a bit seriously, "land somewhere! Go watch television!"

"Our TVs are on," Bart said, still moving.

"Then why aren't you watching them?"

"Because we want to be in here," Dylan said.

Brian walked in the door, smiled warmly at them all. "Hey, you guys! So nice to see you!" He was carrying a green bucket, which he placed under the sink. "Just taking out the compost." Dylan ran over and punched his father in the thigh, and Brian swooped him up and tucked him under his arm. "Let me go get rid of this nuisance," he said, and carried Dylan, who was kicking and laughing, into the living room. They fell on the floor in a pile and started wrestling, and Bart ran in and jumped on his father's back, but tentatively.

"Cassie, carry these salad bowls to the table, it's just lettuce and shredded carrots, I couldn't find a good tomato, and Puck take this dressing, we only have ranch."

They carried the bowls and the salad dressing. Puck whispered to Cassie that he was *so* happy. So Happy.

Over the dinner of salad, homemade, baked macaroni and cheese, and garlic bread, milk for the children and for Puck, they talked about Bart's test scores, very high, and Pokémon. Giengar, the ghost Pokémon. Dylan remembered and went and fetched him from his room; he was indeed transparent. Cassie declared him her new favorite, and so Dylan had to change his own favorite to Rabbitmon. Bart said, with thick disdain, that his name was not *Rabbitmon* but would not go on to say what the real name was, and Dylan started to cry. They talked about Brian's agency, he sold car insurance at cut-rate prices, he owned a franchise.

"How's your brother, Em?"

"He's fine, he's at MIT studying . . . what is it, Brian?"

Brian said, "I have no idea."

"Something with particles? Particle acceler—transmi—I don't know."

Emmy said since Dylan was in kindergarten, she thought about getting a job. She had applied to the new bookstore in Jonah. "It was terrible, the interview."

"Why?" Puck asked, concerned. Cassie could see his wheels turning, in his mind he was writing a chapter heading, The Interview.

"Well, for one thing, the manager asked me what was the last book I read, and I couldn't think of a thing to say, because I haven't finished a book since Bart was born. I've started a few. So I finally answered honestly and said it was *The Cat in the Hat*."

Puck roared with laughter, he leaned back and put his hands on his belly like Santa Claus.

"The manager didn't think it was so funny. He kept asking me very pointed questions about child care, like what would happen if I was scheduled to work and one of my kids got sick, what if their school called, would I be the one to go get them, who would take care of them after school if I was scheduled to blah blah blah."

"I told her," Brian said, "that the workplace is the workplace and home is home."

"Wisdom," Puck said, bowing his head slightly toward Brian, who ignored him.

"And I realized he was right, the manager was right. I'm in a carpool and I have responsibilities, and I have to attend all those school functions and there are snow days, so I'm not getting a job."

Cassie ate. Dylan crawled under the table and lined Pokémon up all around her boots. She and Puck had ten bucks riding on whether Emmy would stay up and talk to them after dinner.

After dinner Cassie and Puck loaded the dishwasher and washed the casserole dish, and it took an hour for Brian and Emmy to get the boys bathed and in bed, to read to them and say good-night, to turn off their bedroom light and see it turned back on seconds later, to reprimand and get water, to kiss them and turn off the light, to see it come back on seconds later. Dylan said his toys were all looking at him. Emmy turned the toys around. Puck and Cassie sat on the new sofa in the living room, sat sort of on the edge of the cushions, which did not give, until Emmy and Brian finally joined them.

"It was good seeing you guys," Brian said, "but I've got to hit the hay. I've got an early golf game in the morning."

"I greatly appreciate your hospitality," Puck said, standing and offering Brian his hand; Brian rolled his eyes but shook it.

"Puck, when you get your license back, come in and see me about insurance. You're going to be considered a high risk at any traditional agency. I'll work with you."

Puck's eyes narrowed. "How kind of you."

"Brian?" Emmy was splayed in an armchair in front of the fire-place. "Do you mind if I stay up and talk awhile?"

"Of course not," Brian said, leaning over to kiss the top of her head. "But I'll miss you. You know I won't really sleep until you're in there with me."

"I won't be long."

"And don't forget that my parents are coming for breakfast in the morning."

"Right, right. I remember."

"And don't stay up too late, you were cranky this morning."

He smiled again, went in to bed.

Emmy rubbed the back of her own neck, closed her eyes a moment, enjoyed the silence of her house. She was terribly lucky; she always said to Cassie, *You can't imagine how it feels to be loved so much*. "You guys, he's right, I really should get to bed."

Cassie stood up, reached for her coat. Emmy stood, too, stretched, put her arms around Cassie. "I'm sorry about your mom," she whispered. "But it was a nice service, the minister was nice."

Cassie gently pulled away. "He didn't know her."

They thanked her for dinner, headed outside. Puck pulled ten dollars from his pocket, and Cassie took it. In the truck Puck said, "I need a drink."

"Hello, my name is Bobby Puck, and I'm an alcoholic."

Uncle Bud ignored the extended hand. "What do you want, Bobby?"

"I'll have a Rolling Rock, and another for my chiquita here."

Puck settled his weight on the bar stool, then glanced at the men playing at the tables around him. "Crackers on Parade," he said, giving Cassie a wink. He bobbed his head and sang along with the song on the jukebox but changed the words to *Sweet Home Indiana*. Bud returned with the beers, and Puck asked him, "Mr. Uncle, would you rather have sex with a dead person or a live animal?"

Bud crossed his arms, gave Puck his fiercest stare, then said, "How dead?"

Puck roared with laughter, slapped the bar. "A fine answer! Cassandra, please do record that in your notebook. How dead, indeed." Bud wandered off; Puck shook his head, drank his beer. "You know I'm an alcoholic, Cassie."

"Everybody knows."

"Kind of you to continue drinking with me."

"I'm not drinking with you."

"No?"

"That's your beer, this is mine."

"I'm a free man or whatnot."

"Yep."

"Not running hither-skither in my Events."

"Nope."

The jukebox changed to Merle Haggard. Puck drained his beer in a matter of minutes, signaled Bud for another. He was wearing a T-shirt under a thick flannel shirt with jeans, and every few seconds he tugged at the neck of the T-shirt as if it were choking him. "Dear old Emmy," he said, "what a full, rich life. And that charming, handsome husband! I almost wish they had their own radio show. So that we might all wake up with them in the morning and hear their conversation over coffee and the morning paper. I'm sure you know what I mean."

Bud brought Puck's second beer, gave Cassie a look.

"Part of the joy of living here is, oh I know what you think I'm going to say, the flatness and the winters and whatnot, but beyond the obvious, the joy of living here is that we never need worry about achieving anything. Surviving the quotidian is frankly enough." He took a long drink, tapped the bottle on the bar a few times, then turned to face Cassie. He grabbed her hands and kissed the knuckles, laughing all the while. Tears ran down his cheeks and onto Cassie's fists. "You've got to get out of here," he said, between kisses, "I love you so much, you've got to go, Cassie, please."

She leaned toward him, brushed his face with her fingers. She saw him climb the ladder to reach her twenty years before, that flash of pale skin. "Okay."

"Please," he said.

Cassie had made the grocery list, there was barely anything in the house to eat, no coffee, no soup or bread, they had one can of cat food left, and Belle had added to the list: celery, pimento cheese. The grocery store was busy, and people kept bumping into her or stopping in the middle of the aisles, and while she was shopping, she was reminding herself that Laura was dead. A stunning bit of news. The soup cans were almost too heavy to lift; taking money from her wallet and handing it to the cashier seemed unmanageable. But she managed. Cassie put the groceries in the back of her old Mazda truck and wondered if pimento cheese had a single vitamin in it, was it actually dairy, could it provide any nourishment to Belle, given that it was orange, like real food. She pulled out of the Kroger parking lot and on to Highway 12. First gear was sluggish, certainly, but it was second gear she would vote Least Likely To Succeed.

She hovered in the turn lane a moment, waiting for an opening, then eased into the left lane, heading toward downtown Roseville. A dark green minivan was trying to pass an old Buick at exactly the same moment and ended up behind her truck. Cassie waved in her rearview mirror to apologize for her slowness; the minivan flashed its lights at her, which even in the broad sun glared in her rearview mirror. Shifting into third, Cassie could feel the truck begin to respond, and looked to see if she could move over into the right lane and allow the van to pass her. The old Buick pulled up alongside her on the right. The driver, who appeared to be in his eighties, was wearing a plaid golf cap with a ball on top and was signaling to turn left. Odds were, Cassie knew, that his signal had been on the past five hundred miles and would remain so until the man died.

The minivan sped up behind her, nearly touching her bumper. The van's windows were tinted; even lifting her sunglasses, Cassie couldn't see the driver. They came to a stoplight. Taco Bell was on their left, Arby's on their right, and beyond that McDonald's, Hardee's, Noble Roman's pizza, with a periodic gas station or dollar store. The driver of the minivan stayed in the left lane behind Cassie, who couldn't merge to the right or get out of the way. When the light turned green, Cassie accelerated as much as she dared in first, and the truck sort of puttered into the intersection before she pushed it into second; the van's lights flashed again, and the driver began to honk. Cassie looked in her rearview mirror and said aloud, "What? Are you an ambulance, what?" By now there were five or six cars behind the old Buick, and more coming. Cassie would never be able to move over before the next light, where the drama would begin all over again.

They went through the third light with more honking and flashing, and then the road opened up for over a mile, becoming residential. As the line of traffic reached the cemetery, a gently sloping twenty-five acres that from a distance looked like thousands of women in spring hats, the minivan passed Cassie in the turn lane. The driver cut too abruptly and too close and clipped the edge of Cassie's bumper. Cassie felt the truck jerk forward and then pull to the side, and realized what had happened. The driver sped past as Cassie reached cruising speed.

For a moment she was certain she had gone blind. Everything on her periphery, the cemetery and the chain-link fence around it, the other cars turned white. Her stomach muscles clenched and relaxed, her chest began to burn, she gripped the steering wheel and gearshift so hard her knuckles lost contact with her blood supply. The van cut back in front of Cassie and slowed down to forty-five, the speed limit. Cassie reached under the driver's seat, veering in the process, and pulled out her tire iron, wishing she had brought her gun. If she had the gun, she'd simply shoot the tires out of the van that second, then wait until the driver either left the road voluntarily or crashed, at which point Cassie would pull him from the wreckage, sling him to the ground, and shoot him repeatedly.

With Cassie out of the way, the van meandered up to the next light, where the driver turned left, passing a Burger King and a Pizza Hut, then a dentist's office and the sprawling high school. Cassie stayed behind it. The van followed the curving lane around the school and turned right on to an old residential street, then right again. The lots got larger, and the houses got uglier; this swath of land had been a farm until sometime in the mid-1980s, when it was sold in half-acre parcels. The faux Victorians under their blankets of vinyl siding, already revealing their cheap materials and shoddy construction, combined with the rows of identical yards, made Cassie even angrier. Her breathing became shallow, her palms began to sweat. She would kill the driver, then burn down the house. Cassie turned left as the driver did, on to a cul-de-sac. The van pulled into the driveway of one of the three houses on the dead end. The house was the yellow of a crayon, with black shutters; the grass was so short it looked tortured. Cassie turned off the truck and was out the door before it stopped rolling. She'd blocked the van in. Holding the curved end of the tore iron in her hand, she took a practice swing, then shattered the van's left rear taillight. It didn't take much.

"Get out of the van!" Cassie yelled, kicking the rear tire. If the driver was a man with a gun, she wanted to get the whole thing over with as soon as possible. No one inside the van moved. Cassie swung the tire iron at one of the side windows, but it didn't break. Raising the iron over her head, she brought it down on the driver's mirror, which bent all the way down to the door but held on. Cassie dropped her weapon and began pummeling the driver's window with her open palms, kicking the door at the same time, shouting, "Get the fuck out! Get out here and face me!"

The driver was an overweight woman in her thirties. Her short hair was curly and had been frosted, probably at home. She wore glasses, and her skin was a strange orange color; Belle used to refer to these women, Cassie suddenly remembered, as Riders on the Pilgrim Holiness Church Bus and Tanning Bed. The woman was wearing a yellow sweatshirt emblazoned with an image of Winnie the Pooh in the honey tree, a child's sweatshirt made enormous by a sinister consortium. That was all Cassie could see, and she absorbed it in a glance. The woman sat facing forward; she was resolute in her refusal to make eye contact with Cassie.

They had probably been at the grocery store together, if not today then on some other Wednesday. Cassie would have barely registered the woman's existence but for the waves of scorn such women often radiated at her. What did they see? Cassie wondered, facing the hostile stares of suburban women out with their children. She kicked the van's door, pounded on the window with her fists, shouted, "You were trying to fucking *kill me* because I wasn't driving fast enough for you? *Get The Fuck Out Of This Van.*" The woman wouldn't look at her, would not look at her, and just before Cassie picked up the tire iron and went to work on the windshield, she saw something in the backseat: a small pink tennis shoe, a white sock. Cassie shielded her eyes and looked in the side window. There was a car seat and a little girl, maybe two years old. Her eyes were the size of walnuts, and she was staring right back at Cassie, not crying, not moving.

Cassie took a step backward as if she'd been slapped. She pressed her fingertips against her temples and said aloud Good God. A cold breeze she hadn't noticed before snaked inside her jacket; the adrenalin that had been propelling her drained away so quickly she felt faint. She walked back up to the driver's window, tapped on the glass, but the woman still wouldn't turn her head. Perhaps she'd had some sort of stroke and was paralyzed. "Ma'am?" Cassie said. "You were driving like that with a child in your car, and this whole time I've been at you with a tire iron, you did nothing to protect her? You *suck* as a mother, your house is hideous, and you do *not* own the fucking road."

She walked back to her truck, slung the tire iron across her front seat, slammed her door. Her head hurt and the palms of her hands stung. She backed out of the driveway and turned around in the cul-de-sac, watching the van in her rearview mirror until she got to the corner, but no one ever emerged. The house was completely still, the last Cassie saw of it.

That night, after Belle had settled down in the living room with a book, Cassie went out on the front porch with a beer. If she'd had her gun with her, she would have killed Winnie the Pooh. She could talk to Edwin, she could talk to Bud or Belle, but what could they say that she didn't already know? She thought about how often it happened that a liar was to two liars born, how tendencies fine or subtle or peculiar thread their way through the genes and out into the world. Her father had an exquisite temper: he was fast, verbally; he struck, he got over it. As a child Cassie never saw it coming, she had to train herself to stay out of the way. When he was on a losing streak, or when he was caught in his own congealing guilt, Laura called him the Mongoose. Cassie took a deep breath, closed her eyes. It had been Laura's temper that unhinged her daughters. Children are like dogs, Cassie thought, they can adjust to the periodic boot to the ribs, even if it arrives for arbitrary reasons and is followed by a pat on the head, but they don't know what to do with someone who stays blank and silent and simmering for days on end. Laura's unhappiness was her religion.

It was a freezing night. Cassie pulled her coat more closely around her, tugged her hat down over her ears. She could see her breath, but the sky was clear and the stars were hard and bright, the beer felt good. A car turned slowly in to the driveway. The driver turned off his lights but left the engine running. "Oh, shit," Cassie said, putting down her beer. It was a sheriff's deputy, taking his time about getting out of the car. Cassie knew most of the myriad ways cops abused the general public, and this was one of them, not getting out of the car. She didn't stand up. The cop could probably see her, in the dim yellow glow of the porch light. She could wait as long as he could. When he finally stepped out of the car, Cassie saw it was only Josh Fellers. They'd gone to school together.

Josh closed the heavy car door, then squinted up at the porch. "Cass? You up there?"

"Hey, Josh."

He walked around and opened the screen door, then sighed and settled down into the splintery rocking chair.

"Don't scoot around on that chair," Cassie said, taking another drink of her beer.

"I won't. I remember it."

"You want a beer?"

Josh yawned. "I'm on duty. For a few more minutes, anyway."

"How's Tracy?"

"She's good."

"The girls okay?"

"They're fine. Growing like weeds. Now, look here, Cassie." Josh reached down and adjusted the volume on his radio. The dispatcher's voice, distant and free of emotion, receded. "Strange thing happened today. A woman named Nancy Cobb was driving her dark green Dodge Caravan on Highway 12 when an older Mazda truck, light blue with a camper shell on the back, began following her and followed her all the way home. Right into her driveway. At which time the driver of the truck, a woman she placed in her mid-to-late twenties with long light brown or blond hair, did with malicious intent attack the van, destroying a rear taillight and the driver's mirror, cracking a side window, and denting the driver's door."

"That is interesting," Cassie said, letting her head fall first toward her left shoulder, then toward her right, popping her neck.

"The driver of the Mazda truck did all of this, and I quote, without provocation."

"Hmmm." Cassie shook her head, as if the ways of humanity were mysterious and perverse. "Did she get the plate number? Of the assailant's truck?"

"Nope. But she says she would sure recognize that assailant, or her truck, in a flat second."

"So she confronted the attacker? Face-to-face?"

"Mrs. Cobb says she was so terrified that she couldn't turn her head, that she refused to look at the other woman for fear of making her more angry."

"She said that?"

Josh nodded. "I wrote it down."

"Doesn't sound like she's got much of a case, if you ask me." Cassie drank the last of her beer.

"You know of many light blue Mazda trucks in this county, Cass? I ask you. My granddad sold me his old Toyota Tercel, and it got vandalized in the first week because it wasn't a Ford or a Chevy, buncha damn rednecks. I had to sell it for scrap, and it was a good car."

"I don't care what people think about a foreign truck."

Josh sighed. Every time he moved, his heavy leather belt squeaked, and the shiny surface of his police-issued jacket made a shooshing sound. Cassie could even hear his shoes. How the police ever managed to sneak up on anyone was a puzzle.

"Three days ago there was a report of a scuffle at a car wash in Jonah, in which a man in a Chevy Caprice Classic pulled in behind a light blue Mazda truck, maybe a little too close, and before the driver of the truck was quite finished. The truck backed up and hit the front of the Chevy repeatedly, then drove away."

Cassie said nothing.

"And yesterday, if I'm not mistaken, around four in the afternoon, you were running through the park, and a man hitting golf balls hit one too close to you, which you then retrieved and winged back at him, hitting him in the thigh. I'll take that beer now."

In the kitchen she got out two bottles of beer; passing the living room again, she glanced in at Belle, who had put her book down and was curled up in the brown rocking chair, doing needlepoint.

Josh had taken off his hat. With his flattened hair exposed, he looked more like the boy she'd known in school, his dark eyelashes and the color high in his cheeks. His ears stuck out just like when he was younger, and they blushed before his face did. "Thanks, Cass," he said, taking the beer. He rested his elbows on his knees, looking out into the dark yard. "In school you fought more than anybody I've ever known. You were in trouble more than any boy, I never quite understood it."

Cassie nodded. "I was a scrapper."

"But you're thirty years old now, Cass, and you've got some burdens on your shoulders. Reports come into the station about you, my buddies hand them over to me to deal with. I stayed late tonight, missed my kids at dinner, to take this report and come talk to you. I did it because your dad got me out of some jams when I was younger, and Poppy gave me a job when I needed it, and you just lost your mom. And you and me has a history, too. I took y'all's side in the fight against Jimmy over Poppy's marker, I went out to the trailer and talked to him and Barbara till they gave it up."

"I didn't know that."

Josh shook his head. "You will always mean something to me."

Cassie tightened her grip on the beer bottle; she wanted to cry, she wanted to thank Josh and apologize to him, and she also wanted to hit him.

"You got any games coming up?"

"Maybe. There's a chance of me going to New Orleans tomorrow."

"Do that," Josh said, pointing his finger at her. "Get out of town a few days, let me deal with this. Then listen, come back and get rid of that truck, I don't care how you feel about it. That truck has you marked like a tattoo. Billy's got a rebuilt Ford Ranger he'll sell for a song, it's a salvage title."

Cassie blinked, clenched her jaw muscles.

"You hear, sweetheart? Let's fix this."

Cassie nodded, smiled at him. "Josh? Don't you think I coulda been a *contendah*?"

Josh laughed, leaned back in his chair, took a drink of his beer. "That's for sure," he said. "You're sure right about that."

Belle was doing needlepoint and weeping. She'd make a few stitches, then wipe her eyes on a tissue, then make a few stitches, then blow her nose. Cassie stood in the middle of the room, looking at the couch where Laura used to sit and read with Belle, they shared a circle of lamplight every evening. Cassie couldn't sit there, never would, so she sat down on the floor at Belle's feet. Neither said anything. Cassie wanted to ask, but she wouldn't, if Belle remembered the fight over Poppy's grave stone, how no one was sure whether Jimmy would even come to the funeral, if Barbara would let him, since Laura would be there, Cassie and Belle would be there, they were the bereaved parties. And how he had come but stayed at the back of the funeral home, had slipped in and signed his name and slipped out again before his daughters could see him. Laura had made all the arrangements, paid the bill, ordered the stone, and while it was still being engraved, Jimmy had ordered them to stop, to change the inscription. He'd wanted it to say Poppy's names and dates, and then HUSBAND AND FATHER, RESTING IN THE ARMS OF THE LORD. That had been a rough time, the monument people calling, and Robbie Ballenger calling, finally the police involved. Laura had power of attorney and would have won eventually, but Jimmy stopped. Cassie knew why now. And so Poppy's stone, in the cemetery with a thousand spring hats, said what Laura had chosen:

Lawrence "Popcorn" Claiborne

1904–1991

An Innocent Man

"I'm going to go to New Orleans," Cassie said.
Belle sniffed. "I think you should, I'm glad."
"I'm worried about you, though."

"Don't be, Jesus, don't use me as an excuse not to do it, I was pretty sure that's what Laura would have done if we'd ever gotten to give her the tickets, she would have said she couldn't go because she couldn't leave me."

"Maybe."

"No maybe about it, it would have been how she expressed her anger at me, we were her excuse for not going every other year of her life, because she was trapped here taking care of us, I would have been so angry if she'd said it this time, if she'd—" Belle stopped, buried her face in her hands, sobbed.

"Belle," Cassie said, resting her head against her sister's knee.

"God*dammit*," Belle said, hiccuped, cried harder.

Cassie stood up, unsure of what to do. Laura would have done nothing, would have let the storm pass. Poppy would have started crying himself. Edwin would have patted Belle on the back, to no effect. Jimmy would have grabbed his keys, here's your hat, what's your hurry. Cassie was on her own here. She bent down, slipped one arm under Belle's knees, the other behind her back, and lifted her straight up; she weighed nothing, her bones were like a kitten's bones. Cassie gathered Belle, crying on and on, then she sat down in the rocking chair, holding Belle against her like a baby. The room was quiet but for Belle's agonized breathing, her sobs. Cassie rocked, rubbed Belle's back, whispered, her own eyes filled with tears, *Are you very very sad?*

SHADOW FATHER

*C*assie chose a guest house outside the Quarter, cheap, painted in a breezy blue that reminded her of a dollhouse Belle had loved as a child. A gift from Laura. The dollhouse, detailed and accurate, sat for a while on a round table in the corner of the living room, its color a surprise against the pervasive blandness of a room that didn't allow for light. At the guest house the owners, sisters named Marcelle and Martine, asked her if she wanted the best room, and without thinking, she said yes; the view from the balcony was of a courtyard so lush and green, the bricks of the walkways were being pushed up out of the ground. In the center a banana tree grew up then sideways, and its branches were heavy with young fruit, each layered against the others like artichoke leaves, smaller than you'd find in a supermarket. Cassie shook her head at such a sight. A banana tree. She remembered an evening a few years ago, sitting late at night around the kitchen table with Belle and Laura, when Belle confessed her ongoing, pervasive fear of water; how she dreamed at night of swimming, and seeing below her body a massive shadow moving slowly.

"But that is—surely you recognize—" Laura began.

"Of course I do, but in this case there's a marriage of the image and the truth, which is that water is an element in which we cannot breathe, and compared to that, the fact of the enormous creatures with their tiny brains who want to shake us like rag dolls and then eat us is secondary." Belle had been wearing, Cassie recalled, special gloves lined with medicine, to treat her eczema and keep her from scratching.

"Oh, I see," Laura had said, leaning back in her chair. "And just where were you born? The *air*?"

Cassie had laughed the hardest, although she couldn't have said why, and even now a sound escaped her throat. But Laura had been right: they were children born in the air, under the flat sky and in sight of the bleak horizon of Indiana. They didn't know heights (except for native trees, and even those were not so tall) or depths. They knew distances, and farmland, the taming of fecundity. Chopping down trees, pulling up stumps, eliminating rocks, plowing and tilling, irrigating; where she lived, they stood so far from what the land had been—an unbroken forest covering the entire Midwest—that barely a trace of the old existed.

But here, and Cassie could feel it right away (if you couldn't feel it, the chamber of commerce would explain it a thousand different ways), the ancient miasma suffused every stone and every breath. This was some comfort to Cassie, who felt that at any moment something in her own blood would rise up, that she would turn a corner and find Laura resurrected, too young to have met her own fate.

*　　*　　*

The air in New Orleans before Easter was so mild it felt like a kiss; hard to imagine, at least in April, the summers Laura used to describe. The temperatures sometimes reached 112, with humidity soup-thick. Drunks used to lie down on the blazing sidewalks and not get up. Laura had stepped over dozens of prone men in her early life, which will prepare one, she liked to say, for the future.

Cassie walked toward Bourbon Street. In the early evening the town felt like any other but more beautiful and more cherished. In a bookstore in the Atlanta airport, she had leafed through a guidebook to Los Angeles, drawn in by the small book's unusual size and cover. The author had chosen to focus on the more prurient lives of the city's inhabitants. There had been plenty to say, but what struck Cassie most was the way each entry ended with: "The hotel in which ——— killed himself in such an unusual manner was itself an oddity; built in 1889, it had three separate towers, and the interior of each was wrapped in dark virgin oak and trimmed with gold leaf. Today it is a parking lot." The mansion of the couple who lent the town the name *Hollywood* is today a parking lot. The early studios: parking lots. The drugstores where starlets languished: parking lots. Not so in New Orleans. Cassie passed a bar that seemed to be tucked into an old blacksmith's shop, and antebellum houses, French architecture, Spanish architecture; she smelled again the cloud of age that hovered over everything. And something else, another undercurrent. She passed the two-story and three-story buildings that had been made into apartments, glancing at their picturesque doors. Most of the doors seemed to be fetching by accident: this one because someone in 1928 had painted it a shocking red and never painted it again. Or this one, with frames of colored glass in clashing tones that would have disturbed the neighbors and been instantly regretted. Most everything ages well, it seemed to Cassie, studying the way the glass had faded unevenly. Even what we most despise in our own time becomes the relic of the lost and is treasured by the later in line. The fires of Time, Time itself, and behind Something, a door, the repository of all those events. There had been so much in Laura's journals, scraps, intuitions. Cassie had spent a long time reading a particular piece called "Acquisitions":

> *Every day the new is made, the novel.*
> *And I read the lists and acquire, it is*
> *my job. Boxes arrive. I empty them,*
> *display them center stage, most*
> *go unnoticed, grow dusty, and are*
> *carried up one flight of stairs. Another*
> *floor. And later another. At the highest*
> *point they are wholly ignored,*
> *no eyes ascend. Nothing is left*
> *in the end but the elevator down*
> *to the basement, the boxes rotating*
> *by age toward the janitor's*
> *hands, the fire. Upstairs, I acquire.*

Laura had not been a building; she had been the city on which her daughters were built, and what had been under the city was labyrinthine and had no map. They had taken it for granted, Cassie and Belle, that they would turn on a faucet and water would pour into their hands. But where did it come from? Where did it go? When something went wrong, they didn't dare descend to fix it. Laura, underground. No one moved behind those closed red doors, no one came or went.

*   *   *

The photo gallery was a stall for time until she was inside it, and then she stayed over an hour. In her notebook she wrote down some of the prints she saw, to tell Belle. Jackie Kennedy in her pink Chanel suit, Marilyn Monroe's wedding to Joe DiMaggio, John and Yoko, every beautiful and strange event made more poignant for having been photographed. And political scenes: George Wallace, Richard Nixon, Martin Luther King, Jr., Bill Clinton playing a saxophone in dark sunglasses. The gallery had what was surely the largest collection of jazz photographs anywhere: Billie Holiday in a curl of smoke, Miles Davis covered with sweat, Thelonious Monk in his dome of a hat, everyone Laura had worshiped. Looking at the pictures, Cassie could almost hear again "Strange Fruit," "So What," "Mysterioso," the songs Laura mourned for. A woman working there told Cassie there was an upstairs, too, and to look around. What was upstairs was even more astonishing: part of Walker Evans's *Let Us Now Praise Famous Men* series, Eudora Welty's Mississippi photographs, photographs dating all the way back to 1917. There were original hand printed Bellocqs, or so the cards said, two of his young prostitutes. A lynching tree.

A man beside her said, "You visiting?" He had a kind face, middle-aged, a wide smile.

"Yes. Do you work here?"

"Too much. I own the place."

Cassie looked at the wall. "I don't know much about photography."

"Do you know what you like?" He had a lot of laugh lines around his eyes; he wore a vest woven from wool in many different colors.

"Only a fool doesn't know what she likes."

He nodded. "What's your favorite piece up here?"

She walked back down the hallway a few feet. "This one," she said, pointing to a portrait of a little dark-haired girl sitting in bed, her eyes round and grave. The wall behind her was painted with a lavish floral scene but was heading toward ruin. The print was small, five thousand dollars.

"Oh, I love that one. Roman Vishniac, the only one I've ever had. I've been here thirty years, and that's it. So I treasure it myself."

The Only Flower of Her Youth, Warsaw, 1938.

"It hardly bears thinking about," he said, shaking his head, "what happened to her. If you like this, I have a couple books of his downstairs. Let me show them to you. I'm Jacob, by the way."

"Cassie." She shook his hand and followed him down the narrow staircase. Downstairs he greeted other visitors, then took a coffee-table edition of Vishniac's photographs off the shelf. On the cover were two little girls caught in some game, gleeful and conspiratorial. *Children of a Vanished World*. He handed the book to an assistant and asked her to wrap it.

"This is on me," he said, handing the package to her. "And take this, too." On the back of a business card he wrote the name and address of a restaurant. "This is where you should have dinner. Tell the goofy guy at the door that I sent you."

"Thank you." Cassie looked at the card, *Epistrophes* on Royale.

"My pleasure." Jacob gave her a slight bow. "Enjoy our fay-uh city."

Epistrophes's owner, Gabe, who looked and sounded like a Brooklyn detective (born and raised in Baton Rouge), took Cassie over the minute she introduced herself. He brought her a bottle of white burgundy, then ordered from the menu for her: fried green tomatoes over fresh mozzarella with a basil aioli, a nearly raw tuna steak with sautéed greens. He explained how the steak had been seared in olive oil suffused with the oils of exotic peppers.

"Is it too spicy?" he asked, sitting down opposite her. "Do you need more bread?"

"It's perfect. I never—I've never eaten this well."

For dessert he brought a goat-cheese crème fraîche with poached pears and a mint leaf, a cup of strong coffee, asked if she'd like a liqueur. She told him she needed to keep her head clear; she was about to visit a landmark in her mother's life, and she was looking for a pool hall.

"Landmarks we've got plenty of; pool halls are scarce. There are a few places in the Quarter with tavern tables, but nowhere around here with nine-footers. I don't know what's happened. It's fallen out of favor."

She said she was looking for a game, mentioned Jackson LaFollette. He told her about a private room in an old hotel, then sized her up, too late to take it back.

"Not the nicest people in the world."

"No," she said, "I wouldn't think so."

Gabe stood up, stretched his lower back. "Gettin' too old for this business." They shook hands, and he told her the meal was on him. "Any friend of Jacob's," he said, walking back toward the bar. She left him a fifty-dollar tip, just a portion of the cost of the meal, then stepped out into the night. Perhaps New Orleans was a real place, or maybe she'd gotten lucky and stepped into the world Laura had conjured, standing in her kitchen in Roseville, in exile. Thirty-three years' worth of longing redeemed was what this city felt like to Cassie.

* * *

She stood outside the Grille on Bourbon Street, studying the facade. Some people were lucky enough to live in Los Angeles and to have their own genesis paved over flat and simple. Others grew up in the shadow of their making (my father was born here and my mother next door); they went to church together every Sunday and married there; (I was conceived and born, too, in this bed my parents still sleep in), and that would have been a terror to Cassie. To Belle. Nothing said run like the fact of her origin: Laura and Jimmy innocent of each other, and then innocent no longer, hell-bent on ruination and their children the evidence they succeeded.

The Grille was a diner as diners should be, shaped like a caboose, a glass door framed in metal, draped inside with twinkle lights. She opened the door and stepped in; the counter stretched the length of the long building, with booths in the front window. On the jukebox Peggy Lee was singing "Is That All There Is?," and at the counter a transsexual was smoking a cigarette and drinking coffee. Her paisley dress, silk and clinging like water, was buttoned up wrong in the back, and she had cut her ankle shaving. A young girl stepped out of the kitchen in an apron and a hair net, and this was what Cassie wanted to see, a girl working. Someone the age Laura had been. Even the transsexual seemed to have been placed as a prop, sincce Laura had mentioned a friend called Beverly who came in every night after eleven and eventually was abducted and left for dead in a bayou. Laura missed her for years, and now here she sat, after a fashion.

To replay the scene entirely, the diner would have to be empty save for Laura, working the night shift, nineteen years old, betrothed to a man of means and questionable character named

Jackson LaFollette. The bell over the diner door, currently missing, would ring, and in would stroll Jimmy Claiborne, beaten and bleeding but on his feet. Laura said his injuries hadn't seemed life-threatening, and she didn't much care anyway.

Cassie sat down a couple stools away from Beverly and closed her eyes. She could imagine him, short and lithe, that spring in his step. He wore, Laura had told her so many times, cream-colored linen pants, pleated and cuffed with a strong break, two-tone shoes, a braided brown leather belt, and a white silk shirt under a cashmere sweater vest. Dance, dance, his feet were always moving, he slid and tapped, jingled the change in his pocket in time. He could whistle the entire repertoire of a mockingbird he kept as a boy: twenty-three songs. And snatches of classical music, isolated for a dramatic rise or fall, a trill. He could sing, do imitations of Bing Crosby or Elvis, but never sang seriously. For a while he'd played a snare drum in a band at a home for Wayward Men, but he gave it up, and Cassie had never heard him play. Legend had it he could cook; he could swim a mile, but she'd never seen that, either. Because he wasn't the sort of man, he might have said, who would take up practicing something just because he *could*, simply because he'd been given a healthy measure of God's gifts, he wasn't responsible for what God had taken it upon Himself to hand out. What he liked to do was gamble. He was wired for a certain sort of risk.

"What can I get ya?"

Cassie opened her eyes to the young waitress, her acne and cheap metal necklace. One of her teeth was slick with the coral of her lipstick.

"Just coffee, black."

"And another for me, doll," Beverly said, raising her cup.

Jimmy sat down at the counter. He was bleeding over his left eyebrow and from his bottom lip. His right eye was starting to swell. A handkerchief, formerly buttercream, was stained with the blood he was trying to keep off his shirt. When Laura approached him, she smelled his cologne, something spicy and masculine, maybe bay rum, and the Sen-Sen he always carried in his pocket, a man who applied Chap Stick every day and was shaved so close his skin was like a boy's. Cassie remembered his smell; she had spent hours as a child categorizing it. *It is like this—no, it's more like this.* Finally she had landed on oranges and whiskey, that was his essence and everything else was extra. He smoked, of course, and wore a tiny bit of Brylcreem in his hair. *I've got places to go and people to do,* he said at the door as he headed out into the night, and left his silent wife reading in the dim living room. Those smells came home with him, too.

"Can I get a chocolate milk shake?" he'd asked Laura, giving her his haven't-I-gotten-myself-into-some-predicament smile. She didn't smile back.

"With whipped cream?"

"There are milk shakes without whipped cream?"

Laura stepped over to the ice-cream freezer—the metal cup would go from warm to frosty in her hand, a swift conduit—and noted, as people do, that the jukebox was playing Louis Armstrong, "St. James Infirmary." The man behind her began to whistle along with the song, but she didn't look at him. She shoved the mixture up under the spinning blade harder than she needed, blocking out the sound. When the blender stopped, he was humming, a sound both scratchy and deep.

The waitress poured coffee for Cassie and Beverly, then went back to wrapping silverware in napkins. The coffee was steaming and smelled vaguely like chocolate.

"This town is full of sonsabitches," Beverly said, perhaps to no one. She shook her head in resignation.

Cassie blew on the surface of the coffee. Laura set the milk shake in front of Jimmy, along with a tall spoon and a straw, and he smiled at her gratefully, then fainted. People fainted in the Grille all the time, or they threw up, burst into sobs, inconsolable. They fought, they fought off delirium tremens, they had heart attacks, seizures, they confessed. It was a busy place. But the rule was that the unconscious couldn't stay. Laura's boss, Badrae, wasn't running a boardinghouse, as he liked to say. So Laura went around the counter and hoisted Jimmy up from where he'd slumped over the neighboring stools, took him under the arms. He didn't weigh much, he was a small man with a light step. She dragged him out onto the sidewalk where he opened his eyes, an even more striking blue-green in the streetlight than in the day, and said, "I don't have any money to pay you for that milk shake."

"Do you know what I mean about sonsabitches?" Beverly asked, looking at Cassie.

"I think I do."

"Mine just kicked my ass out his apahment. Don't have my clothes, my purse, nothin. Says he'll be 'round this way to pick me up in the mahnin. Mmm, mmm, mmm. I think he caught a whiff uh his wife. She in town, I think."

The coffee was rich. Not chocolate. Something else. "That's no good," Cassie said.

"Naw it ain't! I say to him, Look how you do me! I cry like a chald and say Look! But nothin gets through that man. Didn't even have my dinnah, he kickin my ass out."

Laura had thought little of it; the way of the world was the con. But the next night Jimmy had shown up again, what a dresser! How sweet he smelled! And paid her for the milk shake and ordered one of the Grille's famous hamburgers (without condiments: he was a finicky man) and tipped her 300 percent. That was all the story Cassie had ever known, that and Laura taking up and following Jimmy to Indiana not two weeks later, leaving behind her own mother, everything she'd ever known. Wild love, oxygen-depriving passion. Cassie was the daughter of a great romance, if what was meant by romance was wreckage. The story was not diminished by the other cogent details: that Laura had been engaged to another, or that when she finally found Jimmy in Indiana, he was back in his trailer on a wooded lot outside Roseville with his own betrothed.

Cassie finished her coffee, then walked over to look at the jukebox. Beverly remained slumped over her coffee cup; her ass must have been kicked out along with cigarettes and a lighter, because there was a full pack of Kools on the counter, and a disposable Bic bearing the words MARDI GRAS 1998. On the jukebox there was Louis Armstrong; Elvis singing "That's All Right Mama," and Frank Sinatra, Jimmy Dorsey, Julie London, Harry James, Howlin' Wolf, John Coltrane, all on CD now. Cassie looked around at the walls covered with festival paraphernalia, and photographs of strangers dancing with strangers, the green vinyl on the metal stools, the old-fashioned straw dispensers. Whoever owned this place, now that Badrae was surely on the bayou, fishing out his final days, had turned it into a dreamland for nostalgics. People like Cassie, who wanted a glimmer of the long-gone world and would accept these tokens. CDs instead of records, but the songs she wanted to hear: if that didn't sum up the struggle. She felt very little standing in this place, far less than she'd expected.

Cassie slipped a twenty out of her wallet and laid it on the counter next to Beverly's lighter.

"Thank you, baby," Beverly said.

In Jackson Square, before midnight, only a few artists and tarot-card readers still sat at their makeshift booths, some drinking cocktails. They spoke to one another as if they shared a long history. Cassie approached one of the park benches, where a boy with blond dreadlocks and a beard the color of honey sat hunched forward with his shirt pulled up over his head, exposing his back. He looked out through the neck of his shirt as if into an aquarium filled with starving sharks. Cassie looped around behind him. His thin back was covered with scars; if he'd been older, she would have guessed shrapnel. Another sort of war, perhaps, other weapons. Every few minutes he shivered so hard he shook the bench. A black man clutching a brown paper bag noticed the boy and walked across the square and knelt in front of him, offering whatever was in the bag, but the boy couldn't see him.

"Bad, very bad." The man shook his head, then sat down on the bench. After a few seconds he reached up and pulled the boy's T-shirt down over his back, smoothed it flat.

Cassie turned the corner and stopped in front of Saint Louis Cathedral. A sign out front declared that the bishop would say the Easter mass, two days hence. The building was beautiful and imposing but didn't suggest the inhuman power of the cathedrals of Europe, at least as they looked in pictures. Laura had wanted to see them, Belle, too, but Cassie felt her skin prickle with resentment anytime she thought about standing in front of such an edifice, or listening to a bird caught in a spire that a hundred poor men had died to build.

"Read your palm?"

Cassie turned and saw a man standing behind her, smiling in the moonlight. He was short and overweight; his glasses rested on the tops of his cheeks. He wore a long-sleeved red T-shirt with baggy shorts, and sandals with thick wool socks.

"How much?"

He was already walking toward the canvas chair sitting in the middle of the walk in front of the cathedral. "How much do you have?"

Cassie reached in her pocket and pulled out a bill. "Ten bucks."

"Okay," he said with a shrug. "Come sit down. Give me your right palm."

She sat down and held out her hand.

"My name is Alan, by the way." He held her hand only a few seconds, tracing her lifeline with his thumb, then let go. She expected him to say, You will have a long and happy life.

"You are healthy, active, you live strongly inside your body."

"Where do other people live?"

"Oh, they're all over the place. Most live in the past. To dwell in the body is to be fully in the present moment, but that can be a grievous thing, and a lot of work." Alan crossed his hands over his round stomach and looked up at the sky above the church; his chin was soft, and Cassie could easily imagine him as a little boy. "You . . . in terms of style, you pride yourself on being free of . . .

the chains of femininity, do you understand that? You pride yourself on not being bound to a single presentation, but that is a matter of willful naïveté. You need to think more about how *absence* and *denial* are statements as surely as anything else." He stopped and stared with great concentration at what looked to Cassie to be the wisps of clouds passing in front of the moon, silent so long she almost concluded the reading was over. "You live in . . . Pennsylvania, the off Pennsylvania turnpike, no, Ohio. Someplace . . . I can see flatness, desolation. Ohio? Ugh, I'm sorry, but that's just *so* ugly. You live in a world where the spirits have completely flown, there are no voices left, and that causes everyone around you to act out against the . . . well, it's really painful, isn't it." He stared at the sky. "Even here the voices are weakened, it's nothing like it used to be, we all used to feel like radio receivers, voices coming through all the time. We'd spin the dial and listen to our favorite songs. But now it's like they're far away, children calling from a great distance." Alan looked at the sky, not at Cassie; she felt her eyes fill, unaccountably, with tears. She blinked them away. "How do you gain power? This is a question I always want answered, I mean, this is something I look for. You are competitive, particularly with men, and this is in conflict with your feelings of loyalty and protectiveness. You are in search of your better nature, but this competitiveness stands in your way, and you don't know how to get around it. I can see . . . a sort of geometry, a Ferris wheel, ah, ah, you're a gambler." His gaze moved back and forth over the roofline of the church as if reading something there. "You measure your life in wins, but you should be counting your losses. The spirits want me to remind you that chance is the equivalent of death."

"I don't play a game of chance."

He ignored her, turning his head slightly, straining to hear another conversation. "You want to travel, but not very far. Authority, hierarchy, the notion of a superior are all so anathema to you, it's a wonder you're able to function at all. You should avoid run-ins with the police. People talk to you a great deal, even strangers, and the reason is that you appear to stand exactly in between, on the fulcrum of happiness and despair, and this regis- ·
ters to the outside world as a tabula rasa on which they might scribble their own names. You consider your life a secret, and living in a secret is like living in a prison or a drafty old house.

"These spirits, the ones still left, are German, which is a surprise to everyone, all the yuppies and frat boys want to hear is that they should drink more, consume, consume, and they want to hear it in a French accent, but the spirits keep quoting Rilke.

> *To you is left (unspeakably confused)*
> *your life, gigantic, ripening, full of fears,*
> *so that it, now hemmed in, now grasping all,*
> *is changed in you by turns to stone and stars.*

"They asked me to say that to you, I don't know what it's called. You are an orphaned child, this is very clear, but most of us are, and our only hope is to recognize it and cling to one another as best we can, or else harden our hearts to our own orphanhood, which is pointless. There is a world beyond this world." Alan looked at Cassie for the first time since the reading began. "You make me sadder than anyone I've seen all week."

Cassie stood, for a moment she just stood there. She took a deep breath, nodded at Alan, his hands still crossed over his belly, then walked back to the guest house, where she called home to tell Belle she was there and safe, something she'd never done before.

The next morning she chose a coffee shop just outside the Quarter, on Magazine Street, by the smell outside. Inside, the decor was vaguely Cuban, the ceilings were high, and an antique roaster sat in the corner, the brass so shiny it mirrored the bar where she sat. She ordered a black coffee from her server, a sullen young person of indeterminate gender. Cassie had never before confronted someone whose sex wasn't immediately apparent; this child was of medium height and very thin; his/her hair was dyed a dull blue and gathered into two small doughnuts above the ears. His lower lip, eyebrow, and nose were all pierced, and his ears sported so many studs and rings, he could have emerged from the hail of an industrial staple gun. His eyes and lips were dark with makeup, and his fingernails were painted alternately red and black (chipped and fading), but his voice, when he took Cassie's order, was that of a young girl, and she walked like a girl. In her black pants and loose white shirt, there was neither the evidence nor absence of hips or breasts.

She took her notebook out of her backpack and reviewed the notes she'd made reading Laura's journals and letters, and from talking to Uncle Bud. The first sip of her coffee was good but burned her tongue. She twirled a pencil around and through her fingers, a habit she'd picked up from her father, and considered that all of her mother's life had been lived in the same sort of alienation. Of course her mother remembered New Orleans as her soul's paradise, she could hardly do otherwise, but Cassie had been surprised to discover that Laura had spent most of her childhood alone, locked in the little house on Rendon Street while her mother, Gladys Dubuisson, neé Beauvray, silent over thirty years now, spent all day and evening at the LaFollettes', cleaning and cooking for the four boys. When Laura was eleven or twelve, she began to accompany her mother to work, and it was there, in the exquisite ancestral home of the LaFollettes in the Garden District, that Laura had met the LaFollette boys.

Behind Cassie the coffee-shop door opened and closed, and someone took a seat at the counter, leaving two seats between them. She glanced over at the man, who appeared to be in his mid-forties. He was wearing a white seersucker shirt with red stripes and a pair of yellow golfing pants, both well worn, and broken-down running shoes. He threw a driving cap on the counter; Cassie noticed the band inside, stained yellow. She guessed that when the temperature broke 110, this man ended up in a heap on the sidewalk.

"Greetings, Themis!" the man shouted jovially at the server, who gave him a slit-eyed nod. "I'll have the usual."

"Bode, don't shout. My head aches me awful," Themis said, pressing her temples with her fingertips.

"Sorry, love."

Themis set about preparing the man's cappuccino. Bode stood up and pulled a handful of items out of his pocket: crumpled dollar bills, spare change, business cards, lint, Starlite mints—mostly cracked—tattered Post-it notes, and square slips of paper covered with spidery handwriting and what appeared to be mathematical formulas. A nickel rolled Cassie's way down the counter, and she caught it.

"Keep that," Bode said, smiling. "You earned it." His black hair was shiny and badly cut, his teeth were coffee-stained, and his smile was crooked. Cassie nodded and slipped the nickel in her pocket.

Bode patted the pocket of his shirt and pulled more bits and pieces from his pants pockets, then rummaged through the mess on the counter. "You wouldn't happen to have a pen, would you?" he asked Cassie. "Not that I mean you owe me."

She reached into her backpack, pulled out a pen, and slid it to him across the counter.

"Thank you, I just need to make note of this one. . . ." He trailed off. He wrote a few sentences or figures on a Post-it, then folded it up and put it in his pocket. He hummed, drank his cappuccino, wrote more.

Gideon LaFollette, Gladys's employer, was from an old family. A judge. Laura had written in her journal that in New Orleans at that time, there was no distinction between honesty and corruption. The worst politicians, policemen, and lawyers were sometimes the dearest fathers, the most pious Catholics. Gideon's wife, Elise, was a former debutante and morning drinker. Their first-born, William (whose nickname was Bank), became a relentless capitalist of unknown occupation, although Laura had been careful to note that he was cruel to his gun dogs and had never married. The second son, Jared, became a lawyer, then a judge, like his father. The third, Ori, was Laura's favorite—the best friend of her middle and high school years, although he was older—kind and shy. He had become a pharmacist after his mother forbade him to play jazz trombone, his true love. And then there was Jackson, sometimes called Jack-Q (Cassie didn't know why), born five years after Ori and treasured as the family baby; southerners make a cult of spoiling the lastborn. Jack gambled from the sixth grade on, twice expelled from Catholic school for shooting craps. Only his father's influence allowed him to graduate. By the time Laura began to date him, when she was sixteen and he was a year older, he was a pool player of some notoriety, not a hustler but a shark. He lied to everyone about everything. He claimed to be older, to have a pilot's license, to have served as an assassin in West Africa. Laura had written, *He liked to pretend he had seen great suffering.* Cassie knew that after Laura fled to Indiana, Jackson had gone on to become a doctor and to marry a rich, consumptive neighbor, a girl Laura described as see-through. Cassie ordered another cup of coffee and a scone. The story was more in the gaps than in the details, the rich shark cast aside for the poor hustler; Laura's abandonment of her mother and her home. Cassie knew only one other thing: that Jackson LaFollette still lived in New Orleans, at least according to the phone book. He was sixty years old, surely prosperous, respected, and out of the game. Maybe he was out of the game.

The coffee-shop door opened another two or three times, mostly on sleepy-looking young people ordering strong coffee to go. A man joined Bode at the counter, leaving only one seat between Cassie and the conversation.

"Thomas, my brother!" Bode stood up and threw his arms around the newcomer. Thomas sat down and ordered a coffee. Bode seemed beside himself with happiness, and patted Thomas on the back.

"Bode, was I not clear about my head?" Themis asked.

"Foolish of me, sorry. Thomas, do tell."

"No, you tell. What happened with the backer?"

Cassie looked at Thomas, then down at her notebook, then at Thomas again. She ran her thumb lightly along the edge of her coffee cup. He was a tall man whose body was shaped by work: broad-shouldered, with a thick chest and narrow waist. His hands were wide and dry, scarred. His blue jeans, thin with age and washing, were tucked into work boots nearly white with plaster dust, and she could see the muscles of his shoulders moving through his thin white T-shirt. His spine was right there, close enough that she could have touched it, a chain of crescent moons.

"Ah, well, yes, the backer," Bode began. "There's a small problem, a very slight problem that caused the backer to, well, back off."

"I see," Thomas said, stirring sugar into his coffee. His hair was sun-bleached, but there were black streaks in it: a peculiar combination of colors, and he needed a haircut.

"I said to the backer, I said as I say to the many tourists who mistake me for a homeless man, 'I will accept your money.' And then I showed him the machine, which is, as you know, flawless."

"I don't actually know that."

"Well it is, except for this one small problem, which is that it can't be turned on with a living subject inside it, and once it is turned on, a living subject can't *get* inside it. A stumper."

"That is a snag."

"Other men, lesser men, would see the ignition problem as fatal." Bode took a drink of coffee.

Cassie picked up her pencil and began doodling in the notebook, a rectangle, a dotted line suggesting the trajectory of a struck object.

"Let me add, since we're being honest," Bode continued, "that the size of the living subject doesn't seem to have an impact on the results. Cockroaches have died, rats have died, rabbits have given up their rabbit lives. That's as far up the food chain as I'm comfortable going, Thomas, I've got to say. Let go and let God, I say. And I believe I could mention something about tying a knot in the rope that would hang me."

Thomas looked at Cassie, giving her a half-smile as he scratched the back of his neck. "I think, Bode, that you're supposed to tie a knot in the end of your rope and hang on."

"I've never known you to hold with correcting, Thomas."

"No, I don't. Generally."

"But I prefer your way. Holding on to the end of the rope, as you mentioned."

Themis emerged from the back carrying clean cups and looking worse than before, her lips in starker contrast to her pale face. "You want anything else?" she asked the three, generally.

"I'll have another cappuccino."

"I'll have another black coffee as well."

"Me, too."

Themis took a deep breath and closed her eyes. "Je-*sus*."

Bode took a cigarette out of his breast pocket and tapped the filter on the counter, settling the tobacco down in the paper. "All this talk about my machine puts me in mind of the end of the world. What would you like to be doing at the end of the world, son?"

Thomas squinted at the ceiling. "You'll have to give me some time to think about it."

"I myself hope to be either fornicating or defecating. You heard right. There's a lot I'd like to *get out*."

Thomas turned and studied Bode hard, leaving Cassie to look at the back of his head. Bode stared straight ahead, smoking.

"I personally believe people should keep much more in," Thomas said.

Bode nodded. "Where are you from again? Kansas?"

"Indiana."

Cassie didn't say anything. She could meet someone from Indiana—that long, skinny state—anywhere in the world.

"You're probably repressed," Bode said, blowing on his fresh cappuccino.

"Probably so."

In Cassie's drawing the 2-ball was only six inches dead center from a corner pocket, but the cue was behind the 5; the one thing for it was a masse shot, showy and not her strength.

Bode blew a stream of blue smoke, then stubbed out his cigarette. "I've met a couple people from Indiana. They were all deeply troubled but appeared to be normal. Does that describe the situation from your point of view?"

Thomas nodded.

"Another thing I noticed about you Indianaians—"

"Hoosiers."

"Hoosiers, is that once you're removed from your home state, you miss it something fierce. I find that curious, given the facts about Indiana."

"What are the facts about Indiana? Thank you, Themis."

Bode took a sip of coffee. "Flat. Ugly. Stupid. Reactionary. I could think of some more if I put my mind to it."

"Where'd you grow up, Bode?"

"Natchez. A soporific. My heart's desire."

"Tell me three things you remember about growing up there. Just pictures, not feelings."

"Three things. Sure. I . . . hmmmm. Let's see. I remember running through cold sheets that had been hung on the line in the backyard. My granny'd hung them, they smelled burnt with bleach. I remember playing in a wrecked-out 1954 Nash Rambler that was abandoned in the woods behind our house. Would have been a great car if somebody had, you know. The seats got *hot* in the summertime. Is that two? Three: I used to pull taffy with my cousin Ruth. She was skinny and a redhead, had those thyroid eyes. She worked me over, son, past distraction."

"There you go. It doesn't take much, does it, to become homesick. I didn't hear anything about Natchez in your description."

Bode lit another cigarette. "I fear something is amiss in yer syllogism. You're making a generalized statement about homesickness, Brother Thomas, and I'm asking why all y'all Indianaians miss that place *in particular*."

Thomas drew a pattern in the sweat from his untouched water glass, a circle next to what looked like the Washington Monument, and Cassie copied it into her notebook. It was familiar.

"I don't know," Thomas said. "It's hard to pinpoint. Maybe I'll write it down for you."

"Ahh." Bode stubbed out this cigarette. "You'll never do it, you coward." He stood up, stretched, sorted money from the pile of paper on the counter, and pushed Cassie's pen back toward her.

"What am I afraid of, do you think?" Thomas asked.

Bode gathered up his Post-its, his business cards. "You're afraid to admit what you miss most about that godforsaken place. Basketball. It's basketball, ain't it."

Thomas laughed, a big laugh that earned a glare from Themis. "That's it; you've figured me out."

Bode bowed to them. "Have a good Good Friday. Remember the man who died for your sins. Thomas, don't be a stranger."

Cassie studied the drawing of the ball and spire, saw it cast in amber on a black base, left behind by Jimmy. For years it had been on the bookcase in the dim living room, separating Belle's favorite novels from Laura's, and then it had vanished.

"It's the trylon and perisphere," Thomas said, glancing at her notebook. "From the 1939 World's Fair."

"Yes." Cassie nodded. "I remember now." She looked up at him; he was looking back.

The night before she had dreamed she was standing in a clearing in a forest with a fat woman she should have recognized. The woman wore a cape and thick glasses and was carrying a crooked stick. Something about the woman struck Cassie as whimsical and humorous, even as she bred a dense wariness; Cassie backed away from the scene so vigorously that she bumped flat against the wall of the dream, a scrim as dense as brick. First the woman was tatting a black lace shawl but leaving holes, accidental gaps, crazed as the web of a terminally ill spider. And then the shawl was gone, and she was pointing the stick at a hawk, an old teacup, a tombstone, and saying, *Me, me, me.* It was a matter of time. Cassie woke up in a sweat.

" . . . except for the college kids, who consider it a rite of passage to vomit in the street in front of a crowd," Thomas was saying. His truck had been a block away, sitting in direct sun. The temperature was in the mid-seventies and the humidity low, but when Thomas unlocked the passenger door, a blast of heat from inside the truck hit her like a wave. It was an old Chevy half-ton, dark blue with a black vinyl interior.

"It gets hot," Thomas said, unlocking his door.

"What's it like in the summer?" Cassie asked, sliding in.

"Oh, Lord. Every day here, in the summer, is a crisis. I don't know why I stay. Some days are so humid you can close your hand around the air, like this"—he made a fist—"and gather water. This truck is rusty and riddled with salt from living on the Gulf. I probably have a pound of sand in my lungs."

The smell of the interior was immediately recognizable: age, plaster dust, the sharp iron smell of tools, a man's body day after day. The dashboard was gray with dirt. The truck started with a rumble, and they both rolled down their windows and opened the wings. At a stoplight Cassie said, "I think Bode was wrong about Indiana."

Thomas glanced at her. "You've been there?"

"I live there, actually."

"Is that right. Whereabouts?"

"A town called Roseville, in Hopwood County."

Thomas shifted, looked in the rearview mirror. "Never heard of it. A nice place?"

"Some like it. Where are you from?"

"Way down in southern Indiana, near the Kentucky line."

"What's it close to? Corydon? Tell City? Evansville?"

"Close to Mount Vernon. A town called Wellsboro."

Cassie closed her eyes, picturing a map. She couldn't see Wellsboro.

Thomas got on to Highway 10, headed north toward 90, the Gulf Coast Highway. The wind and road noise made conversation difficult. Thomas drove easily, the way Jimmy had, steering with his left hand, his right resting on the gearshift. The sunlight and caffeine worked on Cassie, making her both sleepy and jittery. She looked out the window at the passing scenery, which was flat, swampy, moss hanging from the trees. The truck hummed. If she'd made the trip with Laura, Cassie never would have met Thomas, she wouldn't be in this truck; everything from this point forward in her life would have been different, but Cassie wouldn't have known it, because the days would have felt the same. An oddity. Her thoughts felt like weightless things dipped in something heavier; she couldn't precisely pull them out. She could see her mother as if in a home movie, much younger, pushing Belle on a swing set. Belle's hair, blonder then, sailed out behind her as she flew up in the air, then gathered around her face as she approached the ground. Laura stood still, squinting into the sun and compelling the swing; her motions seemed mechanical, her mind elsewhere. Cassie tried to see herself—was she standing, was she playing?—and then she was falling, she could see her hands outstretched to break her fall.

"Whoa," she said, sitting up.

"All right?" Thomas said, touching her arm. "You jumped."

"I fell." They were in a different place than when she closed her eyes, a two-lane highway running next to the Gulf, fogged in. The water was out there, on Cassie's right, but she couldn't quite see it, and buildings emerged from the fog then vanished again. Thomas had rolled his window most of the way up, and Cassie did the same, feeling chilled. "Where are we?"

"Between Pass Christian and Gulfport. You missed Bay St. Louis. We're heading toward the riverboats. You gamble?"

Cassie shook her head. "Not when I'm bound to lose."

"Good thinking."

They passed large ugly buildings filled with cheap bathing suits and inflatable sharks; seafood restaurants; beachside motels surrounded by trees thick with Spanish moss. And there were houses, estates, behind low whitewashed brick walls, side by side with condominiums, next door to small businesses. A jumble.

"Gorgeous houses."

Thomas nodded. "Those are the ones that survived Camille in sixty-nine. To natives, all time is measured before and after."

Gulfport had a small college right there on the highway, but Cassie didn't see any students. A live oak in front of the building was so large, and had so many elephantine, twisting branches, that a tree house had been built in it and could be seen from the road.

Cassie turned to look at it as they passed.

"The Friendship Oak, that tree is called. Pre-Columbian. A lot of kissing goes on up there."

"You would know, I guess." Cassie gave him a slight smile.

"Not me, no ma'am. I get my information from those far more morally dubious than myself."

They passed a casino designed to look like a pirate's ship.

"What brings you down south?"

She shrugged. "Curiosity. What about you?"

"The same. And I needed to simplify my life."

"But you miss home?"

"Off and on. I've been gone a long time. I want you to see something," Thomas said, turning north on a busy four-lane road. Cassie thought at first that they were in downtown Gulfport, but the town seemed to disappear, replaced by low-slung buildings, one after another. Every other business, it seemed, was a pawn-shop; between them were E-Z Cash windows where soldiers from Keesler Air Force Base were getting advances on their pay. There were body shops and strip clubs, but the vast majority of the buildings contained treasure in hock.

"We like to keep things right out in the open on the Gulf. No messing around with subtlety." Thomas turned around and drove back to 90, went left. The pawnshops were lined up outside the casino doors, too. "We're almost to Biloxi. You ready for lunch? We could go to Mary Mahoney's, it's a place tourists like to visit, but it's still local. I have breakfast there a lot. Close to my house."

"Sounds fine."

"There's another big tree there."

"Well," Cassie said, rolling her window down, taking in the fog. "I wouldn't want to miss that."

They ate lunch in a courtyard surrounded by lacy wrought iron painted white, visited the massive Spanish oak, and went for a walk on the beach. The pale sand stretched the entire thirty miles of Harrison County, Thomas told her, but the water wasn't good for swimming. When she asked what he'd been doing in New Orleans that morning, Thomas said he'd come to find her. "Since it was my day off and all. I mean, I wasn't doing anything else. And what were you doing there, Cassie, if you don't mind my asking?"

She crossed her arms against the Gulf wind. "I went for coffee. It being a coffeehouse."

"Mm-hmm. It still seems like there's something you're not telling me."

"There's a lot of that going around."

They pulled in to the driveway of a lovely house on Reynoir Street, a 1930s cottage. The front porch was wide enough for rocking chairs, a wicker settee, and small wicker side tables.

"This is your house?" Cassie asked, admiring the fresh paint, the oak door, the polished brass numbers on a post next to the steps.

"No, I live in the gardener's shed behind the house. Miss Sophie lives here, my landlady. We've been together seven years."

"So she's like family."

"She is my family," Thomas said, stepping out of the truck. "We should introduce you."

The backyard was a model of order against abundance, the flower beds thick with camellias and vines Cassie didn't recognize. They walked onto the screened porch, where there were more rocking chairs, a brass plant stand, and a table on which waited a green pitcher and two metal drinking glasses. As Thomas knocked on the back door, Cassie could smell the inside of the house: lilacs and something earthy, an undertow.

"Miss Sophie?" Thomas called, opening the door.

"I'm in the sitting room, Thomas," Sophie called. "Don't make me get up."

They walked through the spotless kitchen with its tall cabinets and hulking gas stove, through the dining room, which appeared to have been unused for years, and into the sunlit front room. Miss Sophie was in her late seventies, Cassie guessed, a big woman in a faded housedress. Her right foot was swollen and propped up on a stool; her white hair was gathered into a knot at her neck.

"Oh, Thomas, you have taken a lover," she said as Thomas bent down to kiss her, "if I'd known, I'd have baked a cake." She gestured for Cassie to sit beside her on the rose-colored sofa.

"Miss Sophie, this is Cassie. She's visiting from Indiana."

"How do you do," Cassie said, offering her hand.

"My favorite greeting, so old-fashioned." Miss Sophie pressed Cassie's hand between her own. "I do quite well, except that my circulation is poor and I have to keep this foot propped up. I call what we're sitting on a davenport, but Thomas calls it a couch. What do you call it?"

"I'd call it a couch," Cassie said.

"And this behind my head Thomas calls a doily, but I say it's an antimacassar. How about you?"

"I think I'd say a doily."

"Do you cut the grass or mow the lawn?"

"Mow the lawn. It's my least favorite job."

"We can both agree, I think, that to our left is a rocking chair, and Thomas, you should sit down on it. Let me ask you another thing: say I handed you a green, very mild bell pepper out of my garden. What would you say that was?"

"Where I live, we call it a mango."

"Huh," Miss Sophie said, staring at Thomas. "She's from exactly the same place you are, Thomas."

Above them a ceiling fan whisked around quietly, and in the corner an heirloom grandfather clock kept hushed time. On the table beside Miss Sophie lay a copy of Faulkner's *Light in August*, battered, and with bookmarks in fifteen different places.

"My mother loves Faulkner," Cassie said.

"He is my god," Miss Sophie said, crossing herself. "When I write his name, I leave out all the vowels, so as not to earn his wrath. You go into the city, Thomas?"

"Just to the coffee shop," Thomas said, leaning forward in the rocking chair, his elbows on his knees. In this light Cassie could see how green his eyes were, the sharpness of the bones in his face. "That's where I found Cassie," he said, "drinking coffee, black. I saw Bode, too."

"Ah. Will I get to go back to 1929 after all? I'd like to get ahold of Grandmother's engagement ring before she loses it."

"I wouldn't recommend it as yet."

"I have a dream about 1929, has Thomas told you?" she asked Cassie, who shook her head. "I am on a train. I'm walking the length of it, looking in every cabin for my mother, and there, in one of them, is Joe. He asks me if I remember the party in 1929, when my father wore the Chief tuxedo and gave that young girl a gift."

"What does that mean, do you suppose?" Cassie asked.

"No way to know with dreams."

"I've never heard of a Chief tuxedo," Thomas said, "that's what I say every time we talk about this dream."

"Is your name short for Cassandra?" Miss Sophie's face was barely lined, but her teeth were not her own, and her earlobes were stretched like crepe paper.

"No, it's Cassiopeia."

"My goodness, what a blessing. What do you do in this world?"

Cassie cleared her throat. She had wandered into this living room as if onto the set of a comic opera already in progress. "I play pool for money."

Miss Sophie barked out a laugh, and Thomas sat back in the rocker.

"You're a what, a billiard shark?" Miss Sophie was so delighted she nearly bounced.

"I play American pool, not English billiards, and I'm not a shark. That would be a person who pretended not to be a good player, then stole the money of her opponent. I just announce myself, I say I've come to a place to play their best, and for money, and that person is called. Or I wait for him."

"I'll be damned," Sophie said, shaking her head.

"And I'm the person in my own town other hustlers would come to beat, except that it doesn't happen anymore. There are very few of us left."

"And do they, would they beat you?"

"No," Cassie said. "No, they wouldn't."

Miss Sophie waved her hand in front of her face. "My interest in this is so sudden it feels *lewd*. Well, Thomas," she said, smiling at him, "it looks to me as if you've met your match. The cosmic wheel and all that. Now, go take a walk or visit the library, have an impromptu prayer meeting, whatever young people do these days. I'll make some dinner."

The gardener's shed was at the very back of the property, partially shaded, a clapboard square, a forest-green door, a green tin roof. There were rosebushes climbing a trellis at one corner, morning glories woven through a small fence, and red and white azaleas in bloom all along the sunny side.

"I'd lock this door, but there doesn't seem to be a key."

Inside was a single room with a small kitchen at one end, an enclosed space for a bathroom, everything finished like a yacht. The wide plank floor was scarred, swept clean. On top of an old potting table was a place mat and a silver napkin ring, and at the other end, books stacked six and seven deep, piles of papers and file folders. A double bed with no frame, covered by a threadbare quilt, filled one wall, leaving just enough room for a small night-stand. A matchbook propped up one of the nightstand's legs. On the other wall were an overstuffed chair and a reading lamp.

"I'm at the limits, probably, of how much I can pare my life down," Thomas said.

Cassie walked toward the kitchen. There were three copper-bottomed pans of different sizes hanging from hooks under the cabinets, a French press, a yellow can of chicory coffee. "Did you pare your life down on purpose?"

"No; that was an exaggeration. I came here empty-handed."

The crazy quilt had a faded green border. Cassie lifted up the edge: the backing was old burlap sacks from the Louisiana Sugar Company. She wanted to stay here, if not in this very room, then somewhere nearby and with nothing. On Thomas's nightstand was a lamp with a paper shade covered with fading roses, dark-ened, and one small gold picture frame. A boy and girl on a wooden swing set, both high above a flooded backyard. The water looked to be two or three feet deep. The children were looking at the camera, their faces lit with unguarded joy. The boy was undoubtedly Thomas; there was the same curly hair, the same hardness of the chest and shoulders.

"Who's this little girl?"

"I've lost track of her."

Cassie studied the girl, her dark hair and narrow face. "That moment in the truck, when I fell asleep, I was seeing my sister on a swing set." The backyard was flooded, the children were swing-ing above it. "A town not far from ours used to flood, back in the late sixties, early seventies. Something about the water table, I can't remember. There was a photograph in the paper once, a man canoeing down the main street."

"Interesting," Thomas said, looking in the refrigerator. "Would you like something to drink? There's water, or . . . water, it looks like."

Cassie put the picture back where she'd found it. "You know what, I'm actually— I'm really tired. I've traveled a long way, and I'm tired."

He turned and walked toward her, his hands out as if he was afraid she might fall. "Come here, sit down with me." He pulled the quilt down off one of the bed pillows. "Lie down here. I'll rub your shoulders."

She slipped off her boots, then pulled her shirt out of her jeans and lay down, facing away from the center of the bed. Thomas lay down behind her; when his hand closed around her tight shoulder, she closed her eyes. "Feel this muscle," he said. "Cassie."

"I'm right here."

"There's a mess in my past I'll never make right, but it doesn't have anything to do with women. I just want to say that there was a long time where I did everything wrong, and I've left that time behind me. But at my very worst, I never, I don't—"

Cassie rolled over on her back and looked at him. "You don't have to tell me anything."

He stared at her, his face inches from hers, then pressed one hand against the side of her head. "My hands are rough," he said, looking at her mouth.

"Is Bode building a time machine?"

"Yes, he is. Is there someplace you'd like to go?"

Maybe 1919, when Ralph Greenleaf won his first tournament, beating the tuxedoed billiard royalty of the time. She wouldn't mind being the person losing, as long as she could watch. And she'd love to be in the room with Willie Mosconi, who took over from Greenleaf at the end of his career. With her eyes closed, she could see Mosconi's hands perfectly, shooting as Paul Newman's double in *The Hustler*. Mosconi was another of those men with genetic grace, power. She'd like to be on the set of the film, watching Jackie Gleason—himself a brilliant player—as Minnesota Fats. "It's hard to choose," Cassie said, her eyes still closed.

"I'd love," Thomas said, "now, don't laugh, to be present when Wittgenstein and Popper had their argument. Apparently a fireplace poker was brandished."

"Two philosophers. Not so different from what I was thinking."

Or maybe she'd like to be in New Orleans on the night her parents met—not the moment the battered Jimmy wandered into the Grille, but before that. She'd like to know what hard thing he had propelled his face against, whether he'd won whatever bet he'd placed. Maybe she'd like to meet her mother at twelve, as she was in the photograph she kept on her dresser: thin, dark, secretive, wearing a white dress with a dark sweater around her shoulders, sitting on a tree stump with a Boston terrier on her lap (*Laura and Milkweed*, written on the back of the photograph in Laura's young handwriting). Cassie thought about the look on Laura's face, the way she seemed to be looking directly into the sun without squinting, her ironic smile and crooked bottom teeth.

Or perhaps she wouldn't travel so far back. Maybe, if she could, she'd choose a year ago. She would take any single day before Laura began to make a certain sound at the beginning and end of every sentence, a rough, wet intake of breath, a slight ragged whistle. At the hospital, pacing the floor or sitting next to Laura's bed, Cassie had asked herself repeatedly, *Didn't you hear it?* And she had, she'd heard it the way you might hear something in the middle of the night then turn away from it. An intruder. And hadn't Cassie noticed that Laura talked less and less, had spent more time reading and writing in her journal? She'd told the doctor, *My mother is a moody woman, and discontent*, but what she'd meant was: How do we know which emergency to treat? The doctor, a distracted man who looked barely old enough to drive, whose pupils were irregularly sized and whose hands shook, said, "You'll probably feel some anger at your mother for withholding her diagnosis," said it without looking at her, and Cassie had seen, as if in a vision, him underlining the statement in a textbook on patient care, and she flew out of her chair, her hands in fists. He tried to back up but bumped into the desk in the waiting room. In a split second she was nose-to-nose with him. "You think so? You think I might feel some *anger*, you hopped-up little fuck?"

Or maybe she'd ask to go back only two weeks, to the day Laura collapsed and Cassie couldn't be reached. She'd gone to Bud's in the morning, then out with a work crew laying hardwood floor in a renovation on the other side of the county. She'd gotten off early and driven home slowly, enjoying the weak March sun, nursing the tendinitis in her right elbow with ibuprofen. The wind blew through the truck. She wore a camouflage cap that advertised industrial cable. When she got home, there seemed to be no one there; Laura wasn't in the kitchen, Edwin wasn't visiting, Belle wasn't at the table proofreading someone else's scholarship. Cassie found her sister in the living room with the shades pulled. Laura had spent the day, Belle said, in bed, under an afghan, and finally Belle thought to check on her, to ask if she needed anything, and Laura *had been very sick*, that's how Belle described it. She was worried, too, about a bloodstain on the old carpet in Laura's room, because the EMTs had a terrible time finding a vein. What should we do about the stain, Cassie, should we try to clean it, should we leave it, should we cut it out and burn it, keep it?

"My mother is dead," Cassie told Thomas, who winced. She gasped, crying suddenly so hard she couldn't consider him a stranger, she felt they'd been drawn together by a natural disaster, all boundaries erased.

"Shhhh," he said, pulling her against him, wrapping his arms around her until she could hardly breathe.

Cassie thought he must have lost his mother, too, to live as he did at the edge of the continent. Laura had hoped, she'd written in her journal, that whatever befell her daughters, they would not be damaged at the level of instinct, that exact phrase. Her instinct was to lift Thomas's T-shirt above his head, which she did, he allowed her to, then wipe her eyes on it. "Go ahead and use my shirt," he said. And then she took off her own and lay back down; Thomas hooked his legs around hers and pulled her against him until their bellies were touching. She thought to say, I don't want to go back in time, I want to stop it, I want to stop time. And then she stopped it.

For dinner Miss Sophie made red beans and rice, and turnip greens, served with sweet tea. They sat at the kitchen table, allowing the dining room to go on undisturbed. Thomas sat next to Cassie; he had a light touch, he let his hand hover near her shoulder or on her knee, he wrapped his fingers around the nape of her neck briefly, then removed them. She had never felt such a thing, so fleeting; she felt like she'd been drinking homemade liquor.

Miss Sophie told the story of how she'd hired Thomas to do landscaping all those years ago, and how she'd gotten so accustomed to having him around, she'd asked him to stay. She said she noticed how, of an afternoon she waited at the window like a collie for him to get off his day job. It had been so long, she said, since anyone had *interested* her.

"He knows a great deal," Miss Sophie said. "He has knowledge from some other life, many books. It's private. Tell me more about playing pool."

Cassie looked at Thomas, and as she told Miss Sophie about how gambling had moved to the big cities and behind the scenes at professional tournaments, about how the life of the road hustler was too dangerous, too expensive, about money men, she looked at him. She told Miss Sophie she'd found no first-rate pool hall in New Orleans, a surprise. Laura's life, Emmy's life, all the lives of all the mated women she knew had been warning enough for her, and yet Cassie looked at Thomas and she *loved* him. She was in love with him, it had happened because her guard was down, she hadn't been prepared. No one in the world would ever feel half as good to her again, and that knowledge made her so sad she had to take a drink of tea and ask to be excused. The red and pink tiles on the bathroom floor and walls made her head swim. She splashed her face with cold water and wished fervently for deliverance. She wished at least to emerge from the day without saying something that would give her away.

They asked her to stay, but she explained there was something she needed to that night, and Thomas said he'd drive her back.

After she'd said her good-byes to Miss Sophie, Cassie walked out to the gardener's shed to get her pack while Thomas helped with the dishes.

She looked around, memorizing the details. His books, his dishes, the dents in the quilt where their bodies had been. The photograph of Thomas and the little girl. Cassie picked it up, stared at his face, at the flooded, familiar yard. Without even realizing she was doing it, she slipped the back off the frame and looked at the back of the picture, and there, written in fading blue ink: *Big Rains. Taos and Langston, June 1973*. She reassembled the frame and put it back on the nightstand. So he wanted to be called Thomas; she'd call him that.

"Scoot over here next to me," Thomas said, patting the middle of the bench seat.

She did so, imagining the two of them driving down the back roads of Hopwood County, listening to country-and-western music and watching for drivers with only one headlight. Cassie would say *perdiddle*, and Thomas would kiss her every time, that was the rule. Sometimes she passed middle-aged couples in Chevy trucks with oversize tires—the woman with her long hair in braids, the man unshaven—who looked to be sharing the same seat belt. Often there was a dog involved, and a gun rack.

"If I hit your knee with the gearshift, you might be crippled and have to stay."

She imagined them at the reservoir late at night, cooking bluegill and listening to Muddy Waters, then back at the house with Belle, who would secretly think Thomas hung the moon.

Thomas in Cassie's bed, facing the west window, the thick after-noon light, the pure scent of him gathered against her.

They said almost nothing on the trip back, but she leaned against him and turned her face in toward his neck, let the tip of her nose touch his ear, his cheek, he was her new-found land.

"How can you leave this Gulf breeze, I ask you?"

She could tell the truth, that all she had left was a sister, a thin, dry-skinned, chapped-lipped woman who was alone and would al-ways be alone. But that would sound like an excuse, or a confession.

In New Orleans they passed a man who looked like Jesus, driving a horse-drawn carriage, and a lot of very normal-looking people window-shopping, picking up beignet mix and crab boil to take home to Nebraska as proof of their adventures, and a man who seemed to be seven feet tall with long black dreadlocks. Thomas pulled up in front of the guest house and left the engine running. He took something out of his pocket, a slip of paper, then looked at Cassie a long time. Cardplayers train themselves to control their blood pressure, their respiration; they watch for nervous tics like sudden blinking, they never tap their cards. Some players tend to give away a losing hand, some can't control the news of a royal flush. She could tell him that a law of game theory is that any game allowing for a bluff will eventually give rise to a bluff. She looked back at him without expression.

"This is Miss Sophie's address and phone number. She would make sure I got any message, and she always knows how to reach me."

Cassie took the piece of paper and slipped it into the back pocket of her blue jeans. She had never pursued a man, had never called a man just because she loved him.

"That's all I'm going to say, Cassie."

She leaned over then and kissed him lightly, moving her lips back and forth across his. She didn't know his last name, and he didn't know hers. The truck was still idling at the curb, he was still watching, as she opened the door of the blue guest house and went inside.

Better-dressed women play better pool, it was a fact Cassie had disputed for years and finally gave in to. She showered, then changed into a pair of black cotton pants that fit closely through the waist and hips and loosely through the legs, and a silky white cotton shirt with French cuffs, tucked at the waist. She carried a thin black sweater. Her ankle-high boots, black, had been polished before she left home, but she went over them again. The two-inch heel was clunky but gave her extra height she needed.

It was early for a game, so she wandered into the Quarter, finally stopping at a café on the water for a coffee to go. There were a lot of people on the street, and every twenty feet or so, a musician or a mime. She stopped at the edge of a crowd watching a group of acrobats, six young men from Jamaica wearing nothing but red shorts and tennis shoes, performing breathtaking gymnastic feats. A portable stereo was playing Michael Jackson's *Thriller*, and the five-gallon buckets being passed through the crowd were filled with money.

"Here, sweetheart, have a seat."

Next to her a clown had scooted over to make room. She sat down, then looked at him. He was a fat, sad old clown. His makeup wasn't sad, his actual face was, and he was wearing a pale yellow one-piece clown suit that billowed out in the middle, as if a hula hoop had been sewn in, but it was really his stomach.

"Are you married?" he asked, presenting her with a flower made from a twisted green balloon.

"Depends on who you ask."

"Would you like to marry me?"

"Our careers would clash."

He nodded. "My last wife felt the same." They watched the acrobats leap over one another, and over members of the audience.

"Have you always been a clown?"

"No, no. I used to be a plumber. Then I lost my license and became a pimp."

"A pimp. A ghetto sort of pimp? Did you have diamonds, big hats?"

"Ha! I was a pimp in Oklahoma City. I looked pretty much like I do now, but without the balloons. Had thirty girls at my peak, then I fell in love with one of them."

"That's no good."

"It wasn't. My wife left me and took our kids, and I moved in with the girl, Serena, and she got me hooked on cocaine. Then I became a dealer."

"And all your profit went up your nose, and you fled here."

"You couldn't be more right. So I got here and looked around, and this seemed to be the best option."

Cassie nodded. The clown sat slumped over his big stomach.

"All those girls, thirty girls. All of them dead or missing now, it breaks my heart."

His makeup had funneled into his wrinkles, his face was a moonscape. One of his eyeteeth was missing.

"Can I ask you something?" Cassie said, pulling five dollars from her pocket and placing it in the bucket as it passed her.

"Back when you were married and a plumber, did you see a clown in your future?"

He shook his head. "Absolutely not. I never would have guessed it."

They sat in silence. The crowd began to clear.

"So you're saying that any one of us could become a clown? It could be waiting for any of us?"

"I guess that's what I'm saying." He smiled, sighed, then dabbed at one of his eyes with a purple silk handkerchief he produced out of nowhere. "Spring," he said.

She gave the cabdriver the address of the old hotel; he drove a long way from the Quarter, far enough that she lost her sense of direction. The driver, a middle-aged man who looked like a leprechaun, asked if she knew someone there.

"Not really."

"You know it ain't a hotel? People lives there now."

Cassie shook her head. "I didn't know."

The three-story brick building had probably been anonymous when it was built at the turn of the century, but it had aged into a hulking grace. Whatever had been around the hotel in its heyday had vanished, replaced by warehouses and dark factories. Cassie paid the driver and asked his name. "Eddie."

"Eddie, if I place a call to this cab company and request you, will you come straight here immediately, even if you have another passenger?"

"You're asking me to."

"I'm asking you to."

He wrote his name and a phone number on the back of a

receipt. "This is my cell phone right here. Don't call the dispatcher."

On the hotel doors, the brass handles—the sort that run vertically, nearly the length of the inner edge of double doors—were tarnished, but the door opened with a cushioned smoothness, and the leaded glass was thick, inset in maple. Cassie paused and ran her hand up the flat edge. Silk. These doors had probably been made by craftsmen who charged a fortune, did nothing else and took their time, were arrogant and proud. The lobby wasn't disappointing, although Cassie could see in it, too, the lost fortune. The wide silk rug was threadbare, the horsehair sofas looked beaten; even glancing at them was uncomfortable. But a gas fire still burned in the fireplace—the gentle fire of gas, rather than a tree being consumed—and the seascape oil paintings on the paneled walls had grown deeper with age. The counter was curved, smooth wood with pillars at either end, and there were individual mail slots behind the hotelier, carved out of pine and marked with tarnished brass numbers. Perhaps twenty of the forty or so held mail.

A man came around the corner and noticed Cassie. He was middle-aged, bald on top, and lean, with the long fingers of a cardsharp. His features were exaggerated: wide blue eyes with thick black lashes; a snub nose too snubbed; a wide mouth, dimples. He wore a blue dress shirt and khakis, and could have been anywhere, doing anything.

"Can I help you?" He seemed friendly enough, but that was his job, the reason he was up front. She could be a cop, a vengeful wife, she could work for a bail bondsman or be serving a subpoena.

"I'm here to see Jackson LaFollette."

"Is he expecting you?"

"Not so much."

The man nodded, looked as if he were about to disappoint her. "Do you have some business with him?"

"I'm actually just looking for a game."

"I'll call him. How about you wait here?"

Cassie wandered through the sitting area and into the formal dining room. The pocket doors dividing the two rooms must have been eight feet tall; Cassie pulled the inset brass handle of one, and it slid out soundlessly. The dining room itself was lit by gas lamps, all wood and red rugs, dark furniture, old photographs. She knew pool halls: in her mind there existed twelve distinct categories, including Obsessed With Wheels (subcategories Trucks, Motorcycles); Frank Sinatra (seedy, thin white men drinking martinis); Hank Williams, Sr. (seedy, thin white men drinking whiskey); Cell Division (mostly for the desperate-to-wed); Closeted (gay, unaware of it); and Graduate School (owned by the deadly serious and catering to those with aspirations toward the PBA). But this was new. If she were betting, she'd say that somewhere in this building was the remnant of a genuine speakeasy, not a simulacrum built for investment bankers and their fishy girlfriends but the real thing. Her heart rate climbed, and she closed her eyes and took deep breaths to try to calm it. She loved this place, she loved finally standing in the world where the real rules applied, the rules of form, composure, conversation. She had taken thousands of dollars out of the hands of men who spent game after game trying to get her to bed. Losing and still trying. Periodically she would even say, *You're never going to win this way; I'm going to reject you, and then I'm going to beat you*, but it didn't matter. And then there were men who were violently afraid of losing to a woman, the scariest men in the world. They became dictators, heads of state, bureaucrats, men with deadly weapons, they were everywhere. Sometimes she could pick one out with a look, but they were often charming, they had to have the power to attract in order to dominate.

"You can come this way."

They walked through a door on the opposite end of the sitting room and into a long, dim hallway. On the left were room doors, regularly spaced, flocked wallpaper fading. Everything was quiet. On the right were three doors: one at either end of the hallway, a set of double doors in the middle. They opened those: a ballroom. In the normal course of her life, Cassie never had to struggle to take in her surroundings, because the structure and the trappings were a reflection of the crowd, and the crowd was the same every night: overdressed girls just out of high school, smoking and trying to look tough; young men tattooed with spiders and reptiles, answering calls on cell phones about where they were and when they'd be home; groups of Hispanic housepainters still in work clothes; long-married couples dingy with cigarette smoke and familiarity. There were college kids who tried to distinguish themselves from the regulars with loud, erudite misstatements and exclamations about the equipment; the neophytes, who self-consciously rolled their cues across the table and scraped the chalk over the tip as if scrubbing the bottom of a filthy pan.

But this: the salmon-colored walls ascending into a gold dome, the floor-to-ceiling windows draped in green velvet, the springy dance floor, this was new. Sound—the murmuring of voices, the jazz quartet playing in the corner—seemed to rise above the scene and hover like a cloud. Cassie felt she could ascend and polish out the voices one by one, every note of "All of Me"; vague, menacing laughter. There were five tables, all vintage Brunswicks, covered in the finest Belgian wool dyed vivid green—the color, as Walter Tevis wrote, of money. A heavy wooden beam ran the width of the room over each table, and from these beams hung lamps in green shades. They illuminated every inch of the table.

The bar was at the end of the room, magnificent, mirrored, lined with bottles of liquor and crystal glasses.

"That's Jack, there, in the brown sweater."

She was faced with the wide back of the man, who appeared to have his arms wrapped around the drink in front of him, as a man might nurture his fatal flaw. She thanked her guide and started across the dance floor, taking in and deflecting the stares of the men at the tables, older men, all, and dressed well. The floor felt buoyant; surely the tables were leveled every day. And the air was dry—the humidity that can so affect a game had been removed. She took a seat at the bar, leaving one stool between herself and Jack, and ordered a gin gimlet from the bartender, a young black man who barely met her eye. Jack ignored her, too, giving her time to look at the cue he had propped against the bar; she was surprised to see that it was new, and one she admired, the Meucci Gambler. Black dice and red playing cards were inset in the butt: it was a flashy piece.

"You were looking for me?"

"I was," Cassie said, tasting the cold gimlet.

"Do I know you?"

"We know some of the same people."

"Is that right." Jack hadn't yet turned in her direction. "That's my table behind us."

Cassie carried her drink over to the shelf next to the house cues, CueTecs, fairly new. She took her time choosing, then chalked, tied her sweater around her waist, waiting for Jack to rise, to move at all. Waves of hostility surrounded him; he had the posture of a mean drunk. When he finally struggled off his stool, she saw that he was at least six feet four and weighed well over three hundred pounds, most of which he carried around his middle. He was wearing creamy linen trousers, tailored. Cassie could not abide a wide-assed man, and she decided to beat him regardless of the greater cost. His face, when he finally looked at her, was another shock: underneath the weight he could have been a Barrymore, so finely were his bones composed. And his gray hair, still streaked with black, was wavy and combed away from his face, like a screen idol from his youth. Laura had written of his villain's smile, and there it was, and his gold fraternity ring, the crucifix he wore on a thin gold chain.

"Hundred a game."

Cassie agreed, then lost the lag on purpose. She would know how to proceed from his break. After racking for 9-ball, he took his place, breaking with his new cue; that was one story. She also saw that he was very strong, very drunk. The cue ball broke the rack violently, harder than was necessary for this game, sending the balls flying all over the table. Everything was wide open. The five fell; the one rolled downtable and the two up, with the cue well placed for both shots. Cassie plotted how she would shoot all the way to the nine, given the chance. Jack swayed slightly, pulled a cigarette from his breast pocket and lit it, then let it hang from his lower lip as he bent and sank the one without sending the cue up far enough for an easy shot on the two. He took no practice strokes, and he barely leaned toward the table. Many fat men played as he did, high above the shot. He had a long way to go for the two and would have to make it on a thin slice, but soon enough the two was gone, he made the three on a combination, he sank the four even though he'd stroked too hard. The five was already gone, and the nine was in front of a side pocket, flanked by the six. He made the nine. Cassie glanced at her watch. He'd won the game in seven minutes.

She took her stake out of her pocket and peeled off a bill.

"Thank you, darlin'," he said, walking toward the bar. A cocktail waitress, a young black woman with a stoic expression, met him halfway there. "Where you been?" Cassie heard him ask the woman, in a tone that bore the contemptuous edge of intimacy. Cassie gathered the balls and racked again as he ordered himself a whiskey and a second gin gimlet for her; she had barely touched the first and wouldn't finish it. When he handed her the cocktail, she thanked him, turned to put it on the shelf.

"You a Jew, by any chance?" he asked. "Excuse me, Jew-*ish*?"

Hard, he was going to make this as hard as possible.

"Not so far as I know."

"A shame," he said, mustering a sad smile. "I've always wanted to, you know."

He took the second game without Cassie attempting a shot. She paid him, and he turned and ordered more drinks.

"You know I'm a doctor? Anything ail you?"

"I'm fine, thanks."

"You say we have mutual friends?" *Myoo-chal*.

"One or two."

In the third game he broke without making a shot, and Cassie approached the table carefully, holding her cue at the joint and stalking possible shots. She could see her way clear through the first three balls, then took a safety on the four. Jack was perplexed by the problem—the four downtable, tight against the rail with the six slightly in front of it—and passed as well, but his shots were getting wilder, and he set her up for a difficult but possible bank. He had begun to leave his cigarette burning on the edge of the table, then was unable to pick it up after he'd attempted his shot; the cigarette was too small and too far away. She won the third game.

By midnight she was up six hundred dollars, and the band packed up and went home. The bartender put on a Tommy Dorsey record; none of the players was ready to leave.

"My family practically owns this town, one brother in the bank, one in the pharmacy, one on the bench. Been running this place a long time."

"So you said."

"We know the same people? Somebody sent you here?"

By one in the morning she thought he would fall, but he continued standing. She had seen him drink twelve whiskeys and go through a whole pack of cigarettes. She'd won twelve hundred dollars.

"I live here when the wife kicks me out. These days that's most . . ." He squinted. "What was I saying?"

"You live here most of the time."

"Right. Are you a Jewish?"

* * *

By two-thirty, the other players had gathered casually at the bar and were watching Cassie and Jack. She was up twenty-five hundred dollars. Jack strolled over to the bartender, said a word to him, then walked back. He was having difficulty finding the table. "Double or nothing," he said, trying to leer but unable to make eye contact.

"Give me a minute?" she asked.

"Sure, sweetheart. Take all the time you need." He turned back to his cronies, the men he lived with in this hidden place, who sat silent, drinking. They were impossible to read.

Cassie glanced at the waitress, then headed for the women's room, which had been added as an afterthought and was little more than a closet with two toilets and a pedestal sink. She washed her hands, splashed her face with water. Her chest was beginning to ache. The waitress walked in and headed for the sink; she didn't look at Cassie.

"I'd appreciate it if you'd call this number for me, please," Cassie said, handing the waitress the slip of paper from her pocket and a hundred-dollar bill. The waitress took it and tucked in her apron.

Maybe she'd call him and maybe she wouldn't.

"The king of *Rex*. Everybody important, either me or my mama or my daddy." Jack reached up to rub his eyes like a little boy, and his sweater and shirt, already untucked, lifted, too. Cassie caught a glance of his stomach: purple and mottled with stretch marks. She hoped he'd live ten more minutes. "Say again who shent you here?" The bartender walked up quietly and handed

Jack his money. He pretended to count it, then handed it to a man at the bar.

Cassie placed the cue ball just behind the headstring, close to the right rail, then hit the one just right, sinking a wing ball in a corner pocket. A part of her considered giving up a shot, letting Jack humiliate himself, but ultimately she wasn't that sort of player. All these years—her whole life, really—he'd been her shadow father, the man her mother almost married. Cassie was the child they almost had. She had been able to imagine the possibilities in great detail, the wealth, the extended family, the promise; all children are gifted at picturing such things. But in the end she played it safe and all the way through, and tapped the nine in, just kissed it.

She raised the cue and slipped it into the house rack. Without it, she had nothing in her hands. The man who held the money at the bar gave her a slight smile, then handed her the five thousand. She gave a nod to everyone there, then turned and headed toward the double doors. Jack continued to stand where she'd left him, next to the shelf where twelve untouched gin gimlets had gone warm. Cassie didn't walk quickly; she led with her hips, as Laura would have done, and made her stride as long as possible. You don't know how to walk, forget it, the world wants nothing to do with you; your genes get lost, and there go all your bright-eyed babies.

"Sorry I forgot to introduce myself," she called back over her shoulder. "I'm Cassie Claiborne, Jimmy Claiborne's daughter." She opened one of the double doors and walked out into the dim hallway. Ten steps, she thought, to the parlor, fifteen steps to the door; she made it into the lobby, where the bald man continued to stand guard, before the hall door slammed behind her. She didn't turn around, she counted the steps, sped up maybe a little bit, he was shouting at her to turn her ass around. Jack shouted things about Jimmy that she'd thought plenty of times herself, but they sounded unseemly coming from him. She considered saying so. The brass door handle was cool in her hand, she'd opened the door, she'd stepped out into the night, and Jack snagged her sweater, pulled it hard enough that it came untied and let go; she had taken another step, and he grabbed her around her left bicep. His big hand closed around her upper arm, I'll be bruised there tomorrow, she thought, and that was the last thing she thought, because it isn't right to grab a woman *anywhere*, for *any reason*, and before she'd really planned it, she was spinning on her left foot, her right leg tucked close to her chest, there was no time, but what can you do. The thick heel of her boot slammed into his chin so hard she heard his teeth crash together like dropped dinner plates. His head snapped backward, and the muscle in Cassie's inner thigh twanged like a rubber band.

"Ow! Dammit!" she said, as Jack bent slowly at the knees, went down. His knees hit the pavement, but his eyes were open, so Cassie brought her knee up and nailed him in the nose, not hard enough to break it, but he would certainly feel regret. "Ow, ow, *ow*." She limped toward the waiting cab, thinking how sorry she was to be leaving the windpipe, solar plexus, groin, and instep part of the program unfulfilled. He was *tall*.

"You forgot your sweater," Eddie said.

"Ow, ow, ow," she said, limping back to the fallen man and

gently pulling her sweater out of his hands. "Ow, ow, ow." Her entire right leg was on fire. She wondered briefly if perhaps it had come unattached.

Eddie pulled away from the curb, then turned up WWOZ, where Beausoleil was playing "Blue a Bebe." Laura loved that band. Cassie gave him the address of the guest house on Rampart, then let her head fall back against the seat. After a few minutes he said, "You enjoying New Orleans?"

"It's great," Cassie said. "It's the best."

He lit a cigarette, smiled at her in the rearview mirror. "That's my girl. That's what we like to hear."

The next morning Cassie called the airline and moved her reservation up. She had only one thing left to do, and it wouldn't take long; she could fly out early that afternoon.

In the dining room Marcelle and Martine were enjoying coffee and corn muffins, reading the *Times-Picayune*. "Good mornin'," they said.

"Morning." Cassie limped to the table and sat down.

"What's wrong, why are you limping?" Marcelle, the more matronly of the two, leaned toward Cassie.

"Marcelle," Martine said, lowering her part of the paper. "Don't ask a person that."

"It's okay," Cassie said. "I just pulled a muscle, I think."

The sisters were in their sixties and had matching gray page-boys. Cassie thought they might be twins and could tell them apart only because Marcelle wore lipstick.

"Can I ask if she had a good day yesterday?"

"I don't care what you do."

"Would that be all right, if I just asked that?"

"Go on, ask."

"Did you have a good day yesterday, Cassie?" Marcelle poured her a cup of coffee and pushed a muffin her way.

"I had"—Cassie thought about it a moment—"a remarkable day."

"Splendid," Marcelle said, handing her a small knife and bowl of butter.

"Is there anything else you want to know?" Martine asked without lowering her paper.

"No!" Marcelle folded her hands primly on the table and looked out the dining room window, as if concerned with nothing. "Someone slept poorly last night, I think."

They sat in silence. Martine turned to the sports section.

"Not you, though, Cassie, you slept well enough? You got in quite late."

"She's a grown woman, Marcelle."

"I'm perfectly aware."

"She can come and go freely."

"Of course she can."

"I sort of lost track of time," Cassie said. "I was playing pool."

"Pool! I didn't know people still did that."

Martine sighed.

"They do." Cassie took a drink of her coffee.

"Would you like part of the paper?" Martine asked.

"Now, did you make friends, or, or," Marcelle picked at the corner of her linen napkin, "were they strangers?"

"Marcelle, isn't there something you should be doing? Do you actually still work here?"

"It is Easter Sunday, *Easter Sunday*, Martine."

"I was playing against a man named Jackson LaFollette."

Martine lowered her paper. Marcelle laid her hand flat against her chest; her pink bathrobe seemed to get pinker.

"I hope you won," Martine said, going back to reading.

"I did."

Marcelle cleared her throat, took a sip of her coffee. "Well. Well, that's something."

Cassie peeled the wrapper off her muffin, cut it in half.

"I haven't heard his name in a while is why it's something."

Cassie buttered one side, took a bite; it was sweet.

"He kilt his first wife."

Cassie put the muffin down.

Martine grumbled, shook the paper. "He kilt his second wife, too. Not many people commit suicide by shooting theirselves in the head *twice*."

Marcelle pursed her lips. "And you just know he kilt his dear mother. He was the only person in the house with her the night she died! She was fine, perfectly fine, and then Jack came home for a visit, and the next thing you know."

Cassie sat back in her chair, smiled at Marcelle.

"I think his third wife ought to watch herself, if you know what I mean."

A light, an effervescent light, seemed to fill Cassie's body until she thought she might rise and float away. She tipped her head back and looked at the ceiling, which the sisters had painted lime green, and heard Laura say to Jimmy, heard her whisper in the fierce tone children can pick up from miles away, "Do you have any idea what sort of life I would have had if I hadn't married you? Do you know? Do you know what I could have given *my children*? You took my life and you *squandered* it." Cassie wanted to go home now, she didn't want to wait, she could imagine herself bursting through the door, calling to Belle, asking Belle to summon Edwin, because Listen to this. Edwin would give his small, sweet smile, and in it Cassie would see all the years he'd counseled Laura and tried to track down Jimmy, tried to make things right. But it was Belle whose face she was most anxious to see. Belle, who was a student of history, and thus well acquainted with irony.

"Did he look like a killer, Cassie?" Marcelle leaned close.

Cassie shrugged, still smiling. "Everybody looks like a killer to me."

Martine lowered her paper. "You got that right." She raised it again.

Marcelle looked out the window, tugged at her napkin. "Not me, Martine. I'm not a killer. I'da kilt you by now if I was."

The cabdriver said a storm was coming up, and Cassie said she'd just be a minute. He waited at the curb as she walked to the front of the house on Rendon Street, a lovely little house painted gray and yellow, a marmalade cat asleep on the step, a spider plant dying in a pot by the door. A driveway led into a one-car garage, Cassie hadn't pictured that, and part of the house was built on top of the garage. The backyard was fenced in, but she didn't see a dog. Neighbors were out; one man was scraping a window frame and listening to salsa music, children were riding tricycles across the street. A mother, likely their mother, sat on the porch and watched them, her expression both loving and bored. The sky was very dark, and the air felt progressively denser, almost solid, but

Cassie knew it was only weather, it had nothing to do with grief or the passage of time or a woman's failure to ever make it home. She would be falsifying everything if she turned this street, this sweet house, into something it wasn't.

Back in the cab she asked the driver to take her to the Quarter, then mentioned to him that her grandfather had been a cabdriver.

"Yeah? What was his name?"

"Stanley Dubuisson." He left his daughter, she didn't say, when she was just five years old.

The driver thought a minute, shook his head. "Don't know him."

"I didn't, either."

She barely found a seat at the Café Du Monde; there were tourists everywhere, and the rain had started to fall. She ordered a coffee, then sat very still, there were so many voices rising up, and the rain on the awning, but she let the warm humid air enclose her and listened to nothing in particular. For years she had tried to imagine her world without her mother in it, or without Belle, and had assumed that everything would stop, we don't know how to go on living except by going on. She had seen Laura do so after Poppy died: she got up the next morning and put the coffee on and smoked a cigarette, and they put him in the ground. There were still library books to return, so they returned them, and a garden to plant, so they planted it, but Cassie had known that for her, as much as she had grieved for him, Poppy's death was an intimation of the Larger Death. It is one thing to lose a grandfather, but something entirely different to become a woman without a mother. A woman without a mother. Cassie could almost hear the whistle of that arrow as it shot past her. The rain came down so hard she could no longer see the sidewalk, a few feet away, and the tourists got louder, as if in a contest. She would go home and say to Belle, Our mother was poisoned. Laura was poisoned by her inability to give herself over to her own life, the life she made and shored up every day, and I, Cassie would say to Belle, will not do the same. Belle was Cassie's responsibility now, and she accepted it; one can't be everywhere, Laura couldn't be both at the kitchen window and in New Orleans. I will *stand*, Cassie practiced saying in her head.

And then a man stood up from his table near the street, he walked out into the pounding rain, turned and faced the crowd of diners. He threw his arms out in surrender, he let the rain hit his face, began to sing "Amazing Grace," it rose up from him and rang out in a deep baritone that silenced everyone. The servers in their striped polyester shirts stopped moving, the restless children stopped, all the tourists with their blank expressions turned toward him. Cassie closed her eyes and decided to take it personally, four verses bright shining as the sun. She sat and let the singer grant his benediction, and when he was finished, in the burst of applause that followed, she headed out into the rain herself; as she passed the man, she thanked him and dropped five dollars in the bucket at his feet.

On the flight to Atlanta, Cassie looked at the Los Angeles guidebook she'd purchased at the airport; the history of the city was rich with dramatic and frequent suicides. Laura would have loved it. The flight reached a cruising altitude, and Cassie closed the book and thought of Belle. When Cassie got home, Belle would ask her questions about her trip, and all of them would be punctuated by a certain look Belle had, a kind of knowing sneer. Laura had asked Cassie once, "You know that face Belle makes?" and Cassie had said yes, she certainly did, and Laura said, "Why is it so *dear*?"

Belle would ask, Did you eat well?

And Cassie would say she did.

Did you see interesting things?

Yes, very.

Did you bring me any presents?

Cassie would give her the Vishniac collection.

And then Belle would ask, in Laura's place: Did you meet the Minor Criminals of Louisiana?

Cassie opened her eyes. She would answer: I met a Minor Criminal, yes. And I met an Innocent Man.

She didn't have to wait long for her suitcase in Indianapolis, and she was in her truck by eight o'clock, saying a prayer that it would start. It started. She drove gingerly out of the airport and on to 465, the loop around Indianapolis, soon to be named after David Letterman; she headed for Highway 69 North, and every gear that took, every mile she covered, was a relief. By nine-thirty she was in the dark driveway of Billy and Patty Poe. Their ranch house was dwarfed by Billy's body shop, but all the lights were shining, and she could hear their kids yelling in the living room. She knocked on the front door, and disturbed two coon hounds in a kennel between the house and shop; when Patty opened the door she looked worried and frazzled. She looked like a mother, overweight, her hair untended, drying her hands on a dish towel.

"Cassie? Is everything okay? Come in," Patty said, and through the doorway Cassie could see three children jumping on the living room furniture and gradually destroying a pop-up tent set up on the floor.

"I don't mean to bother you," Cassie said, "is Billy around? I just need to see him a minute."

"Sure, he's in the shop. Go to that side door, he might not hear you knock."

Cassie walked across the gravel driveway, past the barking dogs, the doors closed on Billy's two hydraulic lifts. Around the corner she found an open door; Billy was sitting on the floor organizing and cleaning parts of a dismantled engine, listening to Led Zeppelin so loudly the speakers of his small stereo were rattling. Cassie walked in slowly, trying not to startle him.

"Hey! Cassie!" Billy jumped up, wiping his hands on a dirty shop rag, then turned off the stereo. The buttons were thickened with dust and grease. "I won't hug you."

"Hey, Billy."

"What brings you out here so late? You in trouble?" He was a thin, rangy man with a long face. Cassie hadn't seen him clean in years.

"Naw, not really. Josh says you've got a Ford Ranger for sale."

"I do. He told you it's rebuilt? I got it for nothing."

"A salvage title's okay with me. Is it out here?"

Billy turned on a floodlight, and they walked back out to the yard where ten, twelve vehicles were parked. Right in the middle was a black truck, tall, shiny, immaculate. "This is it?" Cassie said, surprised.

"That's it. I got it at auction. A tree fell on it, I did all the body work myself. Engine was fine, untouched. Everything under the hood is original."

Cassie opened the driver's door. The inside was tan, the upholstery looked new.

"It's full size, with an extended cab. Four doors."

She opened a door on the cab's extension. There were two jump seats, folded up.

"It's got air, a CD player, cruise control, five-speed stick. A bed liner."

"How much?"

Billy scratched his head. He hated to talk money. "The Blue Book is ten. I put four in it, and I'll sell it for five."

Cassie nodded. "I'll give you cash, and you can have the Mazda. The title's in the glove box."

She had to admit, driving home, having long been a person to whom vehicles meant nothing, that she was not altogether immune to the charms of being the owner of a big black truck. Every mile of road felt good; this was Information. Billy had lent her a CD, the Nashville Bluegrass Band, and the combination of the early warmth of the night, the air coming through the truck, the music, made her remember how it felt to be high, the bounty of perception. She had once told Laura that pot made her realize she lived in an analogous world; that all the connections had already been made, the architecture was laid bare, the whole plan was shining up in everything, and all she had to do was look, name it if she wanted to. Laura had said those were the world's riches.

The King's Crossing was as wide and dark as any road. She

passed the Taylors', the trailers, the pond, and pulled in to her driveway. The house was lit up for her arrival, and Edwin was there, his used Taurus, a dull and institutional blue, sitting in front of the garage where Jimmy used to park the Lincoln. Cassie carried her suitcase and Belle's book through the screened porch, the front door. From the living room a man's histrionic voice said, *Ivan had seen the woman before, but he couldn't remember where.* Cassie left her bag at the foot of the stairs and went into the kitchen. Belle and Edwin were at the table, side by side, looking at a stack of documents.

"Look who's here," Edwin said, standing. He had aged well; his Lovely Face was unlined, his eyes were clear. Maybe his shoulders slumped a bit more, his clothes hung loose, but on the whole he seemed the same to Cassie as he had twenty years before. "Welcome home," he said.

"Cassie," Belle said, not standing. And then she burst into tears. She sat straight up, let her head fall back, and wailed.

Cassie sat down across from her sister. "Belle."

Belle had on one of Laura's sleeveless shirts, red, and she wore a white sweater around her shoulders. She sobbed, she gasped for air.

Cassie said, "Belle."

Edwin finally reached out and put his hand on Belle's back, and she cried even harder. She cried much harder than she had when she was unable to attend Laura's funeral, harder than when Poppy died. She cried freely, she was liberated from the world of noncryers.

"Cassie!" she wailed. "I have! something! to tell you!"

Edwin said, "Do you want me to—"

Belle nearly shouted, "No! It's my duty! She's my sister, my life would be a great deal easier if someone in this house would read the *Oresteia*."

Cassie said, "Belle. Is Jimmy dead, are you ill, are we bankrupt? Because all you have to do is tell me."

Belle looked up, gave a last, brave sob, and said, "Edwin. And I. Are married."

They were wearing rings. Thin gold bands that Cassie could plainly see, now that she was looking. She sat back against the chair.

"We did it as soon as you left for New Orleans, I was afraid I'd chicken out if I had to tell you ahead of time, a judge came here to the house, we had the ceremony in the backyard."

Cassie said nothing.

"It was beautiful."

Belle, a mess, tear-streaked; Cassie could see what she had been afraid of, that the two of them, the sisters—who had so little left!—meant nothing to Belle, that Cassie had been excluded. Cassie saw, too, that all the time she'd been in New Orleans, making her pledge to her sister to *stand*, Belle and Edwin had been right here, sanctifying their own pact. In this very house. They seemed so precious to her suddenly, like newborn babies, their unscuffed rings, their subtle glances. Edwin was smiling at Cassie, his same sad, small grin, and that was what finally did it, Cassie opened her mouth and began to laugh, and she laughed and laughed and laughed, tears running down her face, and Belle stood up and they danced around the kitchen, Edwin turned on Howlin' Wolf, and Cassie laughed and laughed.

* * *

In the morning Edwin and Cassie left Belle at the kitchen table looking at the Vishniac photographs. She was still crying, had cried all night. Cassie couldn't begin to unravel what her sister was crying about; she let it lie.

Edwin and Cassie took the documents he and Belle had been studying and headed for Laura's attorney in Hopwood, an old man named Harold Piper; he preferred to be called Hal, but no one did.

"Let's take my truck, Edwin," Cassie said, not giving him the option of saying no. Edwin in a truck. He looked miserable and shy.

"Cassie," he began, clearing his throat, "is there anything you want to, would you like to ask me—"

"Nope," Cassie said, shaking her head.

"Because it seems as if maybe you'd have questions about—"

"I don't."

"I appreciate that you're a private person."

"Thank you."

They drove the rest of the way in silence.

Harold Piper's office was in downtown Hopwood, in a building that was probably a bribe away from being condemned. His office was above a restaurant where Cassie had gone a few times with Jimmy, the Top Lunch and Cigar, a broken-down cafeteria where every day they served the same thing, beef and noodles with a slice of white bread and butter and a cup of coffee. Two ninety-five. Only men ate there. Harold Piper ate there every day. In the back room a card game ran indefinitely, had for decades, low-stakes stuff. High enough, though, to make Harold the sworn enemy for life of Jimmy, which is how Laura had chosen him in the first place.

"Sit down," he said to Cassie and Edwin, gesturing to two moth-eaten armchairs. Harold wanted to look like Mark Twain, or at least like Hal Holbrook as Mark Twain, but his white suit, his white hair and mustache, had all gone the yellow of liver failure, dissipation.

"Cassie," he began, lighting a cigarette, "you know I despise that wastrel of a father of yours."

"I don't have a father," Cassie said, crossing her legs.

"I guess that's legally true. Your mother, however"—Harold leaned back and studied his filthy light fixture—"was another story. A rare, a wonderful woman."

Edwin cleared his throat. "About the will, Harold. As you know, I was privy to the contents, but Cassie—"

"Your mother," Harold continued, "was not only wonderful, she was *surprising*, wouldn't you say? Think about it, Cassie."

Laura and Milkweed. Laura on the bus chasing Jimmy so long ago, because if you perceive something as holy, you will not let it go, you will not defile it; laughing through her wedding night. Laura pregnant, at the mercy of strangers, Laura chasing a tornado through the geometry of rural Indiana, carrying to her grave the memory of a woman who never quite met the horse walking toward her. Apples in her apron.

"Yes," Cassie said. "She was."

"You might be equally surprised by this." Harold raised a pair of half-glasses, bifocals, and rested them on the beaky bridge of his yellow nose. He lifted his head just slightly, focusing. "When your grandfather died, he left your mother the house and land in Roseville and all the contents therein. That house and land have been deeded over to you and Belle, and you have equal shares in it." He took a long hit off his cigarette, blew it out through his nose. "Additionally, he left an insurance policy. Your mother was the sole beneficiary."

Cassie uncrossed her legs, crossed them again.

"Your mother took that money and converted half of it into another life-insurance policy, in her name, with you and your sister as the beneficiaries, and she took the other half and invested it in the stock market."

Cassie raised her eyebrows.

"Some of the investments she undertook on the advice of Edwin here, and they were very safe, and her return was small but guaranteed. But she also bought stocks and bonds under the tutelage of Ernest Pettigrew—"

"*Uncle Bud?*"

"Yes, whose instincts ran closer to the margin, you might say. The bottom line, Cassie, is that if I liquidated your half of your mother's portfolio today, along with your half of the payout from the life-insurance policy, you have about three hundred thousand dollars, after taxes."

Cassie blinked once. "Sell."

Harold looked at her over his glasses. "Why don't we—"

Edwin said, "I really think you should consider—"

Cassie stood up, held her hand out to Harold. "Thank you very much for your representation. Please do as I have asked, and sell my shares." She turned to Edwin, who was looking at her with great concern, a sort of worry he'd perfected over the course of his German life. "Edwin." Cassie shocked him and surprised herself by resting her hands on his shoulders and leaning close to his face. He smelled dry, like Belle. "You are my brother. I never thought I'd have a brother." They looked at each other. Edwin's eyes filled with tears. Then Cassie said, "But I'm leaving this state."

After she had signed what she needed to sign and everything was in order, Cassie and Edwin turned to leave. Cassie said to Harold, "Please call me as soon as the money is available. I want it in cash."

When she got home, she called Jacob at the photography gallery in New Orleans; she called Gabe at Epistrophes on Royale. She told them she was looking for real estate, and they agreed on an old building in the Bywater district, the area of town where everything was moving. It had been a jazz club, and then a studio for a glassblower, and Cassie asked them to call the seller, and then she went to see Uncle Bud. She told him to sell everything, to sell it all and bring the Brunswick and the light with the red glass shade, because they were moving to New Orleans. He looked at her steadily, and she thought she could see him picturing the house he'd never finished, Railroad Street sinking further to seed, the glass room without Cassie in it, and then he nodded and called his attorney.

For days Belle sat at the kitchen table and cried, but at lunchtime Edwin came home from the hardware store, and she heated up soup in a pan, and they sat together at the table to eat it. He checked her arms for imaginary thorns and adjusted the dosage of her medicine, and found a special conditioner that made her hair look normal again. At night they slept in the same bed. Cassie drove in to Roseville and said good-bye to Emmy, who seemed irritated and distracted; Dylan had spilled a bowl of Cheerios the day before and hadn't told anyone. Now they were stuck like barnacles to the dining room floor. She repeatedly asked Cassie, "You're moving *where*? to do *what*?" And then later, "Explain this to me again?" But at the door, as Cassie was leaving, Emmy threw her arms around her and cried some, saying that with Cassie gone, almost nothing of her past would remain. Cassie didn't say anything but wondered where Emmy had gotten the idea that anything of the past remained for anyone, ever. Then Cassie went to Puck's mother's house, and down into Puck's special finished basement, where she found him lying in bed watching cartoons. His computer was on in one corner of the room, displaying a constantly changing, garish configuration of what appeared to be electrical specs. The floor was covered with comic books and science-fiction novels and the artist's notebooks, in which Puck worked on his own, never-ending "Saucy Little Broadcaster." Cassie looked around, stunned by the profusion of disemboweled machines, machines connected to other machines, instruction manuals, pill bottles. She told Puck that she was leaving, then sat with him for an hour as he wept like a fool.

She got up very early and snuck down the stairs and made coffee quietly, then took it out to the porch and waited for the sun to come up. Sometimes, when you leave, you never make it home. You never see the place again. She studied the driveway, the yard, the road, the fencerow, the fields, the windbreaks, the power lines; Laura had drained these things of their resonance, or so she believed. It wasn't so for Cassie. The sight of the hawk circling its prey, the hawk's flight, the racing heart of the mouse, the vole, the rabbit—these things were perfectly real, they were everything. All. She had stood in the pouring rain that last day in New

Orleans, had stood outside Saint Louis Cathedral as the bishop said the mass. He wore a small microphone on his collar, and the homily was broadcast all through the square, to the people with umbrellas who had arrived late and couldn't get in, to the junkies and the homeless and the tourists and their children. *Why did He die?* the bishop asked. *Where is He now?*

Cassie got in her truck. She didn't own much, but it was all there with her. A vintage Balabushka pool cue won fair and square; a backpack from a Boy Scout packed with Laura's letters. A phone number in Biloxi. Her tools, her boots, her clothes, some books; she had a .22 pistol, a Ruger Single-Six, strapped to her ankle. She had three hundred thousand in cash in a metal box behind her seat.

She drove away.

ACKNOWLEDGMENTS

For technical information about pool (particularly the things I wasn't able to learn in a pool hall), I owe a debt to Jeanette Lee, Ewa Mataya Laurance, and Philip B. Capelle, whose books I consulted daily. Writing about pool and writing a novel are two very different things, and I also learned invaluable lessons from David McCumber (Playing Off the Rail), and the incomparable Walter Tevis (The Hustler, The Color of Money). As Martin Amis once said of Elmore Leonard, Tevis is a writer free of false quantities, and I'm grateful for his fine, clean work.

Thanks to Joshua Mann Pailet, who lent me the perfect table.

For a year I spent many nights in bars and pool halls, a condition my children accepted with their usual sangfroid. Thank you, thank you, to the Amazing Kat and Obadiah. Ben Kimmel was equally and always supportive and, along with Don Kimmel, bought me my own cue. (*Sweet.*) To the people who read the fledgling first draft and were generous with praise and suggestions, I reserve special gratitude: Jody Leonard and Lisa Kelly, Deb Futter, Ben, Meg Kimmel, and my agent, Bill Clegg, who is a genius of kindness and professionalism. My mother, Delonda Hartmann, read an early draft and wrote me a letter I'll treasure for the rest of my days. My deepest thanks to the owners of independent bookstores around the country, without whom my books would languish in dank basements (thanks especially to Tom Campbell, John Valentine, Keebe Fitch, and Robert Segedy), and thanks also to the American booksellers, our unsung heroes. Ruth Liebmann, thank you. My deepest thanks to the poet Alan Shapiro. Rachel Pace, you were lovely. Thanks to all the bookclubs who read my first two books. Mary Herczog was with me at the genesis of this novel and let me spend weeks with her in New Orleans. For this and many other acts of generosity on her part, I am deeply in debt. Thanks to Katherine Williams, who lost a fight with a turkey buzzard. Thank you to Dominick Anfuso and Martha Levin at Free Press for your faith and vision, and thanks to Chris Litman. Beth Thomas copyedited the final manuscript brilliantly. There aren't sufficient words of gratitude and respect for Elizabeth Berg. And to my editor, Amy Scheibe: I'd follow you to the end. You are one of my great blessings.

Bud Rains provided me with a model of a really good man.

My nephew, Josh Golliher, first flew a snake kite with me. He is in this book in many ways.

To Bob Jarvis: without you, I'd never know how much a girl could love her father.

Finally, I'd like to thank the people who enliven this daily work: Augusten Burroughs, Lawrence Naumoff, Suzanne Finnamore, Steve Hochman, Patricia Morrison, Matt Piersol, Dorothy and Will Kennedy, Beth Dalton, Jay Alevizon, Susan Naumoff, the beloved Maia Dery and Senga Carroll. I completed the last rewrite of this book at the home of Leslie Staub and Tim Sommer; they traded that week in New Orleans for my heart. And to John Svara, who stood still and studied grace with me.

BOOKSHOP

Other titles available from Harper Perennial at **10%** off recommended retail price.
FREEF *postage and packing in the UK.*

The Solace of Leaving Early
Haven Kimmel (ISBN 0 00 715253 1)   £6.99
....
Happy Accidents
Tiffany Murray (ISBN 0 00 718367 4)   £6.99
....
Eve Green
Susan Fletcher (ISBN 0 00 719040 9)   £7.99
....
Truth and Beauty
Ann Patchett (ISBN 0 00 719678 4)   £7.99
....

Total cost ....

10% discount ....

Final total ....

To purchase by Visa/Mastercard/Switch
*simply call **08707 871724** or fax on **08707 871725***

To pay by cheque, send a copy of this form with a cheque made payable to 'HarperCollins Publishers' to: Mail Order Dept. (Ref: B0B4), HarperCollins Publishers, Westerhill Road, Bishopbriggs, G64 2QT, making sure to include your full name, postal address and phone number.

From time to time HarperCollins may wish to use your personal data to send you details of other HarperCollins publications and offers. If you wish to receive information on other HarperCollins publications and offers please tick this box ☐

Do not send cash or currency. Prices correct at time of press. Prices and availability are subject to change without notice. Delivery overseas and to Ireland incurs a £2 per book postage and packing charge.